PENGUIN BOOKS
SUDDEN SUPERSTAR

Claire Betita de Guzman is a Filipina writer based in Singapore and author of four novels: *Miss Makeover, Budget is the New Black, Girl Meets World,* and *No Boyfriend Since Birth,* which was adapted into a TV series. A former journalist, she started as a news reporter for the broadsheet *Today* before becoming a lifestyle editor for international and local magazines including *Cosmopolitan Philippines* and *Harper's Bazaar Singapore.* She is a member of the Singapore Writers Group and has led talks and panels at literary events in Southeast Asia, including the Singapore Writers Festival. She studied journalism and graduated cum laude (with honours) at the University of the Philippines. She has taken writing courses at the University of Oxford in England and was a fellow in literary workshops in Europe and Asia, including Miradoux, France; Bali, Indonesia; and Tbilisi, Georgia. She is co-author of the poetry collection *Dreaming of the Divine Downstairs* and is co-editor of *Get Luckier,* an anthology of Philippine-Singapore writings. Find her online at www.clairebetita.com.

T0124626

Sudden Superstar

Claire Betita de Guzman

PENGUIN BOOKS
An imprint of Penguin Random House

PENGUIN BOOKS

USA | Canada | UK | Ireland | Australia
New Zealand | India | South Africa | China | Southeast Asia

Penguin Books is part of the Penguin Random House group of companies
whose addresses can be found at global.penguinrandomhouse.com

Published by Penguin Random House SEA Pte Ltd
9, Changi South Street 3, Level 08-01,
Singapore 486361

First published in Penguin Books by Penguin Random House SEA 2023

Copyright © Claire Betita de Guzman 2023

All rights reserved

10 9 8 7 6 5 4 3 2 1

This is a work of fiction. Names, characters, places and incidents
are either the product of the author's imagination or are used fictitiously,
and any resemblance to any actual person, living or dead, events or
locales is entirely coincidental.

ISBN 9789815127997

Typeset in Garamond by MAP Systems, Bengaluru, India

This book is sold subject to the condition that it shall not, by way of trade or
otherwise, be lent, resold, hired out, or otherwise circulated without the
publisher's prior consent in any form of binding or cover other than that in which
it is published and without a similar condition including this condition being
imposed on the subsequent purchaser.

www.penguin.sg

To those seeking self and sanctuary

in this age of social media, this book is for you.

May our quest for authenticity

lead us to heights we never thought possible.

Prologue

'Aaaaaannd, go!'

The production assistant in charge, clad in a wrinkled, grey, T-shirt and looking like he had not slept in days, gave a series of frantic little jumps as he yelled at us from the sidelines, just out of the TV cameras' range.

Nobody moved.

'You, Arya Alvarez! Go! Now!'

I jumped at the sound of my name, but hesitated moving from where I was standing with five other fidgety 'contestants', all lined up in the darkish, cluttered, chaos backstage of the TV studio. Just a few steps away, just beyond that curtained door in front of us, I could hear the slight tittering of, oh— just a few hundred people who were this show's live audience for that day.

Where was I supposed to go again? Straight through that heavily draped door where they built a set to mimic a huge walk-in, two-room closet? Or through the narrow side doors where they said I was supposed to—

'ARYA ALVAREZ!'

I stiffened. 'Wait, I—'

'Go!' Mr Production Assistant yelled. 'Go, go, go, go, GOOOOOO!'

No joke, he screamed that last 'Go' so loudly and so shrilly, he looked like one of those cartoons whose head and tonsils appeared just about to fall off. Thank God there was no audio yet backstage.

Before I knew it, I was being unceremoniously pushed through the heavy curtains, straight into a brightly-lit set. Beyonce's 'Bootylicious' suddenly blasted from the speakers and a voice-over suavely boomed throughout the studio, right as I stumbled into full view of the studio's live audience as well as on the TV screens of *Fashion Fever's* millions of viewers nationwide.

'Here we are with fabulous travel expert and lovely local wander woman Arya Alvarez, who's about to choose the clothes that reflect her style. Will she make it to this round of the show? Will she become a finalist? What's *her* fashion fever?'

A rousing applause came from the live audience—a wild, entertainment-hungry clapping that must have been similar to the Roman crowds cheering in the Colosseum, watching poor souls about to be fed to the lions.

Calm down, Arya, I told myself as I stood on the set, in the middle of the makeshift 'closet' squinting against the harsh, coloured, studio lights that had seemingly come out of nowhere. *You are not being fed to the lions. Just to the thirty-five million viewers of this show.*

Indeed, I was simply being asked to choose a set of clothes that were hung on various racks in the makeshift closet, put on the outfit in the makeshift dressing room, and then do a short runway strut up until the far end of the staged set nearest the audience; for them and the judges to see my outfit.

Simple, right?

Only problem was, I had to do all that in less than five minutes.

This of course was repeatedly emphasized by Mr Production Assistant himself, while we were being herded backstage before call time—all six of us from different professions and walks of life, thrust into the limelight, thanks to this abomination of a TV show.

What Mr PA also never tired of reminding us was that we were *the* contestants for *Fashion Fever*—only the Philippines' newest, hottest, and most-watched reality show. It was hosted by no less than Christian Salvador, who had done more than thirty movies, most of which were box office hits. The show had catapulted immediately to number one on primetime, and winning this would mean one became a household name, *stat*.

Because the six of us weren't professional actors, some of us had to be briefed more than twice about the rigours and requirements of television such as blocking, timing, and of course, improvising. Like, uh, me.

Earlier, when I asked Mr PA again, *exactly* what we were supposed to do when we were on set, I had to endure a massive eye roll, provoked for sure by this question.

Nevertheless, he provided the much-needed answers. 'You enter the closet on the set, choose five clothing items in one minute—this can be a top, a skirt, a hat, a scarf, whatever.

After that, you enter the dressing room—right on the set, too. And you're allowed three minutes to put it on, style it, and make it work.'

'Be careful as there's a booby trap there! Like a dress with no sleeves, *suman*-style. Think spring roll. Or a skirt with a slit on the wrong side,' he continued, with an almost-evil smirk. 'If you pick it, you *have* to wear it, you have to make it work. Or else.'

Or else, what? I wanted to ask out loud.

I knew the answer, of course. You get kicked out of the show.

Now, it was my turn to hide a massive eye roll. If this show ended right now, I would thank the universe, really. And in celebration, I would treat myself to a big plate of *tapsilog* at my favourite joint in Maginhawa Street—never to see the studios of *Fashion Fever* again. And yeah, *tapsilog* . . . strips of tasty dried, cured beef on top of garlic rice and sunny-side-up eggs, a true Filipino breakfast staple. That's my jam.

Not that I'm a celebrity or something, but I almost wished that I was in a normal TV show doing something typical like an interview or better yet, just as part of the audience watching the show. Wasn't that what normal people like me ended up doing when someone took notice of the work we do? Whatever happened to normal TV shows where you sat on couches and talked, then some celebrity would come out and sing or a band would play?

If I thought those were already daunting, then *this* was crazy. Besides, I wasn't even a fashionista or a wannabe model or anything. I was simply a travel manager who worked in an office and occasionally—well, often—travelled as part of my job.

'Arya!' Someone hissed from behind a pile of sweaters in the makeshift closet.

Gah, it's Mr PA again, this time with a wild, panicked look in his eyes.

'Start choosing! Now!'

I gave a start and wildly looked around the closet, the clothes . . . in a blurry, colourful mess before my eyes. How many items, again? Four? Five? My heart started pounding—more at the thought of Mr PA's wrath than my potential humiliation when I come out of this part of the show. I took a quick, deep breath and told myself, *Choose, choose, choose something, Arya. Anything!*

I knew that they were also shooting me from above and showing it on the huge screen in the studio. There was no escape from showing the world every detail of my face, my gestures, and my moves. Which right now, still involved standing frozen in the centre of the closet.

Then, as if possessed, I lunged at the sweaters, grabbing a red one, then a pair of black pants that looked roomy enough for me, then a cream-coloured beanie, and a pair of pointy heels. All this happening as the voice-over gave a running commentary of what I was doing, thankfully drowning out whatever heavy, panicked breathing or guttural, torturous sounds I was probably emitting while frantically choosing the clothes.

I hurled myself into the dressing room right on the side of the set, dropped my stash on the floor, yanked off my clothes, and got ready to pull on the new set of clothes I'd hastily grabbed from the racks.

But what was this?

I stared in horror at the piece of clothing in my hand, a seemingly innocuous red sweater in an of-the-moment graphic print and the softest cashmere material, which would definitely look smashing on me—if I had five arms.

Desperate, I threw down the five-arm sweater and rummaged again through my pile, catching hold of another piece of clothing. With relief, I saw that it was the loose pair of pants that I'd grabbed, the roomy one with the garterized waist.

And one leg.

Oh.

Just my luck, I ended up not just with one, but two booby traps. Just as I thought I had it bad with the five-arm sweater, here I was with modesty issues about the one-legged pair of pants. Did I even shave my legs today? More importantly, will my underwear show? Did I even wear decent panties today?

'Two minutes to go for Arya Alvarez!' The voiceover was louder than ever. 'What's *her* fashion fever?'

I pulled the red sweater on, and by some grace of God, my arms were thankfully pulling through the left and right armholes. I hurriedly tied the offensive extra arms around my waist—maybe they'd see it as a chic obi-belted top? Then I wrapped the fifth arm around my neck, like a turtleneck or a short, knit, scarf. Whatever. As I said, I wasn't that much of a fashionista.

It felt ridiculous. And even with the lack of mirrors, I knew I looked ridiculous.

I inwardly groaned as I pulled up the even more ridiculous one-legged pants. The left part with no leg came up extremely high to my thigh, almost like a skimpy panty, and the fleshy bits of my upper thigh which, as I've now discovered, was

the flabbiest and most unattractive part of my lower body—
bulged out in a dismayingly unflattering way.

An extra loud racket had started up all around me, and
I knew that it was time for me to go out, face the thirty-five
million, and do my runway walk.

This is it, I thought. In my five-arm sweater and
one-legged pants, I was indeed about to be eaten alive by
the lions.

All hell broke loose when I emerged from the dressing
room, with the music and the voice-over so deafening, the
studio spotlights brighter than ever, and the clapping, cheers,
and hoots (and was that a nasty boo?), so noisy and wild that
I couldn't distinguish if they were cheering sounds of support
and delight or screams of ridicule and derision.

I stopped in the middle of the set.

What was I doing here?

I couldn't see anything. Not the audience, not the
cameras, not even Mr PA who must be hyperventilating over
my blocking this time. No, I could only just see the lights and
more lights. And I can only hear one single question in my
head.

What was I doing in a bizarre reality show in Manila?

Chapter 1

Seljalandsfoss, Iceland, 11.46 p.m. The gush of the waterfall could only be described as constant, thunderous, and almost deafening. It emitted a spray akin to the fine, facial cooling mist you get when you spray on a bottle of Evian. There were no lights—except for our puny flashlights, hastily scavenged from the depths of our tour van.

We were at Iceland's Seljalandsfoss waterfall, right by the road and 120 kilometres away from the capital city of Reykjavik—and it looked, sounded, and felt magnificent.

You'd think we were peacefully gazing up from a good, safe distance at this splendid work of nature, taking a million pictures of this famous Icelandic landmark with our iPhones and heavy DSLRs.

But, we couldn't.

Because it was dark. Despite our flashlights, it was very, very dark. Because it was almost midnight.

And because we were standing *behind* this gigantic, raging waterfall, getting mist in every part of our bodies. Talk about

being up close and personal with an indefatigable beast—
this big baby gushed water 24/7, 365 days a year. In fact,
I thought I was going to be totally soaked, not to mention
turning deaf any minute now—

'Darling, come! Let's take a *selpie!'*

A shrill, petulant voice cut above the din. For a split
second, I was relieved. Apparently, my hearing, thankfully,
had not yet been impaired. But, foolish me. I had far worse
dilemmas to deal with—and judging from the insistent,
whine-like quality of the voice, no big bad waterfall was going
to stand in the way of a much craved-for selfie.

I shone my flashlight around the cavernous interiors
from where I was pressed against the rocky wall (that
space just behind the waterfall was our exact spot) and
promptly caught the obnoxious glint of a sequined *turban*—
an outrageous choice of cold weather fashion if you
ask me.

But, Turban Girl—yes, can I call her that?—had been
insistent. She had fought, fiercely, to keep the turban, despite
my protestations earlier that it wasn't enough to keep you
warm in Iceland's late autumn weather, which can reach a low
of seven degrees. For children of the tropics like us, that was
practically like being trapped in a malfunctioning refrigerator
turned on high.

No, Turban Girl had been firm on her decisions—thigh-
high wedge boots over the sturdy hiking shoes that staff at
our hotel were offering to lend her, and a resounding 'No!'
coupled with a fit just before we left Reykjavik, when Damon
suggested they pop in at the North Face boutique and secure
a proper, albeit very puffy wool jacket to protect her from
Iceland's brutal cold.

And so here we were. And no wonder she practically had to be carried up the steps during the brief climb going behind this waterfall, whining constantly about Iceland's supposedly whacked-out weather all throughout our epic eight-hour tour of the island. She even blamed the cold for the loss of one of her precious Shu Uemura fake eyelashes (it was windy in one part of the tour)—which I'm pretty sure was really just due to an under-performing eyelash glue.

'*Selpie?* Darling? Please?'

I inched closer to the wall while trying not to cringe from my dark corner. Baby talk just made saying 'selpie' out loud even worse.

There was some rustling and I could barely just make out the outline of two people huddled close together, one shadowy figure with an arm defiantly outstretched high above in a classic selfie pose.

I tried to imagine what could be the expression on the picture-perfect face of 'Darling'—a.k.a. the uber-gorgeous Damon Loh, a.k.a. Turban Girl's boyfriend, a.k.a. the famous lifestyle host of relatively new TV show *Uncommon Asia*. Which was turning out to be the most tuned-in show of every single girl in the Philippines, Singapore, Hong Kong, Malaysia, Thailand, Vietnam, and Indonesia—well, just about all of Southeast Asia.

Because who could resist Damon Loh's perennial coolness and swagger? That soothing, dreamy voice was enough to send shivers through every woman's spine, especially when he uttered the very mundane words, 'Let's check it out, shall we?'

The way it wafted out of his mouth, you'd think you were being invited, no—seduced into a rose-filled, secret garden with the promise of a lustful, intimate romp. And Damon Loh might as well have been trained in beauty pageant school—he had that unwavering bearing, a composed, tireless smile, and a charismatic enthusiasm whether he was featuring something as ordinary as the latest electric toothbrush or as glamorous as the goings-on at New York Fashion Week in his TV show.

I didn't have to shine my flashlight around the surroundings to know that Turban Girl was now cuddling into the arms of Damon.

For a moment there, I actually felt a teeny, tiny twinge of envy. It was cold, dark, wet, and way past bedtime—and though this was a land that was indeed unimaginably beautiful, it was still a strange land. It wasn't too much to ask for someone to protectively wrap his arms around you at this very moment, was it?

Maybe it was the cold, the dampness, or my irrational envy—but my thumb hit the button of my tiny flashlight and I switched it on, training the weak line of light on whoever and whatever was beside me.

My little light revealed Turban Girl pressing impatiently against Damon, chin determinedly tilted down and lips in an immovable pouty duck face that was, perhaps, what the selfie was all about.

'Just a little more, darling. One more take,' she was almost singing out between clenched teeth—she had to, what with Seljalandsfoss to compete with.

'It's all dark, honey,' I heard Damon murmur. Despite the steady sound of the water streaming, his well-modulated voice wafted out clean and clear.

'Don't be a killjoy! We can ask your crew or someone to Photoshop this, right?' Turban Girl's voice rose an octave higher.

Another cringe from me, from where I clung to the damp, rocky wall—which, in the last twenty minutes we had been standing there after a dark, slippery climb—had somehow become my best friend. I tried not to think of the dreaded climb down, which would be another encounter with the slippery steps in the darkness, along with puddles, mysterious holes, and rocks of all sizes conveniently covered with slimy moss.

I squinted in the dark light to look for our Icelandic guide, Grummi. But he seemed to be transfixed by the crashing and falling of the water in front of us, oblivious to the wet spray and the ongoing selfie shenanigans taking place.

Of course, it was Turban Girl who insisted that we see this waterfall on our way back from a whole day tour of Iceland's main sights. She and Damon were flying out to Turkey early the next morning, and apparently, the hundreds of *selpies* she took at Jökulsárlón, the surreal glacier lagoon, and stunning Reynishverfi, the black sand beach in South Iceland's town of Vik—*still* wasn't enough to lend that glamorous, world-traveller vibe on her Instagram feed.

'I want to see the waterfall, you know? You know, like, go inside? Just like in the magazine?' She'd said earlier in the van in her usual stunted English, just as I was dozing off. I was sitting in the front seat beside where Grummi was driving and was starting to congratulate myself for surviving this four-day trip of organizing, shepherding, picture-taking, and hand-holding Damon Loh and company.

I guess Grummi was just being his typical Icelandic tour guide self when, upon hearing Turban Girl's wishes, promptly turned into the road that led to the grand waterfall that was Seljalandsfoss—at 11 p.m. That was eleven o'clock at night when we were supposedly on our way back to Reykjavik, to our warm, cozy, hotel. I assumed that we were only just driving past the falls, what with it being the middle of the night, with growling stomachs eager for a midnight nosh, and our toasty beds waiting back in the city.

But when Turban Girl started chattering about actually going into the waterfall and wanting to be 'like in the magazine', I knew it was going to be one of *those* trips. Oh, how I know them. So I started my breathing exercises—the ones that got me through many-a-stressful-moment and what my boss, Oliver, would call 'trip bumps' like these.

This is work and I am thankful, I silently chanted to myself, as the hulking form of Seljalandsfoss came into sight and I could hear the faint sounds of gushing water from where our van was slowing down.

This is work and I am thankful, I repeated silently. *It could be worse, really. This is part and parcel of what you signed up for, Arya Alvarez.*

Indeed, this was just part of my amazing work for Isle Z, dubbed as Singapore's number two boutique travel company and most recently, awarded by World Travel Group (WTG) as the Most Outstanding Travel Agency in the boutique category.

Isle Z organizes sophisticated, upscale, tailor-made trips for the rich and adventurous, for celebrities and influencers, and for whoever yearning for a unique, completely different experience, even in a destination they thought they already knew. Yearning for an Instagram-worthy getaway with your new beau? Isle Z can seek out the best, most picturesque yet off-the-beaten spots for you. Need a much-needed sabbatical in a remote Mediterranean villa before being cast in your next movie? We can organize a 'Live Like A Local' trip designed to rejuvenate your tired, cynical sensibilities. Want a solo, soul-searching journey to Bhutan, Nepal, or Bali? We can certainly put together a glamping trip where you can have your fresh cold-pressed green juice every morning and be as comfortable as you want—while you find yourself.

True, Isle Z was number two in the business—a detail that I knew kept my bosses, Oliver Liu and Desmond Chan, on their toes. Seed Travel, a much bigger company despite its name, with three branches in the region, was the current number one. Still, my bosses at Isle Z dealt with it with an admirable level of grace and class, quietly pushing us for better quality work and service—instead of requiring everyone in the company to do a tacky hard sell to get closer to that coveted number one spot.

And I do believe that Isle Z has more heart and soul, which was probably why I also enjoyed the work so much. So thank you universe for having Arya Alvarez at Isle Z! Yup, that was my constant chant.

Honestly? More than being just a job, I think joining Isle Z has saved my life.

But then again, sometimes people just want the simple things, eh? Like climbing behind an Icelandic waterfall, as Turban Girl here wanted.

It was totally safe, Grummi had repeatedly assured us. Grummi must have gone behind this waterfall even as a kid.

And this must be one of the usual things he's been doing all his life: going behind waterfalls, hiking on glaciers, driving along volcanic fields, coasting along in a T-shirt in single-degree weather—indeed a world away from where I was from.

A typical weekend in Iceland was spent fast-climbing hills and mountains—certainly a far cry from my weekends back home in the Philippines, where one's preferred physical activity was lifting sixteen oz bottles of Red Horse beer and sometimes, engaging in a psycho-battle as we shy away yet silently covet that last piece of *liempo*, my favourite grilled pork dish, or *tokwa't baboy*, which was crispy fried pork with even crispier tofu that was so excellent with alcohol, all found everywhere back home.

Back home in the Philippines.

At this sudden thought, I felt a sad, tiny squeeze in my chest.

No use delving into that right now, I told myself, what with this waterfall hanky-panky going on.

Right now, Singapore was home. It was where I now lived and worked, where I got this fabulous job that allowed me by some grace of the universe to go to these exotic places and organize, supervise, and execute trips for important people like Damon Loh and occasionally, the likes of Turban Girl.

It was where I thought I could start a new life—and leave one of the most catastrophic events of my life behind.

Chapter 2

Singapore, 6.21 a.m. The thing with leaving, I realized, in the months that I was trying to navigate my way through my new life in Singapore and my job at Isle 7, is that you always somehow still come back. And the kind of work I did, in the past and at present, involved a lot of leaving and arriving, of coming and going. Take this morning—the taxi ride from Singapore's Changi Airport to the city was smooth, quiet, and icy cold—as per usual. Never mind that by noon, it would be close to thirty-three degrees outside, with the UV index hitting eleven. Manila's weather was definitely cooler, and yet it still amazed me that I could reach my flat in Serangoon, right in the middle of Singapore's heartlands, without shedding a single bead of sweat. I know it would be an exaggeration for me to say that it was as if I was back in Iceland's chilly weather—but Singapore, truly, wasn't called an air-conditioned country for nothing.

'Good holiday?' The taxi uncle asked, his voice rising clear and melodic above the soft tunes of a Chinese song playing on the radio. I only had a glimpse of his face earlier after we'd done the business of shoving my suitcases into the trunk, where I'd had to help with the lifting because he was complaining about his back. Now all I could see from the backseat was his bald spot and pinkish, flaky scalp that hinted at a bad case of dandruff. I felt a wave of sympathy; perhaps he himself could use a holiday. Still, it was nice to be asked.

'Oh yes. It was quite nice,' I said, automatically, the words rolling off my tongue as easily as a spot of cool, green tea. Even if it had been just another work trip for Isle Z and definitely not a holiday, I knew better now than to elaborate. 'Thank you,' I added, feeling expansive.

'So we'll take the PIE, can?' Taxi uncle's head turned slightly towards me, a firmness in his voice. 'There's a jam at TPE, no point in passing there, *lah.*'

I also knew better than to argue with taxi uncles and their preferred routes.

I nodded and sat back with an approving murmur from the backseat. I looked out the window, then only noticing the faint, familiar smell of pomade and Tiger balm as we zoomed past the rest of the Changi Airport terminals and the impressive scenery that Singapore was known for. Like many who've chosen to live and work in this island state, I've grown to love coming back to its clean, almost gleaming highways, to the lush canopies of trees that lined its roads, to the wonderfully dense, bright pink bougainvillea flowers spilling over the city's elevated walkways and along its well-manicured road islands. After more than two years, I had gotten used to referring to the big highways as PIE, TPE, and CTE—these were, after all the speedy routes that brought me from airport to home (and sometimes, from airport to office), and from home to office.

I had also gotten used to 'traffic' being called 'jam' (which somehow never failed to elicit an image of an open jar of sweet, sticky, deep-red Baguio strawberry jam in my head), elevators being called lifts, and saying 'Sorry, I'll be three minutes late. Text you when I reach'—which really is such a great message but can be bewildering if used back home in Manila where traffic, hold-ups, and all sorts of mishaps can happen before we can even say confidently these things for certain, much less give the exact time of arrival to the minute.

I was on my way from the airport that morning after a thirteen-hour flight from Copenhagen, where I flew in a day earlier from Reykjavik. Back to the warm tropics once again, after all these nippy Nordic countries. I really would have wanted that to sound glamorous, but it really wasn't. Not when I arrived at the Danish capital last night at 8 p.m. and, perhaps feeling some leftover boldness from Iceland's jaw-dropping, mythical-looking landscapes and waterfalls, decided to just train it to the city centre. What was, after all, boarding an efficient commuter train compared to climbing behind a gigantic gushing waterfall in near-complete darkness?

Rain was what threw me, I think—I emerged from Copenhagen Central Station to sharp sheets of cold rain, thought nothing of it, and walked, hopped, and dragged my suitcase to my supposedly 'nearby' hotel, turning into a bedraggled mess along the way. When I got there, it turned out that I had booked its sister hotel of almost the same name. I must have been so tired or just rushing that I must have mixed up the two places when I double-checked it before the flight.

Luckily, a taxi was called for me and I was able to finally arrive at the right hotel. So much for walking, so much for bravery. That was the night I learned that 'near' was relative to the Danes—a five-minute walk was more like a fifteen-minute one. I was just thankful that the Danish driver didn't say a thing about the sopping wet umbrella that I'd accidentally shoved into his leather cab seats.

The next day I had to wake up early to make it to my 9 a.m. flight to Singapore. My dear clients Damon Loh and Turban Girl—whose real name, by the way, was Mhaybelle (yes, that's Mhaybelle with an 'H', thank you very much)— had finally left for Turkey. Thankfully, since Damon was staying at his wealthy uncle's villa in Istanbul, who had more than enough household staff to take care of him and Mhaybelle, I was not needed at that part of the trip any more.

And so I was back here in Singapore, ensconced in this icy taxi and speeding towards the indefatigable neighbourhood of Serangoon, where I've been sharing a wonderful little flat for more than two years now with Nhi Tran, my housemate-turned-best friend who was probably the most patient, understanding and fun housemate one could find.

I just needed to leave my suitcase at the flat, take a quick shower (I was an expert at that), grab a quick *kopi* from the coffee stall downstairs, and head to the Isle Z office. I had sort of passed out in the flight, eating a little and then sleeping the rest of the hours, and so I actually woke up feeling strangely refreshed. Thank goodness for that. For some funny reason in our line of work, jetlag just wasn't an excuse.

* * *

'Hey, Superstar! You're back!'

A smooth, assured voice wafted out from one of the chicly-decorated corners of Isle Z, just as I slipped out of the private elevators—lifts—and into the modern interiors of our office. It was five minutes before 10 o'clock, and the Isle Z office was looking calm and sleek as usual, with soft music playing from hidden speakers, bouncing softly on the glass walls, and the soft beige carpeted floors. Plants peppered our office's corners—peppy monsteras and leafy calatheas, hardy pothos, philodendron imperial reds, and a teenage rubber tree that I was fond of checking up on whenever I was there. There was even a green wall on one side. The coolness was a welcome change from the sticky humidity of Tanjong Pagar's streets, where Isle Z's office had been located for the past five years.

Without turning my head, I knew that that voice belonged to Oliver Liu, one of my two bosses at Isle Z. My other boss was Desmond Chan, Oliver's business partner, who started the company five years ago. Desmond, whose fortieth birthday party early this year was held at the Isle Z office itself—he surprised the staff with a fun, Mexican-themed bash complete with twelve different taco flavours and at least two piñatas—was actually, hardly seen in the office. Desmond, who was genial to everyone but definitely much quieter than Oliver, kept mostly to himself and his laptop inside his office. And except for our weekly Tuesday meetings with the rest of the travel managers, Desmond himself was often out at meetings and networking with potential clients.

Oliver came to Isle Z one year after Desmond established it, and the staff who'd been there from the start often spoke about how the small, boutique company really took off after that. There was a certain energy to Oliver, and not just because he was only in his mid-thirties and physically fit. I've always thought that Oliver was the epitome of confidence and smartness, with his excellent posture, a ready smile, and a shock of hair that had a bit of salt and pepper on it at the temples. Poised, too—that is when he wasn't teasing you or saying something outrageously funny about something. He was always dressed, alternatively, in crisp white shirts, or in sharp suits paired with the narrowest slacks I've ever seen, in varying shades of grey. Or black, when he was feeling bored. He was fond of hanging around the reception area, usually with that day's *Straits Times*—he was old school that way, which I found amusing—folded and tucked under an arm. Some days, he had his iPad opened to a page of *Luxe Journeys*, his favourite insider travel trader's magazine.

'Yup, I'm back,' I said. 'Turban Girl—I mean, Mhaybelle did it again.' I threw my hands in the air in mock-weariness.

I watched Oliver's grin grow even wider. 'Aha!' He said, eyes crinkling up at the corners. 'The alluring Mhaybelle has charmed you again.'

I must have sounded a little whiny, perhaps even curt, because Oliver gave a tiny but audible cluck of his tongue. 'Well, now,' he said, in that familiar teasing voice, eyes meeting mine as he flashed a smile. 'Good morning, Superstar!'

'Morning, Oliver.' I couldn't help but chuckle. I raised my eyebrows at him. 'This is becoming a habit, I see. Looks like you're not giving up on this nickname.'

'You bet I'm not.'

I was comfortable with Oliver. I admit, I could still get shy with some of the people at the office, but I wasn't with him. It was the constant travel, I knew, that slowed down my relationships at the office—something that I had always wanted to remedy but hadn't gotten around to. In the more than two years that I've been with Isle Z, I found myself travelling more and more, sometimes with less than twenty-four hours in between, i.e., arriving from hot, T-shirt-weather Bali at noon, then packing thick, heavy winter thermals and clothes for a 9 p.m. flight to London that same evening. I never missed a flight, but I certainly missed office nights out—even the official ones—and themed parties, where partying with the staff and the bosses just meant that you could let loose a little, and that would be okay.

What this really meant was that thanks to technology—emails, video call meetings, WhatsApp group meetings, or even old-fashioned notes left at my desk—I had an efficient working relationship with my colleagues but had never had enough time to personally bond with them. It still made me a little sad to think that I've missed the company's yearly trip twice, the latest of which was in Seoul, South Korea just a few months ago. At that time, I was with a group of other travel agents from Asia, on a familiarization trip to an obscure beach town at the edge of Slovenia called Piran.

It was Oliver who had hired me, and maybe that had something to do with it, because he knew me right from the start of my stay here in Singapore. It certainly helped that I found him to be one of those calm, charismatic people with the rare ability to put others at ease, simply by their presence.

And so surprisingly, I had grown comfortable enough with Oliver to dispel with the usual niceties; I also knew him well enough to know that he loved being dished the most hilarious, outrageous parts of the trip first. The serious reports, he often said, can be reserved for the weekly conference room meetings.

So except for the new nickname I've given Mhaybelle, Oliver knew all about the Mhaybelle-Damon Loh saga. Actually, thanks to melodramatic visits at the office usually initiated and led by Mhaybelle, the whole of Isle Z was quite familiar with this mismatched couple.

'Ah, yes, you were with the alluring Mhaybelle,' Oliver was saying now. He pronounced the name as 'Mah-haybelle.'

'Selfie galore, as per usual, and this time, a midnight trip to one of the Icelandic falls,' I said, walking towards the direction of my desk.

'Predictable, and completely normal nowadays,' Oliver said, not unkindly. 'That's what all first-timers in Iceland want. Except that Damon has featured Reykjavik and Greenland a couple of times already. So this thing with Mhaybelle must be special. What do you think?'

I loosened, a little. Oliver, ever charming yet obviously well-informed, had this effect on people. 'No, I meant we went behind the waterfall,' I glanced at him, feeling my lips shaping into a small smile, despite myself. 'Behind. Seljalandsfoss. At midnight. In the dark!'

Oliver stared at me for a moment, eyes widening. 'Oh, I see!' He started laughing, that deep belly laugh he was so known for. 'You do have the best clients, Superstar!' He shook his head, looking gleeful.

I gave a grunt. 'I do, I do, *I do!*' It was funny, now that it was all over and I wasn't groping in the icy darkness any more.

'Well, then.' Oliver turned serious, drawing in a sharp breath. 'I'm glad to get you here in one piece. Be careful out there.'

I shook my head. 'Don't worry about me,' I said, waving a hand. 'This is just the kind of work that keeps me alive.' I meant it, and I was grateful. This job has given me the opportunity to start fresh somehow, and the chance to be somewhere else other than in a place that had, at that time, been too painful for me to be in. I had always believed that it was this job at Isle Z that had kept me, all these months, from spiralling into someone I wouldn't like or even recognize. This job meant so much to me, had done so much for me. I wasn't about to let anyone down.

When I turned, Oliver was looking at his phone. 'Look,' he said. 'Her numbers are up.' Oliver waved his mobile, then tapped the newspaper on his hand. 'I'm not sure if it's me getting old, but I believe our dear Mhaybelle has been using the wrong hashtag.'

'What? Let me see that.' I fumbled for my phone and opened Mhaybelle's Instagram account, @mhayluvinit. She's gained more than four thousand followers in the past week, a substantial boost that may just have been brought in simply by her association with Damon Loh. There were loads of Iceland photos on her feed, but when I clicked on the latest one, it said #travelsbyIleZ.

'Just a harmless typo.' Oliver sounded amused.

'On all fifteen photos of Iceland.' I muttered. 'I'll ask her to edit it.'

'I knew it wasn't just my failing eyesight,' Oliver said. 'Well, Superstar, you'll just have to forgive this old guy.'

'Oliver. You're funny.' I gave him a look. 'Stop that. It's my bad. Desmond?'

He shook his head. 'No big deal. Desmond is cool. Just keep doing what you're doing.'

The thing was, I wouldn't really call Oliver my mentor. Being sort of an introvert, I had set out to do things by myself, to learn, discover and experience my field of work as it came. Moreover, I didn't enter my field expecting one. No, Oliver felt like a wise old teacher who wasn't in your class, but who looked out for you. Also, Oliver's family owned a tea shop in Chinatown where I bought all my tea.

* * *

The first time I met Oliver was at my job interview. It was not my first time in Singapore, but it had felt different and new the moment I walked into the stylish, compact offices of Isle Z, with its steel beams and glass rooms, black-and-white travel photographs lining its walls, and an unmissable bonsai collection displayed on its own separate table beside reception—not to mention the elegant, graceful Isle Z people who seemingly glided about, speaking in low, even voices. It was a completely new environment where I'd dared to feel I can actually hope for a new start, at a time when I had been feeling hopeless.

Both of Isle Z directors will be interviewing me, Tammy Paul, Isle Z's head receptionist, said. I found Oliver and Desmond in one of the glass-walled conference rooms, looking like a pair of wealthy brothers discussing golf strategies along with their business marketing plan. They had looked me in the eye, enumerated the nitty-gritty of the job, and then proceeded to tell me the perks, the growth, and the irresistible potential of working for this boutique travel company.

A travel manager, they said. That was what they needed. Someone who would create very special, even unusual itineraries for some very discerning people. 'And for some very interesting people, too,' Oliver had said, the narrowness of his eyes softened by the very warm, perennially-amused smile on his lips. They needed someone who would do extensive research to come up with unique, unexpected, and sometimes, very discreet itineraries for high profile people. Someone who could be discreet herself. Someone who was comfortable not only with tailor-made programmes but sudden changes and shifts.

Oliver and Desmond had asked me questions. All had revolved around my knowledge of travel, asking for insights and experiences that I'd apply to different destinations and itineraries to make a trip stand out. And then they had really listened to what I had done in the past, and what I had to say. It was refreshing.

And what I had to say was that I had been through something sad, but I was so ready for this job.

I was hired. There was a flurry of preparations from Manila to Singapore, paperwork to be done, and long lines to stand in. But I welcomed the busyness of it all.

It had not been my intention to leave my home country, but I'd discovered that I could. I had discovered, at that time, that it was only space and time away from Manila—the scene of my grief—that could save me.

Chapter 3

Singapore, 9.30 a.m. How, really, did it all start? If I could pinpoint two things that helped jumpstart and define the kind of work I do now, it would be first, the Philippines' most popular, most-watched *telenovela* actress, Maja Montenegro—star of the chart-topping primetime drama *You're My One and All*—and second, Europe's notoriously-celebrated and equally deplored summer vacation in the months of July and August.

I had been going about my job as per usual—booking clients, researching a destination's newest offerings, and keeping up-to-date with a city's latest luxury experiences. I proposed one-of-a-kind activities or mixed high and low off-the-beaten-path tours, then emailed suppliers and vendors, asking them if they could work with what I've conceptualized. I met with all kinds of travellers who've chosen Isle Z and briefed them on their trip itineraries.

It was Desmond, Oliver's business partner and my other boss, who'd passed Maja's contact details to me. Being from the Philippines, I knew about her, of course. Who didn't?

Filipino soap operas were so intensely loved and ardently followed, you'd most likely catch parts of the previous night's episode being discussed here and there—from the security guards at the mall's entrance to the busiest lunch crowds in Manila's CBD. And *You're My One and All*, which had been running five days a week for close to two years, had so captured the hearts of Filipino viewers that it catapulted Maja Montenegro from a teenybopper minor TV star who couldn't even stand out among her group of young wannabees—to a serious, award-winning actress capable of mature roles and holding her own as a household name in the Philippines. Why, you couldn't pass through EDSA, the city's main thoroughfare, without seeing Maja's face plastered on a billboard showing off a local toothpaste brand's bright, toothy smile or lounging languidly on a cozy sofa, exulting the perks of a luxury condo project.

Maja's schedule had suddenly opened up, Desmond said, after an early wrap-up of the wildly popular telenovela. Her manager had gotten in touch with Isle Z, saying that Maja was to start filming a movie for three weeks in Dubai after August, so this was her only time to get away. But it was Oliver—who as usual, had his ear on the ground and tended to sniff out some insider intel—who had told me that it was Maja herself who had demanded for this vacation to happen and that if she didn't get this particular time off with her family in her destination of choice, she would make it very, very hard for the directors of the show. I didn't want to get into the details.

Yes, Maja wanted to bring her whole family with her. She'd been linked to countless men, most of them, it was often reported, wanting to ride on her current popularity.

No, Maja wasn't committed to anyone at all except Josh Alvan Garcia, her love team onscreen. And if there was another distinct thing about her, it was that she was always surrounded by her parents and a sibling or two on set, even in far-flung places and at hard-to-access filming locations. Guesting stints at noon time shows or FAMAS and Gawad Urian awards night always had the cameras pan on Mr and Mrs Montenegro, neat and smiling and dressed in their Sunday's best, at the front row of the audience. And so, it need not be said that if her family was keen on a full-blown holiday at the Amalfi Coast at the height of the European summer season—then Maja was, too. 'One for all and all for one!' was Mr Montenegro's favourite phrase, whenever TV reporters had the bad luck of missing Maja during press briefings and were left with him as he straggled behind his daughter's extremely efficient entourage. Filipino viewers loved it.

Pressured by tapings and by the upcoming filming schedule in Dubai, Maja and the Montenegro family had wanted to leave as soon as possible, but were also looking for a memorable family holiday, a private Italian vacation for the books. Could Isle Z organize a complete Amalfi Coast holiday—a full Italian experience, the whole caboodle complete with a grand villa, meals at the best and most popular restaurants, a stylized photo shoot with a local photographer in front of the hillside houses of Positano (Maja's special request, and to be released long after her vacation is over) and a slew of city and out-of-town tours like a visit to Pompeii, a cruise to Capri, and scenic cocktails in the hillside villages of Ravello—for seven people?

Sure, I had thought at that time, clicking languidly and scrolling through Desmond's email brief about Maja's holiday. Though I knew I worked best with small groups, solo travellers, or couples, organizing trips for a large family didn't really faze me. Comprehensive, unique, luxe experiences were the sort of job that Isle Z was known for.

I skimmed through the email again before clicking on the attachment, a hasty snap of a handwritten list by Maja of her Italian holiday must-dos—an authentic pizza lunch at Naples, a day tour at Amalfi town, at least two church visits, and the aforementioned shoot in Positano.

The usual. I felt my shoulders relax, my tongue suddenly craving for a drop of hot, ripe *pu ehr* tea, the deep brown liquid soothing my insides as it always does. Tea time, I thought as I extricated myself from my chair, already thinking of the pot of fragrant loose leaves I'd be brewing at the office pantry, where Oliver and I kept our Yixing teapots, along with a box of our tea caddies, measuring spoons, tea dispensers, and spatulas and other tea paraphernalia. My mind was clicking into gear but still relaxed as I thought of large hotels and group activities for the Montenegro family in Italy.

I was about to dash off in the direction of the pantry at the back when a sentence towards the end of Desmond's email caught my eye.

No. I stood in front of my laptop, my hand gripping the back of my seat, feeling my stomach seize.

I was to organize a ten-day trip to Italy's most popular, most crowded summer spot for seven people in . . . five days.

Five days.

I looked at my calendar. It was a Tuesday. Yes, *Tuesday,* I remembered saying to myself in slow-mo, as if underwater. The Montenegro family wanted to leave on *Sunday.*

My head swam.

My first instinct was to say no. Shoot an email to Desmond saying it wasn't possible. Or if pushed, quality would suffer—I'd most likely give them overpriced hotels and crappy tour deals, not the unique, special family experiences they'd been dreaming about. It was already in the middle of summer when crowds were at its peak. I knew from experience that tours, Michelin-star restaurants, villas, and hotels were booked solid.

And yet that day, I brewed my special pot of *pu ehr,* the one that had been fermented since 2006 and recommended by the tea uncles at Wellington Tea in Chinatown, which was actually owned by Oliver's family. I went back to my desk, charged my phone, ordered *siu mai* and congee from my favourite dim sum place, and got to work.

I didn't stop until four days later, when I'd secured not a villa, but a small palazzo for the Montenegro family to stay in. The owners were Italian, but due to a sudden lack of funds, were desperate to rent it out. Nope, I didn't stop until I'd managed to arrange not just a unique cave tour, but a one-of-a-kind dinner and degustation inside a cave made magical with hundreds of tiny lights and crystal chandeliers among an already dramatic backdrop of stalagmites and stalactites. I didn't stop until I'd booked the whole family to listen to Mass at an ancient rock church that looked, yes, just like a magnificently gigantic rock jutting out on top of a hill. After Mass, I'd scheduled for them all to try their hand at making and baking the local *pane* and *focaccia,* and sampling even more local delicacies at the open-air courtyard of only the best-known bakery in town.

It was the perfect Italian holiday for the Montenegros, one that I was sure Maja Montenegro and her kin would love. There was, however, one catch—or should I say a blessing?

It was not in Positano, Italy.

Nope, it wasn't in that beautiful, postcard-perfect yet crowded, over-touristic destination that was overrun, yearly, every summer in July and August by both local and international tourists. All these lovely activities were not to take place there at all. It was, instead, all about to happen on the other side of the Italian map, almost 300 kilometres from Positano, directly east of the Amalfi Coast.

I had booked La Familia Montenegro in Matera, Italy.

Yes, that's right. When I realized that there was no way I could get through the thick holiday crowd in Positano, I decided to shift gears. I emailed my Italian as well as my Asian contacts who were already there, asking about the density of the crowds. They all emailed back with their own version of a single answer—it's hellish. There were day-trippers, cruise ship passengers, home-sharing tourists, as well as influencers and backpackers all wanting a piece of that space. Go to the cities, they said, there are fewer people there. That's just because most of the locals have fled the confines of their own cities to bask in the sun of the provinces.

They were right, of course. A quick check on Instagram revealed candid snaps of crowded monuments, shoulder-to-shoulder crowds, and bunches of people seemingly on top of one another. The beach, even with its colourful summer umbrellas lined up, was swarming with swimmers and sunbathers.

Thinking quickly, I realized that if I wanted to give Maja and the rest of the Montenegro family an unforgettable Italian holiday, then I should just suggest a new destination. I rifled through my old clippings and folders, Googled and read travel blogs on Western Europe—and found Matera, Italy.

After a quick exchange with Maja's personal assistant, who assured me that she'd taken up my suggestion to the actress and her family, plus showed them Instagram pics of Matera and the rest of Puglia, I was given the go signal.

Matera, the third oldest city in the world after Aleppo and Jericho, was a city two hours from Bari, in northern Italy, and had views just as arresting as Positano. Sure, it was considered the shame of Italy in the 1950s, but now it was teeming with cool apartments, award-winning boutique hotels, quaint shops, contemporary museums all built in the natural cave dwellings. It was also near Alberobello, known for its series of white structure dwellings with conical roofs, which I knew Maja would want to use as yet another backdrop for her photoshoot. I even found a dashing Italian photographer who specialized in portraits, to shoot her photographs.

It wasn't that uncrowded. But aside from the dinner inside a cave experience, I had also managed to book them a table at La Nonna to fulfill their Michelin star resto longings. And La Nonna does serve the most sublime pesto pasta and osso buco, according to *Luxurious Magazine*, *Epicure*, *Gourmet*, and *The New York Times*.

Never mind that I hardly slept for three days, as I needed to be on standby in case my Italian contact called, emailed, or FaceTimed. It was a mix of luck, endless hours of texting, calling, and group conferencing on WhatsApp, the internet and yes, said lack of sleep.

In the end it had been worth it. So worth it because Maja Montenegro had *raved* about it. She said it was magical and unforgettable and had been the best quality time she'd had with her family—with the best photos of her life, to boot. Can you imagine that this was the set for the filming of *No Time to Die*? She had not resisted posting on her Instagram account. In fact, she'd gone by herself to the neighbouring towns, and did a whole 'Travel with Maja' kind of thing in her Instagram Stories. An online celebrity magazine had even picked up the story, and then another. Less than forty-eight hours after the Montenegro family landed at Manila's NAIA airport, Maja's Matera photos were splashed all over the internet.

Of course, Maja and her family couldn't stop talking— to reporters, to TV hosts, to online magazines, to Oliver and Desmond—about how organized the trip was, how the palazzo was everything they expected, how the guides I chose to bring them around understood what they wanted, and how the restaurants were so on point, how the caves were wondrous and blew them away. They loved the fact that I was also a Filipino and spoke of how our Italian counterparts were saying that I was a breeze to work with. Maja's Instagram, Facebook and Tiktok were all bursting with content on her Italian trip, tagging Isle Z in almost all posts. And she actually took the time to send a series of glowing thank you emails to Oliver, promising even to send in a flurry of recommendations to her friends and colleagues in showbiz.

This was how we ended up deluged with clients the next summer, to my bosses' delight.

Shortly after a brief meeting with Maja, Oliver sent me a one-liner email: 'Fantastic work, Arya. You're a Superstar!'

It was the first time I was called that actually, that I blushed even while I was reading the email at my desk.

After that, we got hired by Daisy Marie Santos, another *telenovela* actress who'd heard of Isle Z through Maja. This time, however, she was travelling solo to the Isle of Skye and the rest of the Scottish Highlands, and had a personal request: she wanted that I go with her on the trip. She was willing to pay for my airfare, all my expenses, and an extra booking fee to Isle Z—and volunteered to do several mentions on her social media accounts.

I was bewildered at first, really. And a little shocked, of course. I wasn't sure about Isle Z's previous policies, but it was the first time in a long time that a client had requested that a travel manager actually go with them. It had all sounded so strange to me at that time, but I soon realized that it was just the sort of thing a boutique agency like Isle Z would do—this was exactly what a tailor-made, highly-customized itinerary was made of. Most importantly, this was what made companies like Isle Z brave, imaginative, and even innovative in their own way. This was what made Isle Z stand out from the rest.

And then I found myself a little sad for Daisy Marie Santos, who felt she couldn't travel solo; I had done it so many times before, albeit to different destinations. Daisy Marie was known mostly for her rich-girl roles in her TV series but was one of those actresses whom celebrity rags lauded and whose fans, when interviewed, had always supported and praised, referring to Daisy Marie as incredibly down-to-earth, real, and relatable.

Perhaps I had expected that she would be brave enough to go on her own, that was the first issue. Second of all, me? Doing the thing I've been trying to avoid all this time? Sure, I now knew that I could organize and mobilize, free-up cave restaurants and secure little-known palazzos, and generally make things move thanks to the power of email, WhatsApp and all apps and the internet, from the safety of my desk. In between was when I struggled and attempted to deal with my own baggage: trying to (and maybe still failing) get over a break-up, still smarting from my heartbreak, still trying to prove to myself and to my company that I was good enough.

And also, did I really want to be sort of stuck with a complete stranger 24/7 and for *days* wandering about in a city or a place that was completely new to both of us?

To this day, I still don't know what made me do it. It was tempting to say that I had no choice since it was all part of my job at Isle Z. But if you really came down to it, I *did* have a choice—most everyone did. And I said yes. Yes to customizing, organizing, and executing the whole trip, and yes to accompanying Daisy Marie Santos as she lived out her dream of exploring the Scottish Highlands. I got myself and my travel skills together and created a tailor-made itinerary for us that included detailed drives to the Scottish lochs, a luxe excursion to the secret fairy pools at the foot of the Cuillin mountains, a special whisky-tasting at the Talisker and Torabhaig distilleries as well as an exclusive tour to a small, upscale Gaelic whisky distillery, and even a brief art and photography session to catch that famous Scottish light that fell on the mountains at a certain hour. In Glasgow, I'd arranged for us to attend a tiny, exclusive concert by Churches, Scotland's freshest and most famous band, a night out at a super secret club that needed a password at the door, as well as an Art Deco tour and a haggis dinner (which wasn't in the menu at that time) at The Mysterious Pompadour, Edinburgh's best and most expensive restaurant that had a waiting list of two months. I went all out.

Back in Singapore and the Philippines, I wasn't surprised that Daisy Marie Santos immediately told my bosses that her 'solo' trip with Arya Alvarez was the best she'd ever had.

Clients started requesting for me to go with them on their trips after that. It started as a trickle—one or two who were eager to go where no one else had really gone, i.e., to super unexpected and underrated cities and destinations—and yet needed some handholding while there. I actually began to appreciate clients like these: those who wanted something completely different, far from the usual, and who didn't just choose to go on the tried-and-tested route. As part of the travel industry, I appreciated clients who preferred thinking and travelling out of the box.

Apparently, the trend was ditching your own personal assistant—one who had too much at stake and baggage to be much fun and laidback on the trip—and jet off with some stranger (me) at their beck and call.

Chapter 4

Singapore, 11.01 a.m. Du Coup were having a fight. Let me be clear that what was happening right this very minute was a real fight, as hard a fight you can get while—well, while on a video call. Du Coup were thousands of miles away from each other, and from me. But oh, this fight was happening. It was happening right here in my office.

There wasn't a physical scuffle; no one, thank God, was about to be punched in the face because that—and thank goodness, again—just wasn't possible on video. But there were expletives being hurled, clashing in the air like invisible missiles. There were random shrieks of rage (Leia) in between hoarse, lamenting crying jags (Donovan). There was a slew of nasty name-calling, some of which actually made me blush.

What or who on earth, you ask, is Du Coup, anyway? And why are they capable of fighting this way?

I was in-between trips. I was in the middle of what I thought was a benign video call to talk about possible travel destinations with Donovan Tsui and Leia Namohaji, an influencer travel couple best known in social media circles as Du Coup of the Instagram account @iheartducoup. Here was where they appeared, almost daily, in some new beautiful destination as the backdrop, and as surreal as their toned bodies, which always seemed to look effortless. Even with just 725K followers on Instagram, they still were voted this year's 'Best Travel Couple to Follow' by the award-giving media outfit Influencers Inc. Donovan and Leia, both French-Indonesians, met while studying at the Sorbonne University, moved back to Jakarta, and only last year decided to start a couple travel account on IG, joining the thousands of other couples who've decided to try and create an IG feed filled with incredible, unreal photos, videos and reels of the places they love, making money from all that in the process. Right from the start, Du Coup had a signature style when shooting their photos: the images of Donovan and Leia, almost always skimpily clad, draped languidly against each other for a kiss or a provocative hug, were best described as hot, sexy, romantic, and adventurous. They were photos that would provoke you to say, 'Get a room!' But not really—because who wouldn't want to see this gorgeous couple be hot and happy out here in the open?

Du Coup's motto? 'Love travel, so travel with love.'

I had yet to scrutinize the grammar integrity of this sentence, but that would take time and energy—both of which I was certain I didn't have at that moment. It could be funny if only it wasn't so noisy at this very moment, because there definitely was no love going on in here. I winced as I heard another expletive blast from the invisible speakers of my laptop, sharp like a dry twig being snapped into two. I wondered why they just didn't sign off. We could have this meeting next time. When no one wanted to kill another person.

Earlier, while waiting for the video meeting to start, I passed the time by scrolling through @iheartducoup on Instagram. There were three pinned posts at the top of their IG feed—kissing against a backdrop of misty mountains, turquoise waters of a lake, and immodestly green lush jungles. The third one was a drone shot of them spooning on the beige sand, the waters of the sea enveloping them from the waist down as if one wide, beautiful azure blanket. The rest of the posts were more of the same, alternating between photos, long reels and short reels—but always, always of Donovan and Leia locked in an embrace, or cutely spitting water on one another in an outdoor shower, or just Leia draped lazily on top of Donovan on a hammock overlooking what looks like a fairytale forest below.

I had actually gone to work today thinking, another day, another client. Or perhaps it would now be more apt to say, another influencer. Or worse, another fight. Because this had not been the first time I'd been caught in the Du Coup crossfire.

As I said, Du Coup had a current following of 725K. Not bad in my opinion, but who I was to say these things? More than two years ago, I had abandoned and deleted all my social media accounts—Instagram, Facebook, Twitter, and even Snapchat, and whatever half-hearted, candid videos I'd begun posting on YouTube. It wasn't because I completely shunned social media; back in Manila, where, as anywhere, everyone seemed to be living their lives online, I actually enjoyed posting about *me* and bits and pieces of my life. It was where I got clients, too, for the travel agency business that I had started there. And there lies the problem: I deleted all my social media accounts precisely because I had started them all in Manila, and they contained all the posts, photos, comments, and saved articles that painfully reminded me of where I was before—my old life, my past life with Jake.

It was only a few weeks after I'd moved to Singapore and only when I had started securing clients for Isle Z that I reluctantly opened a new Facebook and Instagram account as a research tool for the destinations and bespoke tours I'd wanted to create and offer to them. In contrast to my growing list of wanderlust celebrities and influencers, I only had less than a thousand followers on Instagram, and not a lot more on the rest of my socials. Sure, I'd posted some things out there, views of destinations I found interesting, close-ups and wide shots of possible journeys, and teasing (but not really good) food shots. I had photos and posts that weren't curated at all, but they were careful. Mainly I was careful not to post anything that reminded me of the mess I'd left behind, and of the heartbreak that I was still feeling now. Photos of random things I saw during my trips, some of myself, posing against the view of the mountains in Jungfraujoch in the Swiss Alps, for example, or pretend-sitting on boulder-sized ice on the beach in Jökulsárlón in Iceland. A shot of me in a swimsuit on the shores of a resort town called Limassol in Cyprus that I had liked, just because it looked sunny and the loungers looked a tad haphazard. There was no trace of the sadness I had felt that tended to come and go, even while I was on these trips, even when I was thousands of miles away from Manila, from Singapore. And this is probably why I had chosen these photos and wrote those little posts, precisely, because they were ordinary and everyday; one who'd care to look at my feed would only think that I was just a travel manager who planned interesting itineraries. Not someone who was still reeling from the disappointing events of her life, someone actually desperate to move on, but couldn't.

Enough of that for now, Arya. I thought, catching myself just in time. There was something more explosive going on at the moment, one that didn't involve me for once. And I wasn't liking it—online and in person. Donovan and Leia's angry voices reeled me back into what was going on at the video call on my laptop.

Donovan: 'You have cellulite on your butt. Faker.'

Leia: 'Better than being a dirty alcoholic.'

Donovan: 'If our followers only knew you pay someone to Photoshop your face.'

Leia: 'I'll tell them you like boys.'

Donovan (screams): 'You lying bitch!'

I stared at both of them, looking like caricatures on my screen. But it was very real and it had been going on like this since we've all met up on this group meeting online. And it was getting worse every minute, the accusations getting meaner and sounding more ridiculous. I felt an unhappy flash welling up inside my chest, my breathing getting rapid and slow. *Why didn't they just split,* I thought, *once and for all?* Clearly, this wasn't working. Clearly, they were not the best fit for each other, despite all these romantic, provocative photos.

Also, witnessing a fight this close made me think of the fight I had with Jake, which was the last time I saw him. I couldn't do this. I took a deep breath.

'Guys. Guys! Calm down, please!' I broke in, leaning towards the screen as if that would help me make sense of all this. 'Listen, do you want to do this another time? We can meet next week.'

I saw Leia's eyes widen and Donovan suck air through his mouth, revealing cheekbones that can cut—before two people started talking, loudly, at once. They were at it again.

'Hello! Excuse me!' My voice echoed in my small office and sounded terrifying, even to me. I hung my head and closed my eyes, but kept my voice loud. 'Guys! I am going to end this meeting! I will set another schedule—'

I paused. Something had shifted. Because suddenly, all I could hear was . . . nothing. I opened my eyes.

I hadn't gone deaf. There on my screen were Donovan and Leia, still sitting in their spots—Donovan fidgeting and squirming in his seat, looking everywhere except at me, Leia sitting still, blinking and biting furiously at her nails. They were still there, but they weren't speaking—no, they weren't *fighting* any more.

'Arya,' Leia began, her voice syrupy yet controlled. 'What we really want is to up our IG followers.'

I blinked. Slowly, I straightened up and flicked a stray hair from my face. 'Okay,' I said, still a little dazed. This was not what I had expected to hear, but it got them to stop yelling.

'Leia and I believe that we should do a couple more 'out-of-this world' photos,' Donovan said, as I stared, still trying to process what had happened. He cleared his throat. 'I mean, we have to try harder on making the photos look spectacular. More outrageous. That should do the trick,' he added.

'We've behaved. We just want our numbers up,' Leia said. 'We can do it, even if some of us here can just act like assholes.'

I could see Donovan leaning towards the camera, opening his mouth as if to say something only to close it again as he fell back on his chair.

I sat up straight in my chair, only to feel myself softening once more against the backrest. This was a tall order, even for them. I wasn't an influencer or anything close, nor did I really know exactly how influencers like Leia and Donovan can gain so many followers and earn money from their social media feeds. What I know, from the steady communication and the regular meetings we've had, fighting or not, is that they've worked hard to gain a following for almost two years. And when I met Du Coup, at one of the familiarization tours in Sicily where the couple had managed to wrangle a collaboration in exchange for exposure, they had only reached a half-million followers. The numbers have been steadily climbing since, and that was when they had the wise idea of contacting Isle Z for a more streamlined, yet more focus on unique, bespoke luxury travel.

'All right,' I said, relief evident in my voice. 'Let's get to work. How about the Balkans?' I checked the notes I'd scrawled on a small, grid notepad, the kind I've begun to like since moving to Singapore. It was a far cry from the thick, blank notebooks I kept by my desk in Manila, filled with my usual travel and client notes—but also little scrawls and drawings of stuff related to Jake and me: baseball caps, his ring, the shape of his lips. Yes, I had made sure that even the way I've kept notes and information had changed; I desperately needed it to. I didn't want a reminder. I wanted zero contact.

'The Balkans?' Leia repeated, the apples of her cheeks looking peachy-rosy and her chin appearing so defined and pointy, I wondered if she had a filter installed in her laptop. Wait, was that even possible with laptops? That was the sort of thing this couple would do, but would do so subtly and with such attuned deftness, you'd never know which parts of their photos were real or not. 'Arya, tell us more. Where, exactly should we go?'

'I was thinking Bosnia and Herzegovina.' My tone sounded clear, confident even to my own ears, and for a split-second, I marvelled at how I've wanted to grow into this kind of person, who had grappled with grief of this kind and moved on—well, *trying* to move—to do better things. How I've wanted to be that person who saw beyond herself to help other people. I didn't feel that I was this person yet.

And then that thought was replaced as quickly as it had come. There was work to do. And I had just come from a familiarization tour of the Balkans myself at the start of the year, organized by Tourism BIH, a large group of entrepreneurs and tourism professionals in the Balkan countries in Eastern Europe that specialized in cultural and natural heritage tours. Tourism BIH had been generous and extremely friendly, but thorough. They had been a truly hardworking bunch who urged all of us twelve travel agents from Asia to experience the most luxurious offerings of their cities as much as the grittiest, most emotionally-jarring spaces of their countries. We had clambered up old fortresses and sailed to the many picturesque islands of Kotor, Montenegro, and peered at underground bunkers that were five storeys deep in Tirana, Albania. And then they brought us to Bosnia and Herzegovina. What had resonated with me the most were the stories of the Bosnians.

'We survived hell but we hate no one,' said one of our Bosnian guides, Enes, when we met him in Sarajevo. He told us that when he was seven years old, his mother instructed him to not wear red to avoid being shot by snipers during the war in 1992.

I didn't share this story with the Du Coup couple. Instead, I told them that maybe what their followers were looking for were photos of peace. 'Something that showed tranquility, a new kind of peace descending on you both. Perhaps that bridge at Mostar? And there's also Blagaj, a monastery.'

'Oh.' Donovan didn't try to hide his disappointment. 'What's to see in that kind of place? A monastery? Isn't that kind of wholesome?'

'Yeah, I mean, can we even have our signature kissing photos there?' Leia piped up.

'Oh no, it's not that kind of monastery,' I said, immediately thinking that I shouldn't even have used that word. I reached for my phone and scrolled furiously until I found photos of the last time, I was there on that fam tour. 'Look,' I typed in, attaching the photos I've taken. It was there instantly.

'Oh,' Donovan said, at the same time that I heard an audible gasp from Leia. It was several photos of the spring at Blagaj, right where the monastery was built, surrounded by a dramatic wall of limestone.

'Is the water really that blue? Or is it turquoise?' Leia was peering at the photo on her screen. 'I mean, is that even real?'

'Where exactly is this?' Donovan's face lit up, and you could tell he was already working something out in his influencer brain. 'We can drive here, 'no? Or is there an airport nearby? Do we need a guide?'

'Definitely a kissing photo here, babe,' Leia cooed as if no shouting had happened in the last hour.

'Most definitely, babe.' Donovan's voice had slid into something suave and in control. There was none of the combative edge that had accompanied his tone since the start of that morning's meeting. 'Let's take wide shots and close-ups, with you maybe in a long, white dress. Or you and me, in same-coloured outfits.'

I used to wonder sometimes why they didn't just hire a social media manager if they were having so much trouble getting along. Yet listening to Du Coup now, it almost felt as if they had never needed anything except their own ideas and just the right amount of vanity, style, and self-absorption to grow their following. I certainly wasn't a digital marketing expert. I wasn't a social media or digital anything, actually. The last time I checked my IG feed—two days ago, to be exact, and an eternity perhaps to any influencer—I had a little more than eight hundred followers. And I mean eight hundred, not eight hundred *thousand*.

No, my specialty was scouting out destinations for that unique experience you never knew you needed, but which just might change your life—or at least, give you a brand-new perspective in life.

Chapter 5

Da Nang, Vietnam, 1.30 p.m. My stay in Singapore was brief. After updating Oliver and the rest about Damon Loh's Iceland trip, handling clients from the office like Du Coup, and completing several other trip reports, I had to fly off again after four days for another work trip—and another round of client hand-holding.

Luckily, this trip was a mere two-hour flight from Singapore. It was in the city of Da Nang, Vietnam where another of Isle Z's clients, a celebrity couple, wanted the local experience—in a fabulously first-class way.

Japanese-Irish model slash budding recording artist slash Asian 'It' girl Rooki Sakimoto and her boyfriend, Daniel, have always been fans of Vietnam, having already spent some time in the capital city of Hanoi, as well as Ninh Binh and Sapa further north, just two years ago. It was in Hanoi, Rooki told me, where they had such a grand time clubbing—yes, clubbing, and then taking impromptu cooking lessons, zipping around the city in a rented motorbike and feasting, in her own words, on the best 'amazing green thingy-coloured veggie balls wrapped in lettuce leaves sold by an old lady in a street corner'.

Rooki was just starting out as a model then, and spent three weeks in Vietnam doing several editorials for *Harper's Bazaar* Vietnam and Singapore, as well as a couple of local print ads. Fast forward to now—on top of Rooki's growing number of both print and online magazine covers, ads, brand endorsements, and editorial spreads—she's amassed a whopping three million followers on Instagram, and roughly, just a little less across all her social media channels.

That wasn't all. In one talk show, she was also discovered to have a powerful singing voice, thanks to an impromptu jamming session with the show's other guests who were members of T2, a K-pop boy band that had been that year's breakout hit. Her manager immediately set her up with a recording studio, and in less than a year's time, there she was, promoting her first album, *The Real Rooki*.

This year, Rooki had another cause to celebrate: she had just been chosen to be the main host of Models Asia, Inc., the newest model reality show, 'a la Asia's Top Model'. This spawned a brand-new flurry of print and TV interviews, editorial shoots, magazine covers, TV guestings, and even a cameo role in an upcoming film.

But Rooki was also exhausted. She wanted a break. For the first time in years, she wanted to be away from the crowds, not facing them. There was the option of going back home to Dublin, Ireland where most of her family lived—but with her prohibitive schedule and the tons of relatives who wanted to spend time with her, she found it too complicated and tiring.

Vietnam, of course, served as the nearest and the most ideal mini getaway from Singapore.

* * *

Rooki Sakimoto wanted everything to be first class and uber-comfy—yet still in touch with any old Vietnamese ladies selling green balls on the street, in the event that the craving would hit her. And because vacations such as this one were so hard to come by with her complex schedule, Rooki was willing to splurge.

I steered her towards Central Vietnam, where Da Nang was. I've long heard that Da Nang was dubbed as the new Bali: it had a fantastic beach just five away minutes from the city, a burgeoning club and café culture, and a brand-new slew of luxury coastal resorts. So the planning wasn't too bad—my newfound Vietnamese contacts were eager to please and extremely welcoming of any requests.

I arranged for Rooki and Daniel to stay at the wildly expensive The Forest, a super exclusive resort dramatically built on the mountainside, where all of the suites overlooked the water and the smattering islands nearby. Think of a grand resort in Italy's Cinque Terre but with a tropical, Southeast Asian feel.

The Forest was a twenty-minute drive outside of the city centre—far enough from the crowds, yet near enough as a luxurious base for all the major tourist sights, or simply if you want to hang out and jam with the locals.

I first encountered the resort when I got an email from its publicist, buried along with the rest of my daily email. I was about to move it to the trash when I accidentally opened the attached photo. A full glorious image of The Forest unfolded on my screen.

The resort was majestically beautiful jutting out of the cliffs like that, and the suites were literally shining and done up in the Vietnamese ornate way with tons of quality wood and plush, jewel-toned fabrics. It also looked secluded—just the kind of thing that would appeal to most of our clients at Isle Z.

I shot an email reply for rates and got my answers in less than an hour's time. In fact, The Forest's management was so eager that they immediately invited me over for a look-see a few months prior. And indeed, when I recce'd the place, it was stunning—and seemed normal enough. Well, normal enough for the kind of guests we usually brought in. A splendid, jaw-dropping façade to rival the resorts in Bali, Greece, Tasmania, or the Amalfi Coast? Check. Over-the-top dining room with an abundance of staff and a plethora of the green stuff that Rooki craves? Check. A brass claw-footed tub in the spacious toilet and bath with an all-glass window that had a view as far as the next island? A spacious private balcony with your very own pool for every suite? Check and check. Not one, but two personal butlers? Check! Yep, you'd think that they'd do away with me after confirming that they had two butlers to wait on them hand and foot. But no, they still wanted a sort of personal guide whom they can trust outside of the resort.

And yes, I sometimes forget that in my line of work, 'normal' actually meant 'fancy.'

* * *

'This place is perfect!'

Rooki Sakimoto, looking not a day older than twenty-one, gave a little shriek as she jumped out of the limousine and bounded through the huge ornate French doors that served as the entrance to The Forest's lobby.

'I have a good feeling about this place, Arya!' Rooki called out, as I struggled to emerge from the backseat, just in time to see Rooki gazing about eagerly and dropping the cool façade she usually took on when she was striding the runway or facing the camera.

So there she stood in the middle of The Forest's unbelievably grandiose gold, white, and black lobby, oblivious to the hotel bellboys who'd spent a full minute gaping at her from the sidelines before jumping up to gather her Rimowa suitcases from the limousine's trunk.

I wasn't surprised; Rooki had that effect on people. She was half-Japanese and half-Irish and had almost perfectly-symmetrical features, skin that seemed to glow from within. But it was her genuine enthusiasm for everything about *life*, it seems, that was the thing that charmed the people who encountered her. Top that with an endearing laugh, perfect posture, plus a renegade sense of fashion—and she was undeniably a presence and a vision.

Today Rooki was in outrageously torn white jeans, a white beaded tank top with geometric cut-outs just below the ribcage, gold feather earrings, and huge Chanel sunglasses. Luxe accouterments for sure, but then Rooki could wear anything and still look chic.

She gave Daniel a brief hug, then pulled away and clapped her hands in glee. Rooki was actually pushing thirty, but thanks to, well, good genes—and a fastidious skincare routine despite countless times she'd had to sit in the makeup chair for prepping, shoot under the sun for hours, and walk the runway shows in the most precarious of venues, she looked like she'd still be modelling for decades to come.

I stepped into the lobby and looked around at Rooki's source of joy and newfound current place of rest and recuperation—and noted with unexpected dismay that this time around, The Forest was practically crawling with honeymooners.

Honeymooners. How I had come, sadly, to despise that word. Rooki did too, and so during the planning stages of this whole trip, it was never really referred to as a honeymoon. But it could be, really. It was a mini-getaway, a mini-honeymoon. Everyone was here for an unforgettable holiday with their special someone, to have a romantic time with their significant other, to enjoy, discover and create memories, except—

'Are you okay, Arya?'

Rooki's low, almost husky voice jolted me out of my sudden flash of bitterness.

'Ah, yes, yes,' I answered, as Rooki's concerned face relaxed into its former state of excited bliss. 'Yes.' I tried rearranging my face into a less miserable countenance. 'This place is breathtaking!'

For a moment, I felt shamed that it was my client who was asking if I was okay, instead of the other way around.

Still. It must have been a low season for honeymooners the last time I was here. A few months ago, there were still groups of guests checking in for a girls' night or a bachelor party, big families who took leisurely meals at the hotel's several restaurants. But right this very moment, The Forest seemed to have transformed into Romance Central, with couples blissfully streaming in and out of the grand lobby—and being presented with welcome drinks or flower garlands or a rose or other mushy (but still very elegant) resort treats.

And to think that this was in November, not February. I looked away from a Korean couple dressed in matching pink shirts who'd just floated in, walking hand in hand and stealing bashful glances at each other. Just as my eyes searched for something neutral to look at—say, a plant—I turned my head just in time to see a Nordic-looking couple who'd parked themselves in one of the lobby's plush couches, rubbing noses and laughing at a shared private—and apparently naughty—joke.

I looked over again at Rooki, half-expecting her to be draped all over Daniel and gushing once again at the resort's magnificence. Thankfully, she wasn't. At least, not right now. In fact, she was ignoring him like it wasn't his business to be there. That's Rooki, all right.

'Excuse me?'

I felt a tap on my shoulder. I looked away from Rooki just in time to see a man in preppy pastels and a girl in the biggest straw hat I'd ever seen.

'Can you help us take our picture?' the man asked. In his extended arm was a compact Olympus camera in a leather case.

'*I'll* take your picture!' Rooki cried, grabbing the camera from out of the man's hand before I could even say anything.

I watched in silence as the couple snuggled up to each other, the woman looking up lovingly at the guy's face as his arm wrapped around her waist. They seemed to want to have a picture beside a complicated glass sculpture that was just one of the many works of local art dotting the lobby.

Breathe, Arya, breathe, I told myself. Remember what Tita Celeste always used to say—these are just feelings, and these too, would pass.

It seemed trite to say that I was always painfully reminded of our relationship, whenever I see couples walking hand in hand, arms contentedly entwined, or worse, in cute matching shirts—but I was, really.

With the mini photo shoot going on with Rooki, I was distracted by yet another couple who'd ambled by, arm in arm, with the guy listening in rapt, lovestruck attention to the girl telling him something in earnest. He was even carrying all of her things; the huge pale pink-dyed straw bag, the fuchsia sarong and the striped cream-and-pink hat that was all hung haphazardly from his body certainly weren't his.

Rooki's excited voice broke through my thoughts. 'Is it all right? Is it nice? Check it, check it please!'

The couple bent their heads together and as if in sync, their faces lit up in pleased smiles when the images of themselves came up on the tiny screen.

'That's so cute! This is so perfect! Darling, you look lovely!' The guy gave the girl a brief hug.

Turning to Rooki and me, the woman beamed and gushed out, 'Thank you so, *so much!*'

'You're, ah, welcome,' I stammered out and watched as the two lovebirds made their way towards the elevators. The woman turned and gave us a brief wave before walking on.

Just two years and eight months ago, I was that girl—gushy, starry-eyed, happy, and in love. I was the one charming everyone for a picture of us.

That could've been us, the voice in my head would whisper insistently, whenever I'd see couples like this.

That couple who looked like they had finally found each other could have been us. If only—

No. It was too painful to even start to think about what had happened.

But it had happened. And there was no way I can undo it, no way I can even un-remember it. Now, even after almost three years, I wasn't even sure that I can call myself recovered. Recovered from what?

Heartbreak, hurt, and humiliation was what.

Chapter 6

Manila, Philippines, more than two years ago. Before Isle Z, and maybe before all the heartbreak, hurt, and humiliation, I was actually doing okay. I had a business of my own, one that I'd started partly by accident, and partly out of my love for discovering new places.

Back then, I was managing my own travel agency in Manila. I had partnered with an old colleague, Luisa Santillan, with whom I'd decided to start a small outfit called Tripology Travel. We held a small office at a rented space in Mandaluyong—a formerly old, dark, and decrepit studio that was being used at that time by the landlord as storage for cement and industrial cleaning materials. This was after a reasonable deal on the rent, negotiated by no less than Luisa whom I have unofficially declared the shrewdest Tripology partner, ever—and tons of white paint, bleached wood, and reworked furniture from second-hand stores in Divisoria and Evangelista Street. We only needed this awesome space, plus the combination of hundreds of contacts we've managed to accumulate in one big directory file, and we were in business.

I was proud of what we had started. Tripology was all about accessibility, budget travel, camaraderie, *barkada* and solo travelling. For one, Luisa and I made sure that we spruced up the interiors of the Tripology office so it didn't look like your usual, run-of-the-mill travel agency. It had become a place that our clients eventually gravitated to where there was always coffee, tea, savoury and salty snacks (which had to be constantly replaced as I was also fond of reaching out for a snack or ten), and a world of possibilities about their upcoming trip. I also had albums upon albums with countless pictures of the various trips of my clients—most of which were presents to me, and some of who were only too grateful to provide me with copies of their fabulous honeymoon in Bali or their *barkada* trip in Chang Mai, or a solo adventure in Siem Reap.

I knew that travel wasn't cheap. And for many, it wasn't even a priority. That was what Luisa and I, via Tripology Travel, wanted to remedy. We wanted to start something— easy, budget-friendly customized trips were what first came to mind—and we wanted to do it right. We wanted to go to new places, of course—and we longed to share that pleasure by creating trips that were accessible, easy on the pocket, and definitely enjoyable.

When I think of that, it always brings me back to my own personal story, where perhaps, it had all stemmed from. Even as a child, being in a new place—or just being *on the way* to a new destination—excited me. Or perhaps it was all about movement—the act of going from one place to the next, which felt both soothing and exhilarating. Maybe it all started when my parents brought me to a simple yet unforgettable picnic in Tagaytay when I was six years old.

Yup, it was only Tagaytay—a mere two-hour drive away from Manila. But as a very shy six-year-old who thought the whole world consisted of home, school, the mall, and the street that I played in every afternoon, being in the highlands with a view that promised fresh, cool air, and a whole vibe that was so unlike the city, was like being in a totally different world.

I had dozed off in the car on the way up to Tagaytay. I woke up to the magnificent view of the Taal volcano right in the middle of Taal Lake, which was definitely nothing like I'd ever seen before. Not in the peaceful yet staid subdivision where I lived, or on my way to my school. Seeing that dramatic work of nature, so vastly new and different from what I was used to, made me feel that I had actually arrived by car in a different country.

I actually thought I had it pretty great that the street where my house was had a neighbourhood full of kids who came out to play badminton or *sipa*, where we fashioned a sort of shuttle that we kicked around, by tying a bunch of fragrant *kalachuchi* flowers together every afternoon.

After that Tagaytay trip, however, I wanted to see more. I wanted to see another view. I wanted to see many different views. Maybe breathe a different kind of air, hear a new set of noises other than the neighbours' chatter and the tricycles that whined, daily, through our subdivision's streets.

As I grew up, I also realized that going places didn't even have to cost that much. That fateful day in Tagaytay, my parents didn't even eat in the expensive restaurant that was done up in old varnished wood, crystal glasses, and fancy red tablecloths, manned by a bevy of spiffy waiters.

The sign outside the resto said that it offered the highest, most unobstructed view of Taal Volcano, one that you could enjoy while noshing on its famous Savoury Spaghetti Arriabata and Aromatic Truffle Fries (yes that sounded unbearably exciting at that time). In a much smaller print, the sign also said that it had a wide terrace *for free* that tourists could enjoy.

I knew it was beyond my parents' means when they glanced at the menu posted outside, with the way they shook their heads and wrinkled their noses—all the while exchanging secret smug, knowing looks. The smugness was attributed to their foresight of packing along one of the Alvarez family's irresistible *baon*: a huge Tupperware of homemade spaghetti complete with red hotdogs and gobs of melted cheese, bags of *pandesal* from our neighbourhood bakery, and a precious gift from my *lola*, my grandmother who had a penchant for *ube* macapuno rolls from Goldilocks, the one that was always finished too fast because it was that good.

We took advantage of that free space on the terrace. My parents had packed all the necessary tableware and utensils, down to the little plastic bowls so our spaghetti wouldn't have a chance of spilling. So clever and practical was the way they'd planned the whole mobile picnic—as they called it—that we could've eaten the spaghetti and dessert in a rocking boat in the middle of rough seas.

There was no picnic area at that time, but we made do by enjoying our homemade spaghetti and bread while perched on the thick, solid railing on the terrace overlooking the lake and volcano. And we came home very, very satisfied a few hours later—as if we really did sample that restaurant's sophisticated cuisine while gazing at the magical Taal.

Sadly, what little travel my family did together in the past dwindled as the years passed. And in what felt like overnight, it became totally nil. No family was perfect, of course. But I found out just how flawed mine was, the year I graduated from college. I still believe, until now, that that was the first major tragedy of my life.

My brother and I never really witnessed any open, heated fights between our parents, but that year, my mom announced that she wanted to separate from my dad. 'I want to leave. I want to be on my own,' she told us, so matter-and-fact and calm, it was as if she was merely announcing what we were having for dinner. And my brother and I, we just didn't see it coming. There had been no scandalous screams, no teary arguments, or bitter exchanges, even during the first time we all learned about my mother's intentions.

My mom didn't leave the house. Not right away. But knowing that she wanted to, made it doubly awful. I think my dad was too angry and also too scared to even stop her. He had retired when I started working, and yet because of this, we had to deal with even less disposable income than before. And my mom did leave, getting herself a tiny apartment nearby, and visiting us kids five times a week. But she wanted autonomy. As she said, she wanted to be by herself, to be free of being part of a marriage, maybe. Whatever it was, it made me miserable.

I would have gone through that year morose, had it not been for a call from Tita Celeste, an aunt and my dad's first cousin who'd been based in Singapore for seventeen years. That call was—I've always believed, until now—really sort of wonderful, especially in the midst of all that uncertainty.

Tita Celeste often called us via long distance in the past; now, she called my dad through FaceTime every now and then, mostly when a friend or someone she knew was flying to Singapore and she needed something to be brought to her from Manila. Tita Celeste had been divorced from her Singaporean husband eight years ago and worked for an insurance company.

She was planning to visit Manila, she said on this latest call. But she also wanted to spend time in Hong Kong and Macau for a vacation. 'It's just an hour and a half from Manila, and yet I've never been there!' Tita Celeste had sounded giddy. 'Manila first, then I'm off to Hong Kong and Macau. A vacation from my vacation!'

She was supposed to go solo, she said. Those were cities easy enough to navigate on her own. But in the end, she wanted—no, needed—company. And besides, who would take all her photos?

'That would have to be you, Arya,' Tita Celeste declared. That was how she had suavely phrased her invitation. It wasn't a question, but a statement.

Tita Celeste knew about the problems of my family. It made me think—did she really need a companion for her trip or was Tita Celeste just being sympathetic?

But we didn't talk about my current family situation when we were there. Not once. Instead, we walked the busy streets of Tsim Sha Tsui, fought off pushy vendors in Mongkok, gorged on cheap but tasty dim sum, peered at secondhand designer bags and clothes in obscure shops, and took the ferry across to the Hong Kong side. We capped the trip with a heady tour of the wax museum which oddly, I enjoyed.

In the end, it was because of Tita Celeste that the trip had been so memorable, so full and so enjoyable. She was the perfect travel partner, even if I didn't exactly know what was one in those days. All I knew was that she was with me, and she was curious and spontaneous, easy-going yet organized, patient yet still fun.

I've always believed that that trip saved me. For once, I was focused on something else—being in a totally new environment. Even the smell of the air was different and was worth savouring. In Mongkok, someone had mistaken me for Chinese, speaking to me in rapid Cantonese while Tita Celeste and I were eating noodles at a local stall. Instead of being befuddled, I was thrilled. In fact, I revelled being in a place where people spoke a different language from my own. It felt glorious to be anonymous, and freeing—as if I could choose to be anyone I wanted to, in the next four days.

On the plane ride back home to Manila, I braced myself for the dire situation that would greet me once I returned to my family. I was convinced and fearful that I'd be overwhelmed all over again by the depressing details of my parents' situation and be brought back, so unceremoniously, to the harsh reality that was my life.

I surprised myself by feeling *okay*. I said goodbye to Tita Celeste and slipped in through our front door with my modest suitcase, tired yet strangely alert from the flight, from my and Tita Celeste's activities in the past four days. I saw my family in their usual spots in the living room and the kitchen and felt something akin to acceptance, and a change in perspective.

I wasn't exactly sure what had happened, but there was one thing I learned, after four days of being in another city that felt like another world because it was so different from where I lived—I came back renewed. Transformed. It was as if I'd turned into someone else, someone who was in a better, healthier mental state. Someone who saw things more positively. And I did begin to see some things differently. I began to think—no wonder people wanted to 'get away' all the time. Travel wasn't the answer to your problems, nor was it a real escape. Unless you bought a one-way ticket, you would always be coming home to your realities. But it was a way to pull back and gain a new perspective. It was a way to look at your problems from a healthy distance—and be all the better for it.

That was how I turned out to be the one who was always up for a trip, whether it was just to the next *barangay*, out of town, or just . . . somewhere. I didn't have the money to fully finance my outings. But as I had learned from my resourceful family early on, there *was* always a way—and I made do.

I learned to take advantage of what was there, at that time. Two words: budget airlines. Luckily, my friends and relatives were also quick to catch on. There was always a trip out of town by someone I know because of a low-cost flight, promotion, or a buy-one-take-one deal. Glamping suddenly became a thing, and it started to become cool, staying in spartan yet functional three-star hotels, smart hostels, and affordable boutique inns.

My parents warned me to never mooch or take advantage of anyone's generosity—so I struck up a deal with my wanderlust companions. If friends wanted me to come with them on a trip, I'd offer to do the itinerary and draw the budget for the whole duration of the journey, from flights, meals, accommodations, tips, and activities. In exchange, they were welcome to sponsor half or at least, part of my flight or hotel fare. Sometimes, a few extremely kind friends would offer to shave off some of the flight cost and hotel expense—as long as I can figure out an affordable way (read—without spending too much) to enjoy our destination.

I got used to my friends ticking off their 'required' must-sees and must-dos, as well as their deal breakers when it came to travelling. Because I was constantly creating itineraries, I learned that it all had to work together—a trip's duration, in-between travel times, plane, boat, and bus schedules, and most of all, the funds available. On one trip to the Philippine island of Siquijor, for example, one friend really wanted to maximize her trip down South. After Siquijor, she wanted to see Negros' 'The Ruins'—the stunning, very Instagrammable remains of an old mansion in Talisay—on the same trip before going back to Manila.

I made an iron-clad schedule where we had to take the boat from Siquijor to Dumaguete, board the bus from Dumaguete to Bacolod, and from there, hire a local tricycle that would take us to the Ruins. Classy, eh? My friend balked at the thought of arriving at one of her dream tourist sites in a *tryke*, but we were extremely pressed for time, and it really was the quickest and cheapest way to get there.

We spent a total of twenty-two minutes at The Ruins, and after a quick tour and enough photos and videos for a whole slew of posts on Instagram and Facebook, we made it just in time for our ferry back to Iloilo and our flight back to Manila.

Not all itineraries I've planned were this seamless, of course. There had been dissatisfied ones who thought that my planning was amateur, too offbeat, and just too cheap. I've worked with friends of friends who wanted to have the usual and were not willing at all to go out of the way or make, say, just one more half-hour jeepney ride to see a special, hidden waterfall or a secluded, secret beach. I also had some relatives who seemed to have suddenly forgotten that I'd actually slaved over their itineraries and simply never wanted to get out of their hotel rooms. And then there were those who insisted on seeing *all* the sights of a city in less than forty-eight hours. *New York Times* was always writing about it, they'd say, so why couldn't I do that for them, too?

When I started working in a public relations agency, where I met Luisa Santillan, colleague, and future business partner, work got so stressful that I'd have a need to just be away— and be anywhere else except my little world of office and home. Most of my friends would be busy whenever I'd get this itch, so there were times when no one was available to be my travel partner. I knew then that it was time for me to try travelling solo.

The concept of solo was both daunting and empowering. And it was unnerving—to have no one else but yourself to depend on in such unfamiliar territory. You could say that the highs and lows, the success and the perceived failure of a trip—were, in many ways, on *you*.

But I made do. I really did. And surprisingly, I thrived. Turns out, my natural introversion combined with my learned organization—developed, it seemed, from dreaming up various itineraries for my friends and relatives—proved to be an effective combo. My friends would always laugh because it was ironic that it would be during my solo trips that I would have the most photos. And sometimes, they would turn out to be the most fun, too.

This was the point and mission of Tripology Travel. I've always believed—and have experienced it firsthand, that there was always a way to go and enjoy a place without spending all of your life savings. One just needed to be more resourceful, more creative, and maybe, more patient. Getting up a little bit earlier than the rest helps, too.

The universe must have sensed my undying enthusiasm for budget travelling, because I was lucky enough to have found Luisa who shared my love for travelling on a shoestring—and who was also eager to share the secrets of her many years of being a budget traveller.

I had dreamed of going to so many places at that time. And there had been a time when I was just, well, everywhere. And yet, I had never expected that I would meet the man whom I've always believed was the love of my life, right here in Manila.

Chapter 7

Manila, Philippines, more than two years ago. Maybe what hurts about break-ups is that when you look back at a relationship, it almost always comes with a perfect start.

Jake came into my life when I least expected it. Maybe that should have been a warning, this sudden appearance of a person who seemed too good to be true, at a time when I had been, finally, at peace with my life.

Warning or not, Jake had felt right at that time. Meeting him felt like the reward for all my hard work—on myself, on my career, and on all the meticulous, painstaking effort I've done with Tripology and our clients. Also, it felt so much like a reward for not pushing the universe, for not forcing it to know that I needed someone in my life. A reward for bearing it out, for suffering and even surviving this situation of not having a boyfriend, a partner, or just *someone*.

And it was a reward, maybe, for always wanting, for trying to do good. At that time, I had been so grateful for Luisa and Tripology: the business was taking off, we were young—I was only around twenty-eight and Luisa just two years older—and we wanted so much to give back.

The day I met Jake, I had actually been doing a favour for a client. I was answering emails in our little rented office in Mandaluyong when I got a message from Kirsten, a client I've had since the beginning, just a few weeks after Luisa and I first started Tripology. Kirsten was a *balikbayan,* an architect based in Amsterdam for the past five years, and who was then in the Philippines for a month-long visit to her family. Kirsten at that time wanted to show her Dutch boyfriend around the city and had asked for me and Luisa to arrange several walking tours in Intramuros and Binondo. Kirsten, her boyfriend, and her family had been so happy with the tours, that she'd taken to contacting Tripology exclusively for anything and everything related to travel within the Philippines—from local car rentals to arranging flights and hotel rooms for a group of ten (always with boyfriend-now-husband in tow, and she had a big family) for excursions to nearby spots like Laguna or to somewhere as far-flung as Batanes, at the northern tip of the Philippines.

How did Jake figure in this equation? I got a message from Kirsten who said that a good friend of her husband was coming to Manila, and could I help him find an Airbnb in a good location? The *right* location, Kirsten had emphasized. He was finicky and averse to cookie-cutter hotel rooms, she said and would like to live more locally. Could Arya help this Dutchman find a decent place for a week, one that was near the malls—because he knew that malls had everything in Manila—or at least, places that would be convenient and easy for him to navigate?

I had wondered at that time, why the friend didn't just go through Airbnb himself. Luisa, wise and reasonable as ever, shrugged it off as being careful, even practical. 'You know how it is with foreigners in Manila,' she said. 'People just want the right place, a safe area, especially in a chaotic city like ours. They know that the locals would know.'

Luisa and I were feeling expansive, so I did it—went the extra mile: I opened my Airbnb app and scrolled through as many places I could find in Manila that were available on those dates. I only stopped when I saw a photo of a soothing, one-bedroom condominium done in classic Japandi style: a light-filled minimalist unit with clean lines, a touch of wabi-sabi, and lots of coziness. The price was within budget, too.

We didn't just stop there. I had this great idea of visiting the place, so that we could assure Kirsten and her friend firsthand that what they were getting was a hundred percent comfortable, clean, and accessible. We wanted these kinds of referrals and more foreign clients, anyway. Off I went to Bayview Suites, which was just across from the Philippines' largest mall, Mall of Asia, to look at this fabulous albeit compact apartment.

And there was Jake Hidalgo, condo owner, and Airbnb host, waiting for me.

Actually, I waited for him. But then, you know when you meet people and you can't tell if you were attracted or just pleased with the way they act towards you? That was how it was with Jake. You know those times when you meet people who somehow leave you just feeling good about yourself without really doing anything overt? Jake Hidalgo had been a complete stranger to me then, but that was how he had made me feel.

'Hi, Arya Alvarez? *Kamusta?*' Was the first thing he said, when he found me waiting, ensconced in one of the plush beige armchairs at the modern, gleaming, but busy lobby of Bayview Suites.

It was such an innocuous greeting, one that people in Manila gave each other all the time. And it provided absolutely no inkling that I would be with this man—love him, with all I've got and everything I had—for the next two years.

No, that day, Jake Hidalgo was simply an attractive man in his mid-thirties who seemed responsible yet easy-going, who owned a condominium suite that was right for a foreign client. He had come from outside, clad in faded Levi's and a light-blue collared shirt, and I saw him go through the lobby's glass doors with unhurried ease until he spotted me sitting by myself near the windows. Tan, tall, and wiry, with a muscular face and a strong jaw, he looked like the epitome of good health, and someone who definitely led a non-sedentary lifestyle. What he said was nothing special, but he held my eyes when he spoke and smiled so sincerely, it was hard not to be disarmed almost immediately.

'Thanks for meeting me,' I said, as we walked along the quiet hallway leading to his unit. I had been initially flustered at his handsomeness but caught myself just in time. 'It's just that, I wanted to be sure that your apartment is to my client's taste.' I had already explained this to him through the Airbnb app.

I continued: 'Well, I had time and actually—' I paused, gave him a sideways glance. 'To be honest with you, I wanted to impress my client so they'd book with me again and again.'

He laughed, a light melodious sound. 'Don't worry about it. I'm glad you came.' He brought a hand up his head and touched the tips of his hair as if checking if it was still in its neat, waxed, subtly-spiky style. 'I get it that you'd want to check out the place. I could only wish that future guests would be like this. I'd probably get fewer complaints.'

This time, I laughed. 'I guess that's what the app is for,' I said. 'Pictures are supposed to be enough, 'no? But I suppose there's always something.'

He shrugged in an exaggerated, carefree way that I found boyish, even cute. I was beginning to like his level of candour. 'Renting out accommodation isn't as easy as everyone thinks it is,' he said, and I noticed that his voice, though solid and firm, was also soft, almost muffled. 'You never really know what's going on with people.'

There was something in his tone when he said this and when I glanced at him, I wasn't startled at all to see that there was a sad, almost faraway look in his eyes.

And then he was back to being gracious and candid and somewhat carefree, showing me the narrow kitchen, the minuscule sink in the toilet and shower, and the apartment's only bedroom, decked out in soft beige and grey. He waited patiently as I took more photos.

I watched as he carefully closed the door of the apartment and twisted the lock with slim, smooth, and tanned fingers. We started walking to the elevators.

'So what is it that you do, besides personally checking out Airbnb apartments for your clients?' His tone was light. I was looking straight ahead towards the end of the hall, but I knew that he had turned his head and was looking at me.

'We own a travel agency,' I said. I was proud of Tripology, of what Luisa and I had built. 'We have a small office in Mandaluyong. Drop by, maybe? I mean, if you need anything travel-related. Or just check out our website.'

I reached into my bag for my card case. Suddenly, it seemed very, very important that I hand him my card. 'If I can just give you my business card, then you'll see our services,' I murmured, my hand tumbling the contents of my purse and searching for my card case. *Please, let me not have forgotten it at the office,* was my thought. 'We specialize in budget travel. That's always useful, right?'

When my fingers closed over the small rectangular leather case, it felt like I had won something.

When I looked up, Jake's sad eyes had turned animated, and he was gazing at me with an expression that I couldn't really define. Was it interest? Disinterest? Curiosity? Before I could really scrutinize it, he said, 'Of course it's useful. Saving money is always a top priority for a lot of people.'

I handed him my card with both hands.

We lingered in the lobby, with me feeling that neither of us wanted to go. And yet neither of us wanted to make any drastic, obvious move. Personally, I didn't want to botch up this meeting with anything else other than having a good place for Kirsten's husband's friend. Weeks later, in bed, Jake would tell me that he had restrained himself from asking me out that day because he was worried that he would scare me away.

He went to our office just three days after that. He wasn't going anywhere—and maybe that should've been a red flag right there—but he said he was in the area and spotted our office and why not say hello to Arya?

He invited me and Luisa, casually, for a coffee at a new café that had just opened behind Megamall. But because someone had to be in the office, Luisa urged me to go. 'You know him, I don't,' was her practical reply. And then: 'Go, he might have contacts for us.' Classic Luisa.

Coffee had turned into a two-hour-long conversation wherein I learned that Jake was a business owner like me who owned several coffee stall franchises and two more studio condo units that he'd turned into Airbnb apartments. And that he was into biking and reading and working out. And that despite these regimens, he liked beer and grilled *liempo*. He was charming and talked smartly, especially about his business experience, but he was also quiet and listened when I told him about my own company and the little travels I'd done that started it all. And because the coffee had extended for so long, it turned into an invitation to dinner. There were so many restaurants in Makati, he said. Quieter ones, where we could talk over a really good meal. It was almost eight-thirty in the evening and I said yes because by then Jake appeared to be everything I had always wanted in a person: charming, unassuming, funny and candid, and most of all, responsible.

Conversation flowed, even throughout dinner. Jake was engaging and even more charming. He was curious and asked the right questions. He asked about my passions, my work, and my views on life. We exchanged college stories and work stories—back when we had our first jobs, and now that we were entrepreneurs.

There was still that magical, mysterious quality he had where he listened intently, asked thought-provoking questions, and made me feel good about myself, again and again throughout the night. When he spoke about his work, he felt like a tough guy, someone who had gone through a lot and yet could still laugh and be quietly calm about it.

At that time, it felt as if Jake Hidalgo could do and manage everything. My fault was, I just didn't have a complete idea of the extent of his capability. He was just too good, too smart. And I wasn't willing to let this one go.

My fault was, I had been so undeniably smitten after that. So smitten that I had been the one to invite him to another dinner the following week. I had not only invited him, but I was cajoling and almost insistent. He couldn't say no.

For the first time in a very long time, I had hope for myself, for my life, for love. I had hope that I could actually be with someone. For a moment, I felt the promise of something good, something that might work.

By the time Kirsten's husband's friend had checked out from Bayview Suites, Jake and I were already sleeping together, and I was in love with him.

Chapter 8

Manila, Philippines, more than two years ago. I couldn't believe it at first when I saw it on Facebook. A mistake, was my initial thought reflex. And I told myself it wasn't him—that clean-shaven guy in a sharp, cream-coloured tuxedo with a shock of thick hair, grinning like he was so madly in love as he kneeled before a woman looking so radiant and ecstatic in a sheer lace wedding dress. He was kneeling like a gallant, modern knight and she was laughing like it had been the funniest thing to ever happen. They looked like they were doing a mock proposal at a wedding—funny, perhaps, to everyone there because they had just been married.

Because, yes, they had been married.

Wait, what was I doing looking at the Facebook page of a wedding photography company anyway?

Had I really been scouring for ideas for a wedding, after dating a guy for only seven months? When I sat down with my phone, one slow day at Tripology and seven months after I'd been seeing Jake Hidalgo, I told myself that I just wanted to check what was happening in the wedding world, what the trends were, what was cool, what looked good in pictures. I mean, I really was just curious how they did weddings these days—after seeing some cute reception photos on Instagram. Was that so sinful or unbelievable? Was it really foolishly indulgent, or wisely forward-thinking?

It had been seven months since my first meeting with Jake, and it had been all that I had hoped for in a relationship. True, I was probably over-positive, but that was just how I chose to look at it. I just have never met a guy who was so into me, it was as simple as that. We texted a lot, sent each other selfies, shared the banal details of our lives, the little wins, and soothed each other with what we thought were losses.

We saw each other three or four times a week. Jake would pick me up from the office and we'd have lunch or an early dinner somewhere, anywhere. I would go to one of his coffee stalls, bring takeaway food and eat the meal with him, depending on where he was that day. True, he never made it to any of my familiarization tours or media junkets overseas, but then he had his Airbnbs and his food stall business to attend to.

He told me, frequently, that he loved me. In person, in texts, in emails, in little Post-it notes he stuck on my books or in the car. Jake could be described as a quiet, charming man, but I found him especially expressive in his messages whenever we weren't together and he was just on the other side of Metro Manila, prompting me to think that there really must be truth to that 'absence makes the heart grow fonder' thing. He had bursts of emotions and I felt it palpably in the long, articulate declarations of love he sent to me in Viber and WhatsApp.

In bed, he was milder, softer, and more careful with his words. And the sex? Sex was vigorous and mostly satisfying, the frequency erratic. I was renting a studio apartment on West Avenue in Quezon City, a simple walk-up and I often invited him there. It was at the other end of the city, far from his condo units. Jake hardly stayed overnight, always saying he had work or had some guest staying at his Airbnbs. He lived in Cavite, south of Manila where I visited only once or twice. The distance felt daunting, and I found myself reluctant to visit. And then we started shuttling between his two condo units, using it for a few hours whenever he had no booking. In the end, he blocked out dates in the app so we could use the unit continuously and whenever we liked.

But there had been lapses. Cancelled dates. Wide swathes of emptiness in my Viber and WhatsApp conversations with him, because there were days when I would have no idea where he was. I had learned to tolerate this, to even understand it and so I let it all slide off me. I told myself that no one was perfect and people had a right to have time for themselves without the need to report to anyone. I didn't want to appear clingy or needy, and the truth was, I had never been clingy in all my past relationships, no matter how short-lived. I just wasn't the type. I had always tried to manage everything on my own. Maybe travelling solo helped; I had always thought of myself as someone capable of taking care of herself, someone who was capable of letting go.

If there was one thing I learned from travelling, mingling, and working with all sorts of people is that they hardly change. I mean, you can't change a person. It was either you accept him, tolerate him, adjust to him, or just completely embrace that other person's traits. But I've never believed that they would change and that you could change them.

I was pretty happy with Jake. I didn't want him to be anyone else other than what he is, or at least, what he presented himself to be. Jake seemed like your regular guy who was sometimes consistent, and sometimes not. That sounded typical, right?

But after what happened, there were times when I questioned everything. There were times when I didn't just question him and his actions, but myself as well.

Jake had a Facebook account with nothing on it, except a profile pic that I suspect he hasn't changed for the last three years or so, and a cover photo of some steampunk scene in sepia, with grotesque-looking characters gathered around a dinner table. Scroll down through his feed and there was almost nothing, except maybe an odd article on cars, but that was also a few years old. He wasn't on Instagram.

I was in my office that day with a lot of work to do. And yet, on a whim, I searched his name.

Well, there it was. It was still the same account, with the same old profile photo and cover photo, the same old emptiness. I was about to close the page when I saw a tiny thumbnail at the bottom, a photo that looked like him but one that he didn't upload. It was posted by a photography company. It was of a bride and groom, and I don't know why I associated it with Jake almost immediately.

At first, I just stared at it quizzically. It must be someone who looked like him. A cousin or brother or something, and Jake was simply attending the wedding.

I clicked on the photo. That was when my skin went cold.

This was no cousin or relative. This was Jake. Jake in that sharp cream tuxedo, kneeling before a woman in a white, resplendent, lace gown. The bride. Of course! Jake laughing, arm-in-arm with this same woman, and this time they were looking deep into each other's eyes. Photography by Bautista Brothers, it said. I went to the Facebook page and clicked some more, and there was Jake again, emerging from the grand, wooden double doors of a church, arms on the waist of the same woman.

Facebook had a bizarre way of organizing photos; these were nine years ago.

I started clicking some more. God knows how I ended up looking at more photos, posted by his *wife*. Old photos of them together, new ones, too. That was when I'd learned that Jake had attended a high school reunion with his wife three months ago, all while he told me that he needed to stay in one of his condos, catching up on admin work for all branches of his coffee stalls. Another was a photo of a concert they'd both attended just last month, a concert where they were standing and he had his arms around her.

I was shaking. The photos swam before my eyes, and for a moment, I felt like I was about to float away. Or collapse and slide down my chair.

Breathe, Arya, breathe. Breathe some more. Just keep yourself alive. Just keep your thoughts calm. At the same time, another side of me was screaming at me to leave, to go and cut my losses. It wasn't worth it.

With trembling hands, I fished out my phone from my bag. I brought up Jake's name in my contacts. 'Can you call me?' I tried to keep my voice low and even. 'I need to ask you something.'

I asked him to meet me. At a quiet, sprawling café in Rockwell that was not one of his businesses, because I had suddenly felt so vulnerable. I felt exposed, and also, I felt like a sideshow attraction, the ultimate third wheel that had been taken for a ride. I felt like someone who was used as an experiment, an alternate life that Jake had wanted to try on for kicks.

Most of all, I felt betrayed. It was as simple and as complicated as that.

* * *

'Are you married?'

We were there, right there, in the farthest corner of the café. It hurt me that I had to ask him such an important, crucial question in so casual an atmosphere. But something had clicked in me—a palpable hurt that was restrained, a rage that refused to reveal itself just yet, and most of all, this deep, stinging feeling of betrayal that refused to unleash itself because once it did, the devastation would be so great that I felt it would destroy me.

Jake appeared resigned. He said that they were living separate lives. He referred to her, Debbie, as his 'ex.' Those recent photos of them together? 'Just a show,' he said, almost breezily. 'I'm so fed up with friends asking the same questions over and over again.' What he was sure of, was that he and Debbie had been over, years ago. He said Debbie knew that he was seeing someone. That he was dating someone. He said that Debbie herself might be seeing someone, too. Plus, an annulment had been filed. It was just a matter of time, and he had hoped that the annulment would come through. He had kept it from me because he did not want to lose me. He was scared of losing me. He had planned, many times, to tell me, but could never bring himself to.

We had been going out, and sleeping together for seven months when I discovered all this.

And it made me sad. No, that was wrong. It almost killed me that Jake Hidalgo, the love of my life, was married.

* * *

I should have left him then. Disappeared, blocked him, and established no contact. I should have flown in a rage, walked—no, ran—out in a disgusted huff, and told him and myself, *never again*. Maybe I should have cut off all ties from him, the moment I knew.

It had not only felt like the ultimate betrayal, but it had been deeply humiliating. How could he have devised all those lies? How could he have kept it from me, all this time? How could he have lied to me and still look at me directly in the eye? There had been so many questions and so many terrible speculations.

But Jake had begged me. He had sat me down, again, in private, after that initial talk at the Rockwell café. He had proceeded to tell me, again, everything about his failing marriage. He emphasized, again and again, that it had been over, years ago. Their closest friends considered them separated. There were papers being drawn, lawyers that were working on the documents, and lawyers on standby. They were in the process of an annulment. It was just that, annulment in the Philippines was one long, ugly, and costly process. And so it can take so much time, right?

'But why didn't you just tell me?' I asked, over and over again, my face hot and sticky with tears. My insides, crushed and churning. I had told Luisa that I needed some time off. Inside of me was a toxic, debilitating swirl of frustration, confusion, and maybe even hate. And of betrayal, still.

'Would you have accepted it?' Jake asked me. 'Would you have understood my situation?'

I didn't know how to answer him. What I said was this: 'I would have benefited from the truth. No one benefits from being kept in the dark.'

Jake was pleading. 'I did want to tell you,' he said. 'I just didn't do it. I was too scared to lose you.'

That should have been a red flag.

There would be days when I thought I had made the wrong decision. And there was a moment—a tiny second— at one point in our relationship when it felt that Jake wasn't the one for me. I had felt it, faint but clear, somewhere in my bones. That this wasn't right, that this was in fact so wrong, and that Jake wasn't at all the person for me.

I ignored them. I pushed all these thoughts away, as fast and as hard and as deep as I could, to a place where I could not see, feel or think about them. That was how I managed to choose to continue this relationship with Jake. That was how I survived.

Chapter 9

Manila, Philippines, more than two years ago. I used to play a game with myself when I was still in a relationship with Jake. On weekends, when he'd managed to get away and it would just be the two of us in bed in the condo or on a day trip somewhere near like Tagaytay, I'd pretend that everything was perfect in our relationship. That we were a normal couple—no, an *ideal* couple—who was just spending another cozy weekend together, as couples do. That we were both single and had our own lives, and yet managed to be there for each other. That we were madly in love and that we had been so in love right from the start. That we had a future that was certainly ahead of us.

There were days when I'd pretend that Jake wasn't married anymore.

Come to think of it, there had been weeks where I had managed to push that fact out of my mind, days when I had managed to bury it deep inside my person, like a small, secret box stashed and hidden inside a jumbled closet. In the months that followed, I went on with Jake like it didn't exist, this fact that he was still legally bound to someone else. I still saw him regularly several days a week, spent meal times with him at his food stalls, and spent one day every weekend with him in the condo or in nearby out-of-town resorts like Laguna or Bulacan. I did so many things with him, all as I carefully avoided the topic of his wife, Debbie. I introduced Jake to Luisa and my friends and kept mum on his civil status. No one needed to know that, anyway.

And so maybe it had been my fault, that it all led to this. I had gone in over my head. I had convinced myself that everything was okay. I had convinced myself that this was sustainable.

I had escaped into another one of these daydreams when I let myself into the Tripology office one Sunday in March more than two years ago, my head humming with plans with Jake for the next week. I was in the office on a weekend, planning to get a head start for the next few days, as had become my habit in the past few months.

By this time, I had been going out with Jake for close to two years; I never really stopped, even when I discovered, seven months into dating, that he was married.

Because it was Luisa who now took on most of the fam and educational trips that we were invited to, all the paperwork that our clients and trips required, fell on me. I was only happy to do it; I did my emails in between seeing Jake, drafted up itineraries while waiting for him to finish work, called up suppliers, and confirmed with clients en route to our weekend dates. Jake didn't mind at all.

I had been planning on staying at Tripology for just a half day that Sunday. I had already settled on my chair, and had just pressed my laptop open when my phone beeped.

I knew without looking that it would be from Jake. We weren't supposed to see each other until Monday the next day.

'I need to see you, today. Meet me at Bayview?'

I smiled, immediately switched off my computer, then typed back: 'Hi! Sure, what time?'

'12 noon.'

I thought it odd that he had to say 'Bayview' instead of 'condo', but I dismissed the thought as fast as it came. I was too busy rummaging through my bag to see if I had brought my makeup kit or that tin of breath mints that I kept in my bag whenever I was meeting up with Jake. I reveled in spontaneous get-togethers like these, and that day I was just too giddy to scrutinize his words; all I knew was that I was meeting Jake, that I was going to spend a few hours with him, that I would be in his company and in his arms. All I knew was that that text—and the thought that I was seeing him sooner than expected—sent me into a new high, like a drug hit. I didn't care if I was addicted.

I rushed to the condo from Mandaluyong, pleased that there was hardly any traffic in the city since it was a Sunday. I got there fifteen minutes early, at a quarter to twelve, with enough time even for me to spruce up the place as I was wont to do whenever we met up, fluffing the pillows, wiping off errant dust on the dining table and the kitchen, pouring toilet cleaner into the bowl so that the bathroom smelled fresher. I had thought of ordering in for lunch, but I wanted to ask Jake if he'd like to just go out to the nearby Indian restaurant beside the Mall of Asia where we sometimes went every time we craved something rich and hearty.

Finally, I opened the door that led to the minuscule balcony, the noise from outside blaring and intrusive as it wafted inside the quiet condo. I looked down at the mad mix of cars, jeepneys, and pedestrians, at the jumble of cables and oddly-placed electricity posts, and then at the buildings nearby both old and new. This city was chaotic, and for a moment, I actually felt safe. For a moment, I thought that this chaos and confusion would never reach me at all and I would get away with all this happiness, unscathed. That day, nothing else mattered; I was going to be with Jake.

A sound at the front door. I shut the thick glass door shut, feeling the apartment fall into a heavy quiet again. Thank goodness for this place, I thought, turning back towards the room.

But it wasn't Jake who had come in. It was his wife, Debbie.

I knew because I had scrutinized the few photos of Jake and Debbie that I'd found on Facebook. And how I'd scrutinized them. How I'd run my eyes over every detail of Jake's wife, the one he said that he was leaving. The one whom he had been married to for ten years and had lost all hope with because they were so incompatible. The one he said he didn't love any more because he loved me. The one who was making the annulment process so long and difficult. The one responsible for dragging the whole thing on and on for years. The one who, according to Jake, was about to finally sign the papers and leave them be.

'Soon it will just be Jake and Arya, babe.' That was his constant, if trite, promise. Jake and Debbie were done.

She looked older than she did in the pictures. Of course, I thought, crazily and in slow-mo, as if in a dream. That wedding had been ten years ago. What those pictures didn't reveal was how this woman, up close, exuded strength, solidness, and a certain steely calmness that unnerved me from the very first moment I settled my eyes on her, right now in the flesh. Debbie was tall and regal-looking, with hair swept in a tight ponytail and secured at the nape of her neck, showing off the large pearl earrings on her ears. She was in faded jeans and a white collared shirt, similar to the one that Jake was wearing when we first met. There was a pink tinge on her lips, which looked flaky and wrinkly, as if the lipstick had dried out.

'Are you Arya? Arya Alvarez?' Her eyes were wide, hard and steady.

I didn't answer. My skin crawled, the hairs on my arm standing up.

'Are you Arya?' Her tone fell a notch, and for a moment it didn't seem as if she was demanding an answer from me.

'Yes.' My heart started beating so fast inside my chest, I wondered if this woman could see it.

'It's you. How dare you,' she spat out, her voice a low snarl. 'Gold-digger.'

Gold-digger? For a split second, everything around me seemed to stop and I was hearing nothing else but that word. One word, three syllables. One word, a thousand insults. Because yes, it was an insult to me that my love for Jake, my devotion, had been reduced to something as easy and tawdry as 'gold-digger.'

'I'm not a gold-digger,' I shot back, finally, dismayed that I sounded so feeble. I straightened my back, felt my chin raise up. 'Who are you?'

'Home-wrecker.' The accusation felt like a whip to my face. Her dry lips had twisted into something I couldn't bear to look at. Debbie's eyes were flashing, a vein throbbing on the side of her throat. But she didn't move from her spot. I was afraid that she'd strike me, but she had not taken a step forward or backward. Neither had I.

'I'm not a home-wrecker.' All defence, that was all I've got? Had I really not prepared for this day? For a moment, I let go of my fear to let in the disappointment that I felt for myself at that moment.

But what was I supposed to say? That Jake had told me he didn't love her any more? That Jake had said that he had loved her in the past years but that Jake loved *me*, now? That Jake was so eager to be apart from her? What was my proof, anyway?

'Then what are you, you slut. Fucking my husband.' The venom in her voice. And also, the steel, because she sounded hard, all-knowing and so confident as if she had done this before. 'You're not the first, you know.'

My hands grew cold. Or had they been cold all this time? What was it that she just said? That I wasn't the first?

'I wasn't the first,' said the wife of my boyfriend. There was something wrong in that sentence, I thought, my chest feeling as if a pair of heavy feet was pressing on it. Words that shouldn't belong together.

'I'm not what you think.'

'I know who you are, all right. *You* don't know who am I, and what I can do.'

'Your annulment—' I began. I raised my chin again. 'He told me that you weren't together any more. That it's been over for years.'

'Is that what he told you? And what the fuck do you know about our marriage? Who are you to say that it's over?' She gave a horrible, mirthless laugh. 'The gall of you! Don't you know how to stay away from married men? There are so many of these jerks around the world and you have to choose *my husband?'*

How had she known? Since when? Had this been a calculated moment, planned for days? Or had she just realized that something was up and so she decided to check on their condo? Up until that moment, I only thought of me and her, and not of Jake. I thought if Jake knew—

The text from Jake. The message that was from Jake's phone this morning. That was why there had been something odd there, a kind of formality that I had already felt but dismissed instantly. Because who was I to know that it had been Jake's wife who was answering my texts?

And then another thought entered my mind, and I shivered. What if she was here to hurt me? To kill me? What if she had a gun?

Calm down, Arya. There was still that part of me that was in control, telling me what I should do: *Don't be crazy. Don't be irrational.* I wanted to laugh. This whole thing that I'd done with Jake, this affair, maybe this was what was crazy and irrational. How could I have thought that I would get away with this?

We stood there, glaring at each other for what seemed like a horrifically extended moment, me rooted in the same spot near the balcony doors and Debbie still standing by the front door. Unless she really had a gun, there was still some distance between us.

The thing was, distance had ceased to be the primary issue here when it came to protecting myself. I had the need to leave the room, to leave the building, to leave this woman who was hurling insults at me. Insults that I probably deserved, in a way.

What concerned me at that moment was that I couldn't just run out. I was trapped.

And then she was screaming at me. Took a step forward and started cursing and shouting so loud and so fast, I couldn't even begin to understand what she was saying.

And then the door flew open and there was Jake.

'Jake!' I cried, hoping my voice rose above Debbie's screaming. And then I saw that she was crying.

'Debbie!' Jake had taken one look at me, then at her, and rushed in. 'What are you doing?'

Debbie was starting to crumple on the floor, sobbing and talking incoherently.

He was by Debbie's side in an instant, catching her before she fell completely on the floor. 'Tell her!' She sobbed, hands swiping carelessly at her eyes. Her ponytail had come loose and there was long dark hair tangled all over her face and neck. 'Tell her that you're choosing me!'

I stared at Jake in horror. I looked at both of them, intertwined in each's other arms, crouching on the floor. I wanted to flee but I couldn't stand what I had just seen.

'Jake, what is this?'

'Get out!' Debbie's voice was hoarse, and when she looked at me her eyes were red and tear-stained and so full of rage.

I looked at Jake. His jaw was twitching, and he was breathing hard. 'Jake? Jake!'

'Arya, it's best you leave.' Jake's tone was quiet.

'But you have to tell me what's going on—'

'Please! Arya! Just leave!' His voice had risen to a bellow, panicked and stressed.

There was a hardening in me that had already formed when I saw them together, right here in the condo that they owned in Bayview Suites. And it felt like something had hit me, a sudden heavy, hot air that slapped my face, waking me up. I knew instantly that I had been wrong, all this time. Oh, how wrong I was. And what a fool I'd been. The world was right. Debbie was right. There was no annulment. There never will be an annulment, perhaps, as long as Debbie was in this life. In Jake's life. As long as there was Jake and Debbie, their arms around each other, asking another person to get out.

I rushed past them and I was out of the condo unit in seconds. The hall lights hit me and only then did I let out a ragged cry, just after I'd closed the door behind me as quietly as I could.

Chapter 10

Manila, Philippines, more than two years ago. My room looked like it had been hit by a typhoon. I looked at the open suitcases around me, at the various clothes, shoes, accessories, papers, books, and bric-a-brac strewn on the floor. I still had a lot of packing to do.

My brother came in, carrying a mug of tea. 'Here,' he said. 'Sorry it's just a tea bag.'

'Thanks,' I said, a little touched. I smiled, feeling wan. 'I don't want to go now, because of this tea bag.'

He laughed. 'Well, you said you broke your teapot.'

I nodded and took a sip. 'I know. How clumsy of me, and just before my trip, right?' My Singapore work pass, processed by Isle Z, had just been approved. I had just received my In Principle Agreement that would allow me to work in the island state. I was leaving for Singapore the next day.

'Well,' he said. 'Don't you have another one? Don't you have your whole other collection of teapots?'

I knew my brother was sad, which is why he was still talking about teapots. I was sad, too.

'They're not as good,' I said, my tone mournful. 'And to think I broke it because I was just emptying its contents in the trash.' I shook my head. 'One wrong move and that's it. Broken teapot.'

A single wrong move and everything can be broken. I used to think about that a lot when I was driving, just living my life here—at how a wrong turn of the wheel, a missed turn, or a sleepy blink can be fatal. Everything gone in an instant, just because a single element failed to align itself with the rest of the universe's flow.

But the thing with Jake was that it wasn't just one wrong move. It was a series of wrong moves, tolerated over a good two years. I had known about the situation, and yet I had foolishly forged on, thinking I was invincible. Thinking I'd never be broken. At least, not that soon.

It had been three weeks after that ugly confrontation with Debbie. Three weeks since I had not been with Jake. Three weeks of pain, of confusion, of hurt and humiliation.

Were all break-ups this way? This intrusive, this debilitating? It did not help that I had started seeing Jake's face everywhere. An innocuous encounter—like passing along a random guy in the mall or seeing the back of someone's head during my commute to work—would ignite my insides with a brief, burning flash as I was suddenly reminded of him. Bits and pieces of him and his imperfections started haunting me everywhere and in the people I met daily—the downward turn of the mouth which I used to find so adorable, the small, kind, earnest eyes that I used to marvel at, the broad, bony shoulders that I used to like laying my head on. Sometimes, I believe I can even remember how my hand felt in his. And how it had felt so safe then, holding that hand. Jake had seemed so kind, forthright, thoughtful, and sensitive; maybe what hurt me most was that I honestly believed with all my heart that he was sincere. Simply, I thought he loved me.

Because we were both entrepreneurs, I have always sensed that there was an astute, cunning edge lying underneath him, necessary when doing the kind of business he did in Manila. I had always thought that this cunning was reserved for his stubborn clients, errant employees, or 'bad' people trying to do a number on him. Never had I thought that Jake would use it to deceive me.

Will the painful twinges ever go away? Will there ever be a time when his name would pass through my mind without opening a floodgate of stinging, muddled emotions?

Give yourself time to grieve, everyone told me, during the depths of my break-up. Time heals and it will pass. It won't be easy, everyone warned me, but it will happen. There will come a time when this debilitating pain stops, when the confusion finally ebbs away, and the questions that I used to desperately seek the answers to, will not seem to matter any more. Or so I thought.

After the initial rage, the first forty-eight hours where try as I might, I couldn't sleep a wink, the succeeding almost sleepless nights, food that tasted like nothing—a resigned, profound sadness overcame me like a slow, quiet wave. I had poured my heart, body, and soul into this relationship—and it terrified me that someone whom I thought shared the very same belief and emotions, someone who had grown to be a part of me—was callous, hard-hearted, and narcissistic enough to lie unblinking to my face.

He called me three times a day. Yes, he did. In these three weeks that we were apart, Jake called every day. Even the calls seemed to be on schedule, so typical of his organized, efficient self.

The first thought that entered my mind as the facts and evidence hit me was, 'Why me?' Why had this terrible, heartbreaking, devastating thing happened to me? This person who claimed he loved me more than life itself, had lied not once, but again and again.

'Don't be a victim,' the few friends I confided in always told me. But in those first few weeks and months, I felt like one.

Sometimes, I test the waters and allow my mind to wander through the good times. The idyllic setting of how we met, how our love as I knew it grew. Everyone we told our story to was always amazed at the circumstances, so romantic you'd think they exist only in movies. I myself was amazed every time I'd relive the incidents in my mind.

But then what would inevitably follow was a disturbingly convenient clicking of everything into place. The absences, the strange refusals to stay, the reluctance to show affection in public, the promises that never materialized.

In hindsight, I couldn't swear that I didn't have my doubts then. There were thoughts that sprung into my mind that I had dismissed almost instantly because they seemed so crazy, even unthinkable. I knew it was intuition, yet I had dutifully, gently yet firmly swatted it away. Following your intuition has always been a delicate, mindful exercise and one that I should have developed. Lost in the flurry of the relationship, I couldn't be farther from myself.

I had been betrayed big time and it felt as if no one could truly understand me. Now that I knew, it all suddenly made sense. I had not been chosen.

And now I was here, split from him. What was the feeling, after the grief? After rejection?

Being alone was a gift, certainly not a sin or a shortcoming. But I did feel something during these early days of separation. Something akin to being adrift, of not belonging. Uncertainty was terrifying, especially when it came to love and one's love life. I found myself thinking, if not Jake, then who? Whom did I belong with? Whom will I grow old with? The yearning was so simple. Why can't I have it, just like others did?

Sometimes, I thought it was all over. I would wake up some days and think that that was the day that the hurt, the shock, the despair, and the heart-wrenching grief would finally be past me. I would look at Facebook pictures of him, see him smiling and easy-going, finally looking at ease with his clients or employees—and expect myself to be happy, not bitter. To be at peace, not perturbed. *My* Facebook pictures looked a hundred times happier, more interesting and more colourful. After all, my life was better now, and it was certainly better without him, right?

But there was that old grief, safe and familiar. No matter how much I wanted to be calm and resolute, the truth was my heart jumps in fear, ever so slightly, every time I was reminded of Jake Hidalgo. Long after I had scanned those photos, telling myself that it now meant nothing, that Jake's happiness, success, contentment, or even discontentment was his business, not mine—I would feel that familiar tug of doubt. And then, despite my best efforts, the weeks and months it took for me to train myself, to steer my thoughts and harness my emotions, it would all just unravel, little by little. And then I would just find myself helpless, thinking the thoughts that perhaps I shouldn't be thinking any more. Thoughts like—was there really nothing wrong with me? Could I have done something to prevent this pain? Could I have been more aware? Could I have done something, anything?

Chapter 11

Singapore 8.32 a.m. 'I'm booking you for tonight, and you can't cancel.' Nhi Tran, my housemate and my best friend, was adamant.

I had just slipped into our flat on the sixth floor, closing the wide, wooden door carefully behind me. 'Well, welcome home to you, too.'

'How was Ho Chi Minh and Da Nang? Or did you just come from Hue?' Nhi frowned. 'I swear you've been to more cities in my country in a couple of years than I have my whole lifetime! Can't ever keep track of where you've been.'

'Da Nang,' I said. 'From Hanoi. I slept the whole two hours.' My laugh sounded crazed, and I scratched my brow. 'With Rooki Sakimoto, remember—so I'm pretty sure I flew in from Hanoi. Goodness, even I don't know where I've just come from.'

Nhi got off the couch and twisted her lips, cocking her head to the side so that her straight shoulder-length hair fell like a brown shiny sheet around her face. 'Are you tired? It's about time you spent time with me. Spent time here! Why else would we make a cozy home for ourselves in Singapore if we're not going to enjoy it?' For a moment, she stood by our low coffee table, arms akimbo. 'I'm really beginning to think I should have put an ad, months ago, that said: 'Wanted: housemate who acts like a real human being by being home at normal hours.' What say you, huh?'

'Nhi! Can you not? You know this is work!' I laughed, despite my tiredness. I *was* tired, and Nhi was always just so positive in her own negative-sounding ways. I parked my suitcases by the door, took two wide steps across the room, and hugged her. 'Oof, Nhi-Nhi. You're so fit. Where's the fat? What would I do without you as my forever fitness and life peg? I have two bottles of wine from Duty-Free.'

'Alcohol won't save you next time.' She placed her arms around me, returned the hug, then pulled at the ends of my hair. 'Just kidding, you know I'm used to your schedule.' She let go and stood back to look at me, eyes narrowed upwards, taking a mischievous look. 'It's just that, it's been so lonely here and I'm so fed up with my colleagues submitting sub-par work. I'm about to give a long, stern lecture next Monday, I swear.'

'Go for it,' I said. 'Just don't do it here. Absolutely no lectures allowed in this living room!' I was kidding of course, but I knew how Nhi could be organized and exacting.

'Oops.' Nhi laughed, catching herself. She waved a dismissive hand in the air but raised her eyebrows. 'Seriously, I need BFF quality time with you, or I'm really gonna give you a real lecture. Just like at work.' Her face softened, slightly. 'Thank goodness, the love of my life *lives* in Singapore and actually stays here.'

'That is absolutely not fair,' I flopped down on the couch. 'Lisa works at a Singapore public relations agency. Of course she can be here all the time.'

I had not known Nhi, or her girlfriend, Lisa, at all before I came to live in this apartment. In fact, I had not known anyone at all in Singapore when I first moved here, after having packed up everything I could, gathered whatever material parts of my life I thought were relevant to the new life and new job I would have in this island state. Singapore was only about four hours from Manila, but it was true—it meant a whole new life for me. It was a life away from Jake and all that we had shared when we were together.

The truth was, it hurt to stay in Manila. It was as if the whole city had conspired, teasing and nudging me until I fell off the cliff, unawares. Because Jake had his Airbnbs and coffee stall business, he almost always never travelled. Desperate to be with him, and perhaps always insecure that he might go back any time to Debbie, his wife, I realized only belatedly that I had also kept myself from leaving the country, even if it had been part of my job and my business. I only realized, so late in the relationship, how I had chosen to stay in Manila, instead of going overseas or out of town, on the trips that I needed to do. I started passing fam tours to Luisa. I declined invitations for private, educational tours by various tourism boards. I arranged all my meetings with military precision, juggling schedules and maximizing half-hours so I would have time to meet Jake, or at least, drop by one of his stalls where I would eat lunch or dinner. I did all the paperwork for my clients and I was thorough—as long as the legwork was only in Manila and the surrounding areas.

It had all been my fault, too. I had failed myself, and Luisa too. I had failed my business. I had let down so much, and all that I had worked for.

I had always believed that I fled Manila because could not be at the scene of my heartbreak. But it was also this: I fled because I could not be at the scene of my failures.

* * *

I found Nhi through Oliver. A lucky streak and another lucky sign that there was hope that things might go well for me in Singapore. Because my employers were aware that I had transplanted myself here, Oliver suggested the services of his real estate agent, Sammy Wong. Fortunately, Sammy knew that there was a flat that was about to be available in one of the quieter streets of Serangoon, and not too far from the MRT.

'A quiet, residential area in the heartlands, with excellent connections to the city,' Sammy had trilled as if he himself was doing a live ad for the place. 'And don't forget, it's six minutes away from the station. I can't get you a better deal than that.' He assured me that I was getting the space for a reasonable price—prices of real estate in Singapore at that time were, thankfully, stable.

I signed the papers after a single viewing. I remember still feeling dazed. And I remember marvelling at how fast things moved in Singapore. I never realized how laid back we all were back in Manila, and how the simplest things took time. But here—well, the cashiers were done before I was even rummaging through my bag to locate my money to pay for my groceries.

And so the apartment search had been quick. Painless. Needed a viewing? It can be done today or first thing tomorrow. Papers needed to be signed? It was easy to do it online or hop on the train to meet. Emails needed to be answered? In Singapore, it felt normal for people to reply within an hour.

I had vowed to keep up. This kind of life was something completely new—and I wanted it. The wound that the experience with Jake had left in me had, at that time, still felt raw. Feelings of humiliation and shame were still swirling strongly within me, and I knew that I had made the right decision to leave and be somewhere else. Here. I wanted a total change of atmosphere because I was desperate for a total change of life. I wanted a life where I can live without Jake.

Until now, I still thank the universe that it was Nhi who turned out to be my housemate. I still thank the universe for her previous housemate Charie, who had to leave five months earlier because she needed to take an urgent job in London, and so had created the space in this quiet Serangoon flat I would soon occupy.

Nhi, who had moved here from Ho Chi Minh City five years ago to work, had become not only a very good friend but a friend and sister for life. Schooled in Zurich and Taipei, she had been working as a communications manager for several sister boutique hotels in Singapore. I had been amazed at her shrewdness, at her ability to juggle her work schedule, manage her mostly young staff, and still spend time with Lisa.

I can't recall the many times we've had heart-to-heart talks, talking about anything and everything. We looked out for each other. With Nhi, I knew it was a safe space.

And sometimes I really wished I was as organized and as wise as Nhi. 'Bah,' she'd say whenever I'd complain about myself. 'You'll get there. You do need to know that you have to do something over and over—and *over* to get it right, right?' She was outspoken and sharp and witty and never failed to keep me on my toes.

Yes, Nhi wasn't only my best friend, but a shining example to me. Nhi was the best example, in fact, that I could also thrive in another city other than my own.

* * *

'Shall we order food?' Nhi was a total sloth on her days off and today wasn't an exception. She stretched her pale legs out on the sofa. 'Or walk to the hawker?' She squinted and blinked, then said: 'How about pizza? Shake Shack? Maybe we walk to the hawker, buy tasty local stuff, then order pizza and beer. And get chocolates from 7-Eleven.'

That was Nhi. She adored junk food, though she'd never made Lisa and I forget that she still had high standards when it came to food and its right flavour—didn't matter if it was street food or a Michelin star resto—and so almost always dictated what was worth feasting on. She can also cook a mean Filipino *adobo,* going all-out generous with the vinegar, garlic and soy sauce that were the main ingredients of this pork dish.

Also, I've lived with her for close to three years, and she's never gained weight.

So now it was dinner time. 'So? Ar?' Nhi was getting impatient. 'Pizza and beer, but need tasty local. Ah, maybe a stingray—and then we pop in 7-Eleven for chocolates? Ooh, or ice cream!'

It always amazes me how easy it was to buy food in Singapore, and yet we still manage to make it complicated.

I gazed out the window and looked at the very clear, cloudless blue sky that was fast becoming muted by the fading evening light. Everything seemed to have an orange tinge, which made the blue appear deeper. It looked postcard-perfect to me.

I shifted from my sprawled position at the end of the couch. 'Nhi-Nhi. How about a drink? Like, we shower and get dressed?'

Nhi didn't move at all from her position. 'Don't you have travel fatigue?' She raised her leg, and did some clumsy leg-ups. 'Aren't you supposed to sleep it off? Or take it easy? Don't you need to stay home because of jetlag or something? Why do you even want to go out?'

'Come on, Nhi, it was Vietnam. I don't have jetlag,' I grinned. 'But even if I did, I still say—fuck it, let's go.'

In an hour, we were actually being led to the bar inside Birds of a Feather, a bar resto along Amoy Street. Nhi and I quickly showered and dressed, putting on flats and patting on makeup. Another plus for Singapore: it was so easy to get out, and so easy to go back. I knew we would make it back to our flat way before midnight.

'There's something about you,' Nhi said. 'I know you just came from my country. I know you don't want to talk about it.'

I hardly discussed Vietnam with Nhi. Actually, I hardly discussed any of my trips to any country with her. Sometimes I ranted about a celebrity or two. But mostly, it was as if I'd become too soaked of everything during my trip, that I had lost all interest to even relive it. It didn't matter any more where I came from, if it was Vietnam or some European country. Time with Nhi was 'letting it all hang without pressure of talking' —and sometimes, that was just the way I like it.

So mostly, we just hung out in front of the TV or watched whatever was new in Netflix.

'So?' Nhi nodded gratefully at the barman, who placed two pints of icy cold Leffe Blonde in front of us.

'I got reminded again.' I took a long, deep, noisy breath.

'Ugh, I hate that sound.' Nhi frowned. 'Please. Talk to me.'

'Why is everyone in Vietnam all coupled up?'

'What?'

'I was in Da Nang, The Forest. I couldn't stand everyone.'

'Honey. That's a honeymoon place. You don't expect solo travellers or backpackers there, do you?'

'I would have liked that honeymoon with Jake.'

'Jake, again?'

'Why, who else would it be?'

'It's been—' Nhi paused. She was smart enough to stop herself and sit back, have a sip of her beer.

'I know, I know.' I had knocked back a few big gulps, and I was feeling heady.

'But, Arya.' Nhi's voice turned pleading. 'You know better than to be affected by those things. I mean, you see them here in Singapore. Or any city you find yourself in. Why, I'm sure there are lovey-dovey couples right here—'

'Still.' I didn't mind if I cut her off. Nhi was Nhi, she would understand my frustration. 'Still,' I repeated. 'I would like to be part of a couple.'

'Oh, Arya.' I felt Nhi's long, slim arms around me. 'I wish I could give that to you.'

'It's what I want,' I mumbled, resting my head heavily on her shoulder, my mouth full of her brown hair.

'Only you can make it happen, my dear Arya.' Nhi's voice was muffled as she patted my back. 'Just you.'

Chapter 12

Kusatsu, Japan, 2.01 p.m. The first thing that hit me was the putrid, heavy smell of rotten eggs, heightened by the sight of visible steam rising from a vast pool of light blue water, so light-coloured it appeared icy. It was corralled by rocks and a decidedly unappealing cement fence. Yubatake was what this hot spring source was called, right smack in the middle of a haphazard-looking mountain town in Japan called Kusatsu. The gushing hot site was the source of all the steaming, mineral-rich water of the onsen baths that made up most of the town of Kusatsu, four hours away by car, south of Tokyo.

It was a week after my Vietnam trip with Rooki Sakimoto, and I was away from Singapore again. This time, I was on a familiarization tour in Tokyo and Kyoto, specifically to learn about the onsen baths of Japan. No celebrities this time. Instead, there were eight of us from different travel tours and agencies in Singapore, the Philippines, Malaysia, and Indonesia. The Tourism Board of Gunma Prefecture, who sponsored the tour, even threw in an irresistible extra, to make sure we would all make it to this four-day tour—they scheduled the trip at the end of cherry blossom season, the last few days that the flowers would be in bloom in areas outside of Tokyo, and just as the *hanami* crowds were thinning.

For now, it was onsen time. 'So,' Helena Lim of JNB Travel in Singapore was saying, wrapped tightly in one of her woolly shawls, languid against the railing that surrounded all sides of the Yubatake. 'I dare say this is Japan's best onsen town. Well, it's the largest, after all.'

'Just *one* of its best,' Serene Chan interjected, wrinkling her nose. 'Helen, yesterday's hot spring water's already got into you.' She, too, was leaning against the railing, gazing at the hot spring field. She tied and retied the string that held the hood of her sports jacket the front of which was printed in big, white letters: Intrepid Tours SG. She waved a hand in front of her face as if there was an insect she was trying to swat off. 'Do you think the other Japanese baths smell as . . . interesting?'

I was a day late for this trip. I had arrived from Vietnam a week before but had to meet with another client, the Singapore–Indonesian socialite Baby Goh, on the day we were supposed to leave for Japan, which I realized I couldn't re-schedule. A minor mess, but given the erratic nature of my clients' work, had not been the first time it happened. Helena, Serene, and the rest of the fam tour group had already arrived in Kusatsu the day before, travelling for four hours to this town from Tokyo by van. Meanwhile, I opted to do a commute, taking a series of different trains and buses from Tokyo to reach the famous spring town.

It took me more than four hours to finally arrive, welcomed warmly by the reps of Gunma Tourism and my fam tour mates. I was grateful for this group. I had known Helena just months after I was hired at Isle Z, and she'd introduced me to Serene and some other agents, a warm gesture that I felt was incredibly sincere, and very much appreciated. It was my first time working overseas, and it did wonders in easing my trepidation about meeting new contacts. Familiarization tours were definitely one of the perks of working for a travel company, and I'd joined several when I still had my own travel agency in Manila. The ones in Singapore, though—and maybe because I was working for a company whose focus was on luxe but unique travel—felt more expansive, more global, more adventurous, and definitely more eye-opening than the ones I've experienced before.

'Arya? Babe, you still have your luggage,' Helena was saying now, straightening up. She narrowed her eyes and did a quick scan of me from head to toe, as if seeing me for the first time. 'I can't believe you declined Mariko-san's offer to pick you up by car in Tokyo,' she said. Mariko, whom I've only communicated with in emails and a Zoom meeting, was our point person and host from Gunma Tourism Board.

I waved a dismissive hand, rolling my carry-on suitcase so it was behind me. 'Oh, no worries. It was just three hours from Ueno station,' I said, touching my nose. The smell from the hot springs, as was the steam rising from the spot, seemed to thicken and intensify. 'Two hours and forty minutes, to be exact,' I said.

It was more complicated than it sounded, and I had to take two trains and a couple more buses to finally reach Kusatsu, but it had been a good distraction. Despite the nature of my job, there were instances when I still craved to be alone, to catch my breath, and this had been a good opportunity. It gave me time to think, even as my train from

Ueno was climbing higher and higher into the picturesque mountains of Gunma Prefecture.

'The views were great,' I said. 'Did you know that the train is at the side of the mountain?'

It was not my first time in Japan—my first time had been on another fam trip to Tokyo and Osaka when I was working in Manila—so I had few qualms about taking public transport and doing a long, major commute. But there was also another thing that I wanted to test out. As the train to Kusatsu passed through postcard-perfect scenery, I thought of how Jake and I had planned a trip to Japan ourselves, as a two-year anniversary thing. A treat to ourselves, especially as how my then travel agency, Tripology, had just secured a bunch of new clients. At that time, despite Jake's status, I had so much positivity in me that I believed so many things were worth celebrating. And Jake—he had always been a homebody, checking-in guests at his Airbnbs, finishing his rounds at his stores, and then heading straight home, a routine he said he did for years. When we were together, I had thought that admirable and disciplined, and he was not a travel person at all, so it had been special.

* * *

'Women on the right, men on the left.' The diminutive Japanese auntie didn't actually speak English, so I may have just imagined that. I smiled and gave a small bow as she handed me a tiny piece of paper that was my entrance ticket.

'Women on the right,' I murmured, as I moved away from the counter and trailed behind a couple of Japanese women in pastel sweaters, shuffling to the end of a queue at the far-right side of the building. Because I was a day late, I had to play catch-up with the rest of the group on the onsen schedule, and this particular onsen, Sainokawara Rotemburo, according to Mariko-san, was where I needed to start. The largest one in Kusatsu, it was just a fifteen-minute walk from the centre of town and from the hot, steaming springs of Yubatake.

It was also Mariko-san who'd instructed me on certain things about the onsen baths, echoing what was already in the PDF file that was sent to the travel agents going on the trip. It contained all the information we needed, including onsen etiquette. Because this was a mixed-gender onsen, Mariko-san said, there were separate hot pools for the men and women. The views of nature were to die for, she'd added. And there was one more thing that Mariko-san said, that I couldn't quite recall.

'No swimsuits!' Someone was speaking in clear, well-enunciated English, down the line behind me. 'You need to take off *everything,*'

I already knew this, having skimmed through the Tourism Board's PDF file on the six-hour flight from Singapore to Tokyo. I had never tried it, but I've always heard about the onsen and the hot springs in Japan, even during my first trip here.

Right now, it felt like an intimidating concept, even though I was sure that my body was craving for something to relieve it from the tension that had been building up since, well—since I fled Manila and everything that I knew and had grown up with, apparently. I realized that I had barely taken days off, especially in the past year, when client after client, and trip after trip, were assigned to me by Oliver and Desmond.

And then, a more pressing thought—would they really make us soak in forty-degree hot water? Naked? With all these other people?

The queue had loosened up and I was ready to go through the entrance that would lead to the shower rooms and the hot springs. Just a nondescript door, with a cloth curtain attached as a single sheet from above, gently flapping and touching the heads of the women who were streaming inside.

'*Sumimasen.*' A petite Japanese woman squeezed past, after laying a demure forefinger on my upper arm and gently pushing me aside. That was when I remembered Mariko-san's advice—bring a towel. For modesty, if you prefer. 'Just pop it on your head once you're in the onsen,' she said. 'Towels should never be dipped in the water.' I could see a whole wall of lockers against the wooden, cabin-like walls of the room.

I turned away from the group of people who were queueing and pushed my way back. Towel, I thought. I need a towel.

When I returned to the front desk and asked, the Japanese auntie directed me to a vending machine at the far end of the room. I sighed with relief. I felt even more assured when someone walked past me carrying what appeared to be a wide, full-fledged towel in her arms.

Only in Japan, I thought, happily surveying the vending machine's current wares: flimsy-looking umbrellas, tumblers, white collared shirts, and yes—towels, packed neatly in a square cardboard box. I had some Yen in my bag, and punched the correct button, easily slipping the coins in the labelled slot. After a moment, the shelves shift inside and my packaged towel dropped down, ready to be retrieved.

Success! I thought, bending down to grab the box from the cavity below. I felt a surge of relief, and finally, excitement of trying the onsen for the first time. I imagined myself safe, and all covered. It would be all right, it would be fun! A learning experience. I love my job!

I smiled again as I passed by the receiving area, hurrying back towards the locker and shower rooms. The bulk of the onsen bathers had gone through by this time, and I found myself sailing into the door and into a room filled with women who had already stripped down and getting ready for the therapeutic soak. Around twenty women were there, stashing their clothes inside lockers, walking about, tying their hair, and waiting for each other. There was a wide opening on one side of the room where I could see women on very low stools running a hand-held showerhead on themselves. Further, I could glimpse the blue water of the famed Sainokawara Rotemburo. I hung back at the edges, unnerved. Thankfully, no one paid me any mind.

I watched as if in a trance, women sealing their lockers shut. Don't overthink this, I told myself, and then I had a jolt—and a sudden, almost irrational fear of not being able to secure a locker to put all my clothes, my phone, and my little bag in. What if I left my clothes out here and someone took them? Somehow, I feared more about losing my clothes at this time, than my wallet. In any case, I couldn't let that happen. I stepped forward and grabbed the first locker door that was within my reach.

I quickly shrugged off my pants, peeled off my jacket and shirt until I stood in my underwear. I closed my eyes and, in a swoop, removed my underwear. There you go, a voice inside me said. That wasn't so hard. And anyway, I now had a towel. I can cover the bits that needed to be covered if I really was feeling shy.

I shook out the towel from its box, only to discover that it was size of a table napkin. A small, square table napkin. A face towel—only, my face was actually bigger than this piece of terry cloth. My butt certainly was.

I glanced at the clock on the wall. It was getting late in the morning and I had work to do—meaning, more onsens to try and more travel partners to make friends with, so I could make the most of this fam trip for more clients at Isle Z.

There were English instructions on the inside of the door, on how to properly lock it. After a little jiggling and two or three failed attempts, I finally managed to turn it the right way, with the right pressure.

A quick shower with soap, and I was ready for my very first soak. The onsen, shaped like a round, sunken pond, was huge. But what was incredible was the view of the trees surrounding it. It was freeing to be so naked under a full sky, gazing up at a forest.

They were not lying when they said it was forty degrees in here. The women were sitting, talking, and laughing out loud. Some had their towels folded neatly and placed on top of their heads.

I closed my eyes and lowered myself into the water. It felt scalding at first, but after a minute felt soothing as if my pores had submitted to the heat and the steam and the smell.

I stood up after a couple of minutes, feeling an incredible kind of calm. My eyes almost drooping, I made my way to a rock where some of the women were sitting, some staring into the forest, others talking softly to each other. I settled myself beside them.

No one had a towel bigger than mine.

Chapter 13

Kruger Park, South Africa, 6.32 a.m. 'Is that our guide?' I heard someone ask. 'Or is that a cheetah?'

I tried to ignore the thick, fearful tremble of the voice that floated above our open-air jeep and into the still quiet of this wilderness, as I, too, tried not to jump at the sounds of rustling—right now, somewhere in the direction of two o'clock, a distinct but oh-so-hidden quivering in the dry, brown bushes of South Africa's famed Kruger National Park.

Think of the onsens, I told myself, *instead of wild lions.* Or cheetahs, which was what our little safari group was currently looking for.

It's been two weeks since my rejuvenating, albeit awkward hot spring bath experience in Japan, and for a moment, I almost wished I was back there in my birthday suit, soaking up the tranquility—and forty-degree onsen waters of Kusatsu. But here I was, at the very heart of one of South Africa's largest game reserves, home to 2,800 lions and only 200 cheetahs, which was why our guide had to go and look for one for us.

We were in the middle of a clearing, all six passengers in that Jeep—four of us from different travel agencies in Singapore travelling with two journalists, which was common practice on fam tours. Janssen Ong was an editor for an online magazine called *LuluSpeaks* in Singapore, while the other journalist, Ricky Deng, was a travel reporter for a newspaper in Taiwan. Around us, baobab and umbrella thorn trees towered above, while sickle and pistol bushes lay thick on the ground below. Our South African ranger and guide, a tall, blond, broad-shouldered man with a fuzzy beard called Johan, had still not returned.

We felt like orphans.

'It's only been ten minutes since he left,' announced Janssen, raising a thick wrist and tapping the face of his black, bulky watch. 'I saw him do a left turn when he reached that tree over there.' He had been doing a running commentary on just about everything since we started our game drive early this morning.

There were more sounds, and they didn't appear as faint as they did earlier. 'What's that?' I craned my neck to see where the rustling was coming from. More importantly, I strained to see what the rustle *was*.

No one wanted to answer me, it seemed.

'Is he back?' Someone asked again. This time, it was Helena. Good ol' Helena who almost always never missed a familiarization tour. This particular one was to several luxe safaris in South Africa, and the kind she'd always declared she'd never pass up. I wasn't sure, though, if she signed up for this: to be left alone, exposed, and vulnerable in a low, open-air safari jeep in the middle of an African game reserve—

where we all knew the thousands of animals who live here. We've seen four of the Big Five, and the cheetah, though not part of that list, was exceptionally beautiful, and rare. There were also the wild dogs.

'There could be lions here,' someone was saying now, forgetting about the rhinos, the tigers, the leopards, and the hyenas.

'Most likely,' Janssen piped up. 'I mean, there are thousands of lions here. Almost three thousand, if I can recall correctly.'

'Shush,' admonished Ricky Deng. 'Johan's still searching for the cheetah, remember.'

'If he hasn't yet been eaten by one.'

'We could be eaten, too.'

Nobody said anything after this.

I was distracted. I was ashamed to say that I couldn't really focus on the gravity of the situation—was it really serious, being left alone with five other people in the middle of a game reserve without a professional ranger or was it fine, I wasn't sure. And so I sat limp at the back row, listening to the nervous banter that my five other safari-mates were exchanging to diffuse the fear, the worry—or perhaps they were just revelling in the thrill? Not that there was anything overtly thrilling about being on your own in the middle of wildlife.

'Whatever happens, don't go out the vehicle,' was Johan's last words, when he set out to find our cheetah.

We were all booked—'camped'—in a safari lodge in Kruger called Wanatu Satu Safaris, complete with an infinity pool, a sprawling deck overlooking the reserve, luxurious tents equipped with marble sinks, thick, fragrant duvets, nubby sisal rugs, and an outdoor shower—besting even your typical five-star resort. About five hundred metres away and from the safety of our electric fence, we could see a watering hole that was, to our delight, actually regularly visited by elephants, a mother-and-baby rhino, and a dazzle of zebras at random times of the day. We always felt a thrill when the babies make an appearance—baby elephants, who were constantly helped by the adult elephants, short young zebras already graceful and a standout among the group.

The plan, when we all woke up at 4 a.m. for our morning game drive, was to look and finally see the cheetah. The thought of this magnificent cat, who's been elusive the past three days, had only whetted the appetite of my group who'd suddenly seemed to discover their inner hunter, working through a checklist of the animals they've seen, all on a little booklet provided by Wanatu. The plan was, for our guide Johan to stop the vehicle, and find us a safe spot where we can wait while he goes off into the dry bush to follow what he declared were fresh paw prints of the elusive cheetah.

'He's near,' Johan had declared just before he left, kneeling down on the ground and pointing to a faint smudge on the ground. I couldn't really see it, but then, my mind was elsewhere.

I was in the middle of Kruger Park in South Africa and my mind was on Facebook, of all things. Back in Manila, we used to laugh about priorities, whenever we logged on to Facebook or Instagram Stories to record what we thought looked good or amusing or funny—never mind that there was a more pressing problem at hand. And I wasn't the type who freaked out without Wi-Fi. But at that moment, I found myself wishing that I was connected to the internet.

I must have dreamt something bad that morning because I made my first mistake of the day—logging on to Facebook without meaning to. I had meant to open another app, one that was related to travelling in South Africa, but my phone was sticky and so my fingers had caught. Facebook flashed open on my screen. And then I thought of Jake, as I do, on and off since the break-up, and even though I haven't even thought about him for weeks—maybe even months. There must be something about being out in the wild, that sense of courting danger, of daring—our safari lodge was luxurious in all aspects but at the end of the day, was actually merely a series of tents that flapped vigorously when the wind blew a little too strong, and moreover, it was built at the edge of that frequently-visited watering hole. Because I found myself taking a deep breath at the same time I started typing in Jake's name, that name I've said for years, the name I thought would be with me forever.

And so there it was, Jake's feed, still visible and available to me even if we weren't Facebook friends any more. He hadn't blocked me, nor I him—for what? Social media had felt so puerile compared to what we'd gone through that day at Bayview Suites, the day of the break-up.

And maybe there was something about seeing the animals up close—all magnificent, still somewhat wild and free in their natural habitat—because I felt strong, unfazed, even empowered. Certainly, I was strong enough to take on whatever right now. And after maintaining zero contact with Jake all these years, perhaps I deserved a kind of break from my disciplined restraint.

It was easy to scroll down, of course. And there it was: a photo of him, sitting at a long table in a restaurant that looked a little familiar, several plastic buckets of San Mig Lite bottles and plates of *crispy pata* on the table. Nothing special—he was having drinks and bar chow, just *pulutan* with a group of friends. It seemed so innocent and well, *normal*, at first glance.

My second mistake was zooming in. Jake wasn't just having drinks with friends, he was having drinks with friends, *with* someone. Upon closer look—and I zoomed in as close as I could get at the dark hour of 4 a.m., curled up in a pathetic ball at a corner of my fabulous safari tent—I could see that he was sitting beside a woman who wasn't Debbie, his wife. Nothing wrong with that—except that she had her hand splat firmly on a body part that belonged to Jake, and so close that it looked like it belonged to her, too.

Her hand was placed squarely on his thigh. Her hand. On Jake's thigh.

I had laughed at first, pooh-poohed as if it were one of those fake news photos they've Photoshopped to death. They must all be friends, everyone in that table was. But my denial mode, already feeble in the first place, crumbled in less than a minute.

Her hand was on his thigh.

The photo couldn't be zoomed in any closer, so I couldn't tell how far up his thigh her hand was without looking at a pixelated mess. But it was enough.

I should've closed, as quickly as I could, that little white and blue window on my phone. I really should've. But I didn't. In less than a minute, I had scrolled down, with the meticulous care of an artist putting the final touches on his work—because I was afraid of accidentally pressing 'Like' on a photo or a post that was two months or two years ago—and realized that he had been with this woman who was not his wife, for quite some time now. Almost a year, to be exact. It was sad and amazing that I sometimes struggled to add up prices and projected expenses for my clients, but could calculate the exact time frame my ex-boyfriend had since replaced me.

That hand-on-thigh photo seemed to be their signature photo. Just like the couple influencer clients I had, Jake and this woman had mastered a certain vibe in the way they appeared in pictures that they posted on their feed. A subtle vibe, one that kept people like me guessing—a photo of themselves, posing with a smaller group of people in Greenbelt, this time with Jake's hand on her shoulder. Typical *barkada,* because another guy also had his hand on the tip of her elbow. A picture of a badminton group where Jake was kneeling in front of the woman, as a way to fit everyone in the photo, I suppose. Perhaps they were, indeed, just a group of friends with the same hobbies—and Jake did have a good number of hobbies. A shot of the both of them having a meal in a plain-looking restaurant, a view of Quezon City behind them. A hotel? A rooftop resto-bar? You couldn't really tell if it was romantic or platonic—no one was holding hands, no one was touching a body part.

But that hand-on-thigh photo. As much as I wanted to be all right, to not be affected by this new image of my ex, I still felt a crushing squeeze in my chest and a hollow ache at the pit of my stomach.

The truth was, Jake had moved on. And it felt that I still haven't. And, why haven't I?

That morning, I almost didn't go with the rest of the group to the game drive. I almost went back to bed—it was, after all, a ridiculous time to be up and about, trundling through a game reserve before dawn has even touched the wild. How easy it had been to fake a headache or pretend I had diarrhea, which always seemed to work. It was certainly easier than dealing with this kind of emotional pain that almost felt physical: a sharp shot from my heart, every time I thought of Jake, that seemed to sear me from the insides.

When Jake and I broke up, I had always assumed that he was going back to his wife, Debbie. That we had fallen apart because he wanted to pick up the pieces of his own broken marriage. I had thought that he chose her, instead of me. A noble thought. An extremely painful thought then. Now that time has passed, and I'd had time to really mull over what had happened, why would I think that? Why on earth did I think that? Was it the fact that he said that he and Debbie were getting an annulment and I believed him? Just like I had believed him when he said that it was all over with him and Debbie, that everything was done.

I hadn't even entertained the thought that he was dating again. Silly me, I hadn't even thought that he was telling the truth about leaving his wife.

Here it was, almost three years after and the truth was, it still really, really hurt.

* * *

'He's back, he's back!'

They sounded like giddy teenagers, but I could sense the relief in their voices. I turned to see Johan walking briskly towards us, his face lit.

'Did you find it? The cheetah?' Janssen's voice rose above the rest. 'Can we take pictures?'

'Praise the lord, you're back!' Helena looked animated. She eyed the rifle that was on Johan's shoulders. 'You really shouldn't have left us, you know.'

'Johan, my man. Do we have hope of seeing the cheetah today?' Ricky Deng asked. 'You did find something, didn't you?'

'I know where she is,' Johan said, a smug smile on his face, revelling in all this attention. He quickly hopped on the vehicle, laying the rifle gently on the front seat.

A charged yet still nervous energy continued to ripple among us in the jeep.

'You know she's a she?' I asked, Johan's statement echoing faintly in my ears. My mind was elsewhere, and I wasn't really thinking.

But Johan just smiled again as he started the engine, and didn't answer.

* * *

Two hours and three false alarms later, we still haven't seen our cheetah. Johan had driven to three different directions, and not one was even near the spot where he left us. It was already nine o'clock, and we'd been out since 4.30. My stomach was grumbling, looking for breakfast.

Johan finally steered the jeep towards the direction of the lodge.

'Do you think we'll see her tomorrow?' I've been hearing this question all morning.

'This afternoon.' Johan's confidence was formidable. There were two game drives each day, one at 4.30 a.m., and the next at 3 p.m.

Back in the lodge, all thoughts of the cheetah fell away, as my phone started its beeping and lighting up: emails,

WhatsApp messages from clients, reactions to my previous days' Instagram and Facebook stories. Not that I had that many friends. Since starting work in Singapore, I have kept my circles and connections more professional than personal.

We were having our buffet breakfast in the main dining room. Ricky Deng made a beeline towards the mimosa bar, pouring himself a generous flute of champagne topped with just a dash of orange juice. Bottles of South African wine, all of which were inclusive in this package, were on display and kept cool in a special refrigerator in one corner, free for anyone to partake.

I wasn't feeling hungry. But I sat down beside Helena, who was arranging her various little plates. 'I need to get bread,' she said, pushing back her chair. 'And more coffee. I only had a teeny espresso before our drive!'

I leaned back and opened Jake's feed again. There was a new comment on that photo. A series of three hearts, from Thigh Woman.

My stomach felt hollow. Carefully, I downloaded the photo, and sent it quickly to Nhi via WhatsApp.

'What's this?' Was her immediately reply, less than a minute after. 'And why?'

I sent her a crying emoji.

'Babe! Not this again.' Annoyed, angry emoji. The one with the big frown.

'It's Jake's new girlfriend.' I wasn't sure, of course. It just felt good to rant with someone and someone who wouldn't think you were shallow or stupid for thinking of an ex in the middle of, well, *work*.

'So?'

This was the good thing about Nhi—she never took the bait. She downplayed everything first. And then, when she thought that it was needed, she'd strike.

'I can't believe he's moved on.'

'Then let me block him for you.'

'No!'

'Yes.' Nhi wasn't letting up. 'I know your password.'

I stared at her words on my little screen and was almost tempted to not reply to her at all.

Another beep. 'Just promise me you won't look at his feed again' was Nhi's latest message.

She made sense, of course. 'Okay,' I typed back, meaning it.

'Arya.' A new message, still from Nhi, flashed on the screen.

'Yes?'

'Be kind to yourself.'

Chapter 14

Svaneti, Republic of Georgia, 7.03 p.m. Angelique van Leuven was drunk, yet the food kept coming: hunks of stone-oven bread, steaming bowls of a pungent meat stew called *kharcho*, multiple plates of thick, sticky cornmeal porridge, platters of crispy, charred pork roasted and smoked on Saperavi vine twigs. The food had materialized from the kitchen, along with the smiles and gentle proddings in Georgian from the dark-haired, apron-clad women who had made them from scratch.

It wasn't just Angelique—upon closer look, it seemed that everyone at this table was drunk. Except, well, me. I'd only taken a small glass of the cloudy, orange-coloured wine that had been brought in and then poured at the table, a curious sight because the wine was in big plastic jugs, the clunky kind used for mineral water back home. I'd later learn that all the alcohol served at the table that night was brewed and fermented right in our host's own cellar.

And the food kept coming.

It had only been six days since my South African trip, when Oliver told me about going to Tbilisi, Georgia, with

Angelique van Leuven. A little too tight, but I was glad that it was with Angelique.

'And she wants to go to the mountains up north, in Svaneti,' Oliver had said. 'Some remote town in the Caucasus she's kind of obsessed with. Ushguli, I believe.'

I already knew that. Angelique had been messaging me for days leading up to the trip. No hiking, she said, for which I was glad. Just a look at the Caucasus and some time with the locals in Northern Georgia. In the village of Ushguli, as Oliver said.

'This is so, so *shwerichoosshhh,'* Angelique was slurring now, waving a piece of meat in the air, much to the delight of our Georgian host.

'Yes, delicious,' I echoed, quickly pulling down her arm. Angelique gave me a watery smile, swiping her lip clumsily with the back of her hand. Yes, the *mtsvadi,* hunks of pork smoked and roasted right before the feast, tended carefully by our host and our guides from Tbilisi, was indeed one of the most delectable pieces of meat I've ever tasted in a long while.

We were in Svaneti, in a small clearing somewhere at the foot of the Caucasus mountains, that long, glorious mountain range separating Russia from the Republic of Georgia, where we've been staying for the past five days. We were in the middle of a supra, a traditional Georgian feast prepared by the locals in the village of Ushguli. We had sat down on a long table, and watched as local specialties were served, local wine poured continuously into quaint little glasses. At one point that evening, someone had brought in an old horn, yet another vessel from which the wine was to be drunk.

We had scaled a hill and gone back down the other side to reach this house, which featured a spacious backyard peppered with walnut trees and a tiny vineyard. Like the rest of my group, I had been floored since we'd arrive after ten hours, driving from Georgia's capital town of Tbilisi to the town of Mestia, 670 kilometres away.

We were all still reeling from the majestic views that had greeted us when we arrived, almost breathless at this village that felt so high up in the air: snow-capped craggy mountains so magnificent and grand and *so close,* it felt as if you could just reach out and touch them. Tall towers loomed at every corner, some reaching six-storeys high, a defensive dwelling of the Svans, known as the bravest Georgians, according to our guides. They also spoke often and constantly about Mount Ushba, pointing out one of the Caucasus mountains' highest peaks on every pit stop and walk.

You'd think I was immune to this, but I wasn't. Svaneti, surrounded by mountains of the Caucasus up to 5,000 feet high, was nothing I'd ever seen before. To say that this place was mystical was an understatement. It almost felt like an open-air museum, surreal with its snow-covered slopes and sprawling alpine meadows as the backdrop to those imposing Svanetian towers. It felt almost like going back to the European Middle Ages.

Our posse had travelled all the way here because of a single person: Angelique van Leuven. Yes, this was *the* Angelique van Leuven, a vastly popular, multi-hyphenate celebrity whose star and popularity had continually been on the rise in Singapore, Southeast Asia, the Middle East, and Europe. Her online deets were in the millions. As in, Instagram followers—eleven million. Twitter followers—4.1 million; likes on Facebook Fan Page—935K. TikTok—two million.

Born in southwestern France, and raised in Singapore, Oman, and Jakarta, Angelique was first a fashion designer who'd trained at The Royal Academy of Fine Arts in Antwerp, Belgium, and finally, in acting in New York. Coming back to her roots, Angelique was first known as a theatre performance artist at Singapore's Repertory Theatre. In between, she had taken up another Master's in Fine Arts at Dundee University in Scotland. After auditioning and starring in *Satori Story*, a Japanese film on enlightening and the martial arts by world-class director Shohei Oshima, Angelique became not only known as a force in the art world but also as a promising actor. *Satori Story* went on to win eight awards at Sundance, as well as at the Berlin Film Festival, the Raindance Film Festival, and the Busan International Film Festival. Angelique shuttled between countries filming movies and then travelled some more to hold art exhibits for her contemporary paintings. Was there anything that Angelique couldn't do?

Our Georgian guides had not understood a word she'd said but had been smitten.

Earlier, we had been climbing hills. My thighs were still throbbing in fact, as I recalled the steep slopes I'd had to scale to get to this place. In front of me, I saw figures bounding ahead as if they had the grace and nimbleness of mountain goats and the speed and deftness of influencers. But Angelique van Leuven was no mountain goat, nor was she a hard and fast influencer out in the wild. From my slippery perch, I caught her bounding easily from the muddy path to perch on a rock, tossing her legs in a ballerina-like kick, the long locks of her hair seemingly intact from the light mist that was spraying from the sky. She looked like a goddess. Well, she was a goddess—according to the eleven million followers she'd amassed on Instagram.

'Come on!' Angelique's voice was like candy, sweet and tinny. 'We'll be late!'

She had insisted we climb up this hill and then go down back on the other side, refusing the horses—yes, horses—that were offered to us by young, hardy-looking Svans with round grey eyes and reserved smiles, on the way up.

And thank God we were finally here, feasting as the Georgians do.

'Should we just go home?' Jojie, Angelique's makeup, hairstylist, and personal assistant was asking me now, his voice a stage whisper. A small plate of something meaty and saucy was handed to him and he took a bite, the brown rich sauce dripping on the table. He rolled his eyes and gave a soft, breathy grunt. 'Or maybe . . . not?'

I nodded, not exactly sure myself. I looked around at the table, grateful for the cool air that nipped at my face. I watched as that night's Tamada, the toastmaster, raised his glass and started a toast in Georgian.

I wasn't supposed to be here. Or at least, that was what I had planned—to not be anywhere but Singapore in the next several months. I had felt a shift, after the Vietnam trip with Rooki, and after that South African safari, where I had messed with Jake's feed on Facebook. It had struck me that what I was again beginning to feel was that I was spread too thin. I had told myself that I felt this way when it came to work, but the real issue was I had begun to feel vulnerable again, exposed, almost attacked. In Vietnam, I had taken the flight back without Rooki and her boyfriend Daniel, who had both decided to travel back to Ireland. I had checked out from The Forest by myself and boarded the plane with a lingering ache and a not-so-healthy longing. I had flown back from Cape Town to Singapore disturbed and uneasy from what I'd seen in Jake's Facebook.

Nhi was right—I needed to protect myself more and prevent further injury. I was aware that the past year had been filled with extensive planning along with trips to destinations I could only have dreamed of. Being in honeymoon destinations such as The Forest in Da Nang and constantly seeing couples being together, looking happy and content, looking like everything was so right, had opened up the memory of Jake and myself—not just of what we had, but what we could have had. For some reason, I was afraid that this time, I may not get out of that frame of mind, out of that state, as quickly and as ruthlessly as I had when I was desperate to get out of Manila, out of my old life. It had been like cutting off a body part.

I didn't want to cut my body in half. I didn't want to lose any part of my body any more.

So I told myself that I would focus more on staying put in Singapore, creating itineraries, discovering new suppliers, and meeting new clients at the office—doing all the other tasks that I've also come to love with this job. Plus, I had also signed up with a new tea club in Holland Village, which exchanged tea by mail and met twice a month. It had been Oliver who had forwarded me the email about that.

'I'm so glad you're here.' The air had become still and I felt smooth, long arms envelop me in a hug. I realized that it was Angelique, and that surprisingly, she wasn't slurring any more. 'Thank you, Arya dear!' She declared, at the same time that I felt those same arms release me.

I watched as Angelique threw her arms up in the air, as if she were on onstage and about to present something. 'Thank you for saving me!'

I wouldn't exactly say that I saved her. And she was still massively drunk. I grabbed the small, but newly-filled wine glass in front of her and downed it, the cool orange liquid feeling sour and grainy as it made its way down my throat. Better for me to get a little tipsy than Angelique sliding deeper into a state of being completely, black-out drunk, I thought. She leaned her head on my shoulder, and I felt a deep wave of sympathy.

'Of course, An,' I said, and it struck me again how I was of nickname basis with such a famous client. But this was work. It had all been work, and my clients have become jobs. There has been no time to realize what else they could be but people who were willing to spend money, a lot of it, on a unique experience somewhere in the world.

Angelique had always taken a special liking to me. She'd started a vlog on YouTube last year with her boyfriend, Wil Lin, who was already a seasoned food vlogger. She had envisioned a couple travel vlog and was desperate to produce content. Naturally, she gravitated to travel. Never mind that there were hundreds and thousands of couple vloggers already.

She had asked me to put together a trip, designed specifically to attract followers and jumpstart her new online venture. She was wise to think that it didn't mean that if she was a popular actress that her vlog would take off. She loved travelling and had always felt she hasn't travelled enough. Could I come up with an itinerary of all the cool but unique places, different but not alienating? Due to her last three films, where she played a housekeeper, a hard-up factory worker, and a struggling nurse overseas, her fans had associated her with being humble, down-to-earth, and most of all, simple.

Only problem was, Wil Lin, who was one half of her travel vlog—broke up with her. Unbelievable but true and known only to us, to this particular circle who had travelled with her to Tbilisi, Georgia.

Angelique lost no time deleting all old videos in her channel, creating instead a brand new one that focused on solo travelling in the most underrated cities in the world. 'This would be a fresh start, Arya,' she'd told me. And I knew then, why Angelique had been successful all the way. She never stopped, she moved on, albeit messily. But she did the work.

I gave her an itinerary, in which she was completely involved. And now she had Georgia.

'Go with me,' she said when we were gearing up to leave Singapore, putting everything in place for her Georgian trip. Not one soul had known how devastated she'd felt. 'There's an extra ticket, anyway.'

I told her what every travel manager was supposed to do. 'I could cancel that for you,' I said. 'Get you a partial refund.'

She had laughed at my face. A sad laugh, I knew. 'I don't need a partial refund,' she said. 'I need company. Support.'

I didn't ask any more why there were no close friends or family who could come with her. I knew, from working with celebrities for close to three years at Isle Z, that it was not uncommon for them to have very few friends. I learned, eventually, that when you have that kind of fame or money, it was hard to find someone to trust, and friendships you could fully invest in.

And anyway, I was required by my bosses to go.

Angelique was recovering from a break-up, and to tell you the truth, I was relieved. After the Vietnam trip with Rooki, I didn't think I could any more stand being around couples. At least, not for now, when my senses were hyper-alert and my emotions were on overdrive. It was a sort of comfort that Angelique and I shared the same experience—Angelique knew how it hurt to have to lose someone. Never mind that her heartbreak happened just two weeks ago, and she was still, dangerously, on the rebound. Or that mine happened nearly three years ago. It was still a time when we lost someone. Gained something, yes, although Angelique wasn't yet sure what that was, exactly. I wanted to tell her that I was okay with this. That, like her, I was trying.

In the more than two years that Jake has been absent from my life, I had tried going out with other men, too. I had gone on dates with guys where we stayed beyond closing time in restaurants and cafes, dates where we peered at art in out-of-the-way museums, watched movies, drank in rooftop bars, and tried craft beer. I had tried to be normal, saying yes to invitations to dinner and drinks.

Until I didn't. Truth be told, if one were to ask me about those dates, I wouldn't really remember; it was all just a blur. Nothing stuck to me, the way Jake and his presence did. Because the hurt was still there, and I still could not let go.

When I first read about Tbilisi, the capital city of the Republic of Georgia, I thought it was one of those obscure, hard-to-pronounce places where no one really lived, but that people dug up and then name-dropped, whenever they felt they needed to project an image of coolness or creativity, or worse, exclusivity.

But there it was, in Oliver's email—Tbilisi, Georgia. The fact that it was Oliver who'd sent it already meant that this was something. A place where I was supposed to do my job, but also, a place that was worth going to.

Never would I have imagined that travelling to Georgia, travelling with Angelique van Leuven, would shake up my life in a way that was all so new to me.

Chapter 15

Svaneti, Republic of Georgia, 9.17 p.m. It was drizzling, but no one seemed to mind. Except me—I placed a hand on the top of my head, not surprised to feel that the knitted cap I was wearing was already damp. I felt a touch of panic. My mother always told me that I had to protect my head, that a mere sprinkle of rain, the slightest sign of dampness on one's scalp was enough to trigger a sore throat, a cold, a bad cough. The last thing I wanted was to be sick because as usual, this was not a vacation. My mother was back in Manila where I wasn't. And this was work. Oh yeah, this was work.

I walked—no, I skidded down a few steps—because there was no real clear path and all I could see directly in front of me was mud. Pure, brown, slippery mud. I looked around to check who else thought this was normal, to be out here in the open, vulnerable to slashes of rain that were about to drop, to the wind that was picking up, to this non-existent path that was actually a clear danger to inexperienced hikers like me. Who else thought this was okay?

Was I the only one who noticed that it was already raining? And that if we don't get off this hill now, we'll be stuck here forever? I was out of breath. The figures slowly got smaller, and I could see my little group in the distance. Angelique was leading the pack, as usual.

We were on our way back from the supra, walking on Ushguli's strange paths and taking on hills once again, to get from one place to another, in this isolated village at the foot of the mountains. We were heading back to our inn, and though the sky was still light, the walk felt lonelier than ever. Maybe it was the wine, the rich, heavy dinner, or the fact that everyone in our group was already way ahead of me and I was one of the few who were straggling behind.

I felt a rustle behind, and I turned, as carefully as I could to see what it was.

It was only Sasha, one of our Georgian guides.

'Let's never come back here,' he said, his English a low drawl just like the others. He took a deep breath and wiped his brow.

'You're the only Georgian I know who'd say that,' I said. 'Although, I've only been here for five days.'

We stopped under one of the towers, just as a woman emerged from behind a wooden fence and walked slowly down the path towards us. A red and white scarf was wrapped around her head, and another shawl in a checked print draped on her shoulders. She was wearing a long skirt and thick, knitted gloves. She went over to Sasha, calling out to him and then proceeding to talk in low tones.

'This woman, she wants to take a photo with you,' Sasha said, with a little shrug. He fished out a cigarette from his back pocket and lit up.

'Oh?' I said, taken aback. It was not every day that the locals wanted a photo with visiting tourists; in fact, I've always believed that it was the other way around. Still, I looked at the woman with curiosity, and smiled. 'Okay,' I said.

The woman smiled back, moving so she was beside me. 'That's good,' I said, putting my arm around her as Sasha snapped a picture.

'There's a man here that she thought you might want to meet,' Sasha said, as I broke away from the woman.

'Really?' I nodded at her, then gave another smiley shrug. 'Thank you,' I said. Turning back to Sasha, I asked: 'What man? And why does she want us to meet him?'

I saw Sasha bend his head down to speak to the woman, pursing his lips as she spoke and he listened, intently.

'Oh. Oh, Arya.' He swivelled his head towards me and threw up his hands. 'I don't really understand the Svan language. I'm sorry.' In a lower voice, he said: 'She may not be in her right mind. She might just be making things up. I suggest we just move on.'

The woman was still looking at me with an expectant smile.

'Sorry,' I said, shaking my head. The woman nodded, as if understanding, and ambled away in the direction of the town.

'What was that all about?'

Sasha frowned. 'Nothing, really. I was afraid that she would ask for money.'

'Really? Is that how it is here?' I pulled my bonnet down even further so it covered my ears.

Sasha looked sheepish. 'No, actually.' He looked towards the town; the woman had disappeared. 'Do you still want to explore?' He looked over to our group, who now appeared very tiny in the distance. 'It's no point catching up, anyway. But don't worry,' he said, his round, rheumy eyes looking kind. 'I'm here.'

He pointed to a little dwelling, a low house with a few yellow plastic chairs out front. 'You see that small restaurant? I can wait for you there if you want.'

I nodded, gratefully. I walked along the snow-covered path, trying not to step on animal manure that seemed to be everywhere. I had wanted to take photos of the towers, the houses, the furry white pigs, the horses, the complicated structures of some of the village homes. I peered beyond a wooden fence that seemed to make a boundary between the village and the foot of the Caucasus mountains.

There was a man in navy blue pin-striped pyjamas sitting close to the ground on his haunches, head bent down on a wide piece of whiteboard laid down on a low table. Even from my spot, I could see his hand slightly moving back and forth on the board as he drew something, then shaded it intently and meticulously. Even from afar, the movements felt precise, and meticulous.

An ordinary scene. What struck me was that he had a potted plant in front of him, containing a slim bush barely a foot tall, with thin leaves that looked silver at first glance, but was actually a cold, faded kind of light green.

When I went closer, I saw the painting that he had made. I was right—there was an amazing precision to it, a certain confident accuracy.

I couldn't help but speak. 'Hi,' I said. 'This beautiful plant—you really painted it as it is.'

There was no reaction from him. The man continued doing tiny brushstrokes on the painting. After a minute, I said, 'I'm Arya.'

The man looked up, not saying anything. His eyes looked droopy and glassy, I wasn't even sure if he was seeing me. I became aware of the silence, every sound disappearing, as if we were suddenly ensconced under a blanket.

Somehow, I felt compelled to know his name. 'I'm Arya,' I repeated, more loudly this time. 'And, sir . . . you are?'

The man opened then closed his mouth, looking like he was about to speak but then decided against it. Finally, he let out a small sigh, looking down on his painting. 'Dave.'

I was startled that he didn't have a heavy Georgian accent. 'Are you Georgian?' I paused. 'Svan?' I wasn't sure I even pronounced it right.

The man looked into the distance, not saying anything at all. It was as if he didn't hear a word that I said.

'Sir? Sir, excuse me?'

Then, he spoke. 'What do you think of this?' He nodded vigorously towards his subject, that silvery bush. 'This plant, endemic to Georgia. Do you think I should put more shadow on it, this way?'

'I'm sorry?' I was startled by the question but I heard him, clearly. I looked down and ran my eyes over the painting, carefully. Then at his subject.

'There's no need to put more shadow,' I said, finally. 'It looks almost translucent, which is why it's so beautiful.' I surprised myself by saying this.

'Yes, yes,' this man—Dave, was murmuring. 'You're right, you're right.' It was as if he was in a trance.

And then his head was bent down again, eyes staring intently at the surface of his work, the hand doing those tiny brushstrokes again, repeatedly.

'Sir?' I asked, unable to tear my eyes away from the movement of his fingers on the painting. 'May I—can I take your picture?'

I thought I saw him nod, ever so slightly. But even if I wasn't sure, my thumb had started working as if on its own, and my phone camera had started clicking. Quickly, I swiped, then pressed to take a video.

From my phone screen, I saw Dave look up once, eyes focused on something in the distance, lips pressed together as if deep in thought. And then he stood up, gave a small nod goodbye, and went inside.

Chapter 16

Singapore, 9.30 a.m. A case of Georgian wine was waiting for me when I slipped in at the Isle Z office, four days after I returned from Tbilisi, Georgia. Six bottles of Saperavi, encased in a white cardboard box printed delicately with Georgian script, from which dangled a floppy card in fuchsia and gold.

'*Gamarjoba* and *Gaumarjos!* From Angelique,' it read in the actress's signature flowing script.

'Looks like it wasn't just you who was moved by a city called Tbilisi.' Oliver's voice, smooth and slightly teasing, sailed past my ears. 'And Svaneti, of course.' I turned and saw him standing behind me in his usual tailored white shirt, and a sedate pair of greige pants. Today's tie was a splotchy Pollock-like print.

'Hey, Oliver.'

'Hello and victory to you!' He grinned and patted the rolled newspaper under his arm, silver cufflinks glinting like little jewels on his wrists.

I raised my eyebrows and shot him a questioning look.

'What?' he said, in mock-defence. 'That's what it says. And also, I can see Angelique's writing from here!'

I let my face soften. 'I know,' I said. 'The trip—it went very well.'

'I'm sure it did. And you do know what *gamarjoba* and *gaumarjos* mean by this time, right? Knowing you, you must have picked up the Georgian language in two days.'

'Not really,' I said, blinking. 'The consonants drove me crazy.'

At this Oliver let out a bellowing laugh, the box in his arms steady. 'I'll put this in your desk,' he said.

'That's kind of you,' I murmured, thankful that I didn't have to lug the bottles myself. After that trip to Georgia with Angelique, and all the hill-climbing that it involved, I didn't think that I was in shape at all.

'Tea?'

'Of course,' I said, my insides relaxing. Just the thought of warm, fragrant tea felt refreshing. I flashed Oliver a grateful smile. 'Later?'

'An ureshino,' Oliver crowed. 'Or Georgian wine!'

'As long you have a wine-opener on hand,' I said.

'Of course we do,' Oliver said. 'I'm just kidding, Superstar. We don't want you to drink here.' He burst into laughter.

I continued emailing our suppliers and reading through my backlog, until afternoon that day, thinking just how lucky I was to have this job. Yep, I wasn't taking anything for granted.

* * *

I was walking home from the MRT, contemplating if I would buy a bowl of laksa or a plate of char siew pork—something delicious, savoury, and most likely bad for my health—from the hawker centre, or attempt to cook something healthier. The trips and the lovely foreign meals overseas, wonderful as they are, had been complete with full meals and were definitely taking a toll on my body. My slacks felt tighter at the waist, plus I had started feeling weak and lethargic in the afternoons. That morning, I'd had to forgo wearing a favourite pencil skirt because it wouldn't close at the button.

I remembered Nhi Tran and the huge salads she would do, tossing two big bowls for us whenever we felt bloated—usually after a three-day weekend or after Christmas. Too bad she was overseas right now, away on a work trip for two nights. I paused and sent her a text, asking if everything was cool in Melbourne and for her to please sleep early and drink less, knowing that she won't. Just the usual banter.

I crossed the street, bumping into a couple who were holding hands, causing them to break apart. I was on my own tonight.

'Sorry,' I mumbled, already knowing without looking that they'd immediately come together again, naturally gravitating back to each other, like magnets. I remembered how Jake would refuse to let other people go through between us, steering me determinedly to one side just so people wouldn't ram into us and cause us to lose our grip on each other. Then, I had thought it silly, corny but still romantic. Now there was no one who was being corny and romantic; why had I ever taken that for granted?

I looked at the thickening crowd on the pedestrian walk and suddenly felt lonely.

My phone started vibrating from my pocket, just as the light turned green. I fished it out to check.

'Arya dear!' It was Angelique van Leuven. The message was full of hearts and kissing emojis. 'Did you get the wine?'

'Yes!' I texted back. 'Thank you, An. So kind of you. Shall we open a bottle together soon?' I meant it. I was truly grateful to have known Angelique, to have the opportunity to travel with her. I smiled at the thought of Tbilisi, of Svaneti.

I remembered that guy, Dave. The strange guy who was simply painting a plant, but who exuded such mystery. Or at least, that was my impression. It really could have been the whole vibe of the place, that community called Ushguli. Or maybe it could have been just me, overthinking things as usual.

There was no more response from Angelique, which was typical and not at all surprising. Despite her secret break-up, the woman was deluged with projects and surely had a myriad of other things to do. I thought about our trip to Georgia again.

I continued walking towards the direction of our flat, which was a straight line from the station and less than a kilometre away. I passed by the coffee shop where I used to take-away dinner, saw that it was heaving with people at this time in the evening. I glanced at my watch. It was only 7 p.m., and I was feeling creative. Why not cook something? I decided to pop into the grocery, an idea brewing in my mind. Angelique, of course! On top of everything, Angelique also had a cooking channel on YouTube where she shared and prepared mostly plant-based dishes. This was a perfect time to try and see if I can do one.

It was quiet when I arrived, with a breeze that was blowing in. Typical. Our apartment had wide windows which we never cared to close. It opened to a view of lush leopard trees which belonged to the condominium right across, but thankfully still provided shade and a cool breeze whenever I was home.

I had taken a detour to buy the ingredients from the list I got in one of Angelique's videos. I hummed as I unloaded the canned beans, carrots, and potatoes on the narrow kitchen counter, thankful once again for this cozy flat. Nhi was into interiors as a hobby and had taken the time to get us a new sofa and a coffee table, and rugs that were all just the right size and height. In fact, this apartment we had been living in had remained simple but tasteful. I can still remember when I first arrived and it was just a kitchen, a dining table . . . and a blank space in the middle.

I propped my iPad on the bare kitchen table and pulled up Angelique's Instagram account. On my phone, I opened her YouTube cooking channel, Angelique's Nest, and typed in 'vegan bean stew.' A very attractive thumbnail of a yummy-looking bowl of beans, artfully topped with parsley came up, with a photo of a smiling Angelique standing in front of a plant-filled kitchen. I played the video and peered more closely.

Two million views. *Huh,* I thought, as I took out garlic and onion from the cupboard, then started peeling the carrots. Why was I even surprised? I knew that Angelique was wildly popular online, why wouldn't she be in yet another platform? The video was posted ten days ago and was twenty-five minutes long.

I looked at the clock on the kitchen wall. I needed to do this fast if I wanted to eat soon and not regret getting my dinner *tapao-ed.*

And then I remembered Reels. That was shorter. True enough, Angelique had a ninety-second version of her bean stew!

By 9 p.m., I was sitting down and ladling myself a big bowl of Angelique's version of cannellini bean stew. It wasn't bad at all. After taking several satisfying spoonfuls, I opened my phone, scrolling through the photos. The latest ones were of Georgia: the listing balconies of Tbilisi, the towers in the village of Ushguli in Svaneti, Angelique looking over her shoulder, our Georgian guide Sasha smoking while climbing the hill, my shot with the Svan woman, and the Caucasus mountains behind us, Dave peering over his work, videos of Dave doing brushwork.

I slurped more of the thick soup, opened Instagram, and chose one of the Tbilisi photos to upload. 'In Tbilisi, there's a gem in every corner,' I wrote in the caption. It was up on my IG feed in seconds, the balconies' latticework clear and visible in the photo. I clicked on the nifty arrow on the upper right so I could share the post in my Stories.

I was about post another pic, this one of the old towers in Ushguli when Dave's photo caught my eye. It was a good photo, with Dave properly framed, and his arm angled just so and very naturally towards his canvas. A truly candid shot of a painter at work. Why not, I thought. I've been posting too many landscape photos, anyway. So I scrolled down further, chose a couple of pictures of Dave seemingly in deep concentration, and then included the video that I took, with the silvery plant in view and a glimpse of his work in progress.

'A village in the mountains, an artist at work,' I wrote quickly. I didn't really know who he was, but he was surely an artist if he was painting something.

It was in my feed in seconds, and I did the same thing as with my previous post of Tbilisi—I pressed the nifty arrow on the upper right so Dave's photos and video would appear in my Stories. I checked again, out of habit, that they were all properly posted, and clicked my phone shut.

* * *

'Look at my Stories!'

Angelique van Leuven again, at 4 a.m.

I took a cursory glance at her message and gave a little grunt. I had recently updated my phone and had forgotten to turn on Do Not Disturb, which I've always set from 12 midnight until 7.30 in the morning: midnight was when I usually, finally dozed off, and just before eight in the morning was when I've finished with at least one tea, saving the other kinds for later in the morning.

Angelique was talking about Instagram Stories, of course, and it was funny and flattering at the same time how Angelique wanted me to view hers, despite having eleven million followers who were probably already looking, dissecting, and screenshotting them less than a moment after she'd posted it. A smattering of my celebrity clients follows me on Instagram, Angelique being one of them, my one thousand followers—mostly travel suppliers, tour guides I've met all over the world, friends from way back, and travel clients—feeling like a speck to her millions.

I looked sideways at my phone again, the screen of which was glowing a bright white. When the screen light went off, just a moment after, I was fast asleep.

Chapter 17

Singapore, 7.15 a.m. I was up by six the next day, strolling through the well-tended lushness of one of my favourite spots in the city. The Singapore Botanic Gardens, truly, was one of the few places where I didn't mind being without my phone, which I'd forgotten still charging at home.

It had been a disaster, the first time I set foot at the Botanic Gardens. A ridiculous thought, I know—because how could one go wrong with such a beautiful place, with such easy access to greenery and with so much nature just within an arm's reach?

It had nothing to do with nature, of course. At that time, two years and eight months ago, it had everything to do with me.

Fresh from Manila, just starting work at Isle Z for only about a month, but still smarting, hotly, from my break-up, I had somehow agreed on a walking date with a guy I'd been set up with. This had been arranged by a former colleague, Stella Cruz Ng, who used to work for another travel agency in Manila and with whom I've previously travelled with in fam tours, but who was also now living in Singapore.

It had sounded so good, and had been so much-needed at that time—an old-fashioned blind date but with a wholesome, healthy twist. He and I were to go walking early in the morning at the Botanic Gardens, which could possibly extend to a cozy coffee after . . . if things go well. And things promised to go well. Henry, the guy Stella had set me up with, was an expat and a gym rat who liked nature, lifting weights, and checking out new breakfast spots in the city. He was also single. *I* was newly single. Suffice it to say that I had vowed to not to commit the same mistake again. Well, I was trying, at least. And somehow, I had placed it in my head that one solution at that time was to actively go out on dates, which was why I'd been exceptionally eager to go out with this man. And except for the physical fitness part, which I admit, I had zero interest in, it seemed like a reasonable match. I wanted to move on, I told myself. I had to move on from Jake. Dating, blind or not, seemed like a good way forward.

Henry appeared cheerful and confident, and hailed from Wellington, New Zealand. He was broad and muscular and had a tanned face, taut cheekbones, a very energetic smile, and bulging calves.

I was all for strong calves. But I should have bailed at the first kilometre. For one, Henry walked too fast. So fast, that, if only it weren't such a cool, twenty-four-degree morning, I would have thought it rude. He was a full head higher than me, so you can imagine how much longer his legs were compared to mine. And, was it normal that I only mostly saw his back in those first few hundred metres?

Secondly, I slipped. Literally slipped and fell on a sloping, narrow path just before we reached the Botanic Gardens'

Swan Lake. We had been walking for fifteen minutes and I wanted to do a mini short-cut, carelessly crossing a flower bed and getting my sneakers caught on a wobbly rock. It certainly didn't help that it had rained a few hours before, in the early morning, and the ground was still looking slick in a lot of the paths. Perhaps I had been desperate to catch up. Perhaps I wasn't used to walking—because while Singapore was a biophilic and pedestrian-friendly city, who actually walked in Manila? The usual reasons were what I've grown up in and have known my whole life: broken, non existent sidewalks, alleys teeming with questionable characters ready to pounce on your first vulnerable move, and air pollution in the form of thick, black CO_2 smoke.

Or perhaps I was just clumsy because my ankle twisted when my foot landed on that errant rock which caused me to topple, heavily, into that flower bed. Perhaps the Botanic Gardens at that time had just been one slippery path.

'Are you sure you sprained it?' This Henry had the nerve to ask, when he finally bent down to look at my leg. This was only after I saw him reluctantly turn around—probably looking for the source of some startled shrieks that I didn't know had turned into high-pitched yelling, all coming from my direction. All coming from me.

'It hurts, it hurts,' I'd wailed, like a baby. It did hurt. I had gashes on my elbows and palms as I tried to soften my fall, to no avail.

'Ah, well,' he said, looking around, as if conscious of who else was seeing this. And then he started laughing, the kind of laugh that, until now, I've always thought, was *at me*.

I *was* sure I had sprained my ankle. By the time I'd taken a Grab home—sans Henry—it had swelled to the size of a baseball, leaving me unable to walk properly for the rest of the week.

* * *

The memory of that date—or non-date, two years ago was already conveniently blurry in my head. It's been laughed about and even almost forgotten. Thankfully, my friendship and walking dates with Stella have stayed very much the same.

'I can't believe you left your phone at home,' Stella was saying now, raising her arms above her head in an exaggerated stretch. She whipped off her Ray-Bans, showing me eyes with thick lash extensions, raised eyebrows. 'And you left it on purpose!'

I've known Stella to be on regular fam tours to Singapore and Malaysia for the travel agency she worked in Manila. So it was no surprise that a year before I even *knew* that I'd be moving to Singapore to work, Stella had already met Luc, a French guy who imported wine in Singapore. It intensified to a long-distance romance, and Stella, forty-five and fitter than any millennial, now had a husband, a landed house in Bukit Timah, and a French cellar that Luc had built. Luckily, I also became the main beneficiary of their wine, with Stella treating me with a bottle or two of the vino they'd amassed on their trips back to Luc's hometown in Alsace.

'Come to think of it,' I said, as we turned towards the wetlands and walked on the bridge that opened to the Eco Lake. 'I never bring my phone here.'

'Good for you,' Stella said in a singsong. I watched her bend over to stretch her hamstrings, palms digging into her thighs. 'At least you don't have a problem being without your phone for a few hours.'

I nodded. I'd tried bringing my mobile and even a thin, pocket-sized notebook during our walks before, only to realize that I was actually already too distracted by the Gardens' vibrant cornucopia of plants and flowers. A good kind of distraction because I actually felt an energizing kind of calm—if that made sense—looking at trees and leaves and vines. Anyway, I had not only almost forgotten my walking date with Stella that morning, but I'd completely failed to charge my phone last night.

I did a half-hearted stretch, bending over as she did, and attempted to touch my toes. When I straightened up, I saw that Stella had paused from her stretches and was now standing under a tree, distracted by something on her phone.

'Come on, Ste,' I called out. 'I'm getting hungry. And you said you had eggs Benedict for us at home?' I could also use a mimosa; bubbly and freshly-juiced oranges were always, *always* available at Stella's.

'Sure, sure,' she said, eyes still trained on her screen. 'Of course.' It was easy for her to dismiss these things nowadays.

'Can't wait for the mimosas—'

'Hey—wait a minute!' Stella brought her phone close to her face and squinted at the screen, as if she was having trouble seeing. 'Isn't Angelique van Leuven one of your clients?'

I remembered that Angelique had messaged me last night. 'Well, yes.' I had forgotten to reply to her, and I couldn't answer her right now, of course.

'She shared one of your Stories,' Stella said, her fingers scrolling up and down the screen. 'On Instagram.'

'Oh?' It must have been a mistake; Stella might be looking at something else because my clients—and even Angelique—almost always never shared the stuff I posted on my Instagram account. 'And so?' I was already just thinking of the hearty breakfast that I was about to have.

'Arya. Didn't you hear me? Angelique shared your post in her Stories.' There was a tremor in Stella's voice that I didn't really recognize. 'And she shared a bunch of other stuff you posted. The artist guy.'

'Okay.' I was only half-listening. My stomach was rumbling.

'She linked it all to your post.'

'Oh-kay. So?'

'So your post now has more than 10,000 likes.'

What?

Chapter 18

Singapore, 10.44 a.m. When I saw the numbers, I thought my Instagram account had been hacked.

Not that I know exactly what happens when an IG account gets hacked. Seriously, I was clueless. I hadn't been paying attention to the nitty-gritty of social media, busy as I was making the hundred and ninety-ninth change in my clients' meticulously customised itineraries, or breaking up real-time fights of travel influencers, not to mention the travelling, the back and forth to Changi Airport for yet another flight for a fam tour or with a client. Would it be like on Facebook where all your friends would be sent a malignant link to a scam website or a porn site? If your account was hacked, wouldn't it disappear or be deleted, like how some Instagram celebrities complain about being unable to access their own accounts?

Ah, to disappear. There was a part of me that half-wished that maybe this should've happened to my IG instead because with my puny following—less than 1,000 as of my last check, a couple of days ago—and my hundred or so half-hearted updates ('Cypriot rosé by the beach,' I wrote in a post three weeks ago, with an awkward photo of a sweating wine glass against yellow-and-white striped umbrellas), it wouldn't really be catastrophic if I actually lost my IG account. I would just start over with a new one.

Unlike, say, Angelique van Leuven and her 4,000 posts, and most especially, her heaving, magnificent eleven million followers. What would she do if *her* account was hacked and lose all that following?

But no one's account was being hacked. No one was losing followers at all—in fact, someone seemed to be gaining a shitload of followers by the minute.

What had only happened was that Angelique simply shared my post on Dave. On Stories on Instagram. Where she has eleven million followers.

So I guess I have to stop thinking that there had been a glitch, or that my IG account was broken. I guess I should have expected the 10,209 likes that I just saw on my post on Dave on my Instagram feed.

Oops, it's now 11,803 likes.

12,671 likes, just after a minute.

13,720 likes.

15,878 likes—wait, what was happening?

I stared hard at *the* Instagram post again at the very top of my feed, the one I had posted just two days ago. Dave stared back at me—well, actually, he merely gave an almost desultory glance in my direction while I was taking the video, before going back to making tiny brushstrokes on the painting in front of him. I swiped right and saw the other photos I had included in the post; Dave in a more relaxed position, sitting back and staring at his work, Dave dabbing his brush intently mixing colours on his palette, a zoomed-in shot of the silvery plant he was painting, a glimpse of the painting he was doing, a work in progress.

Were there really thousands of likes every thirty seconds?

I tapped the little heart icon on the upper right corner of my screen, the little red dot on the side, like a tiny round medal that signaled there was new activity in my account now a constant, now never disappearing. I tapped it again and again, IG's version of refresh—as if I was in a trance. The numbers were jumping by the thousands each time my finger hit that little heart.

Was this really my Instagram account?

More importantly, who was Dave—I mean, Davit Nadibaidze?

'THE Davit Nadibaidze is here!!! With fresh art!!!'

This was what Angelique van Leuven had written in her Instagram Stories, in the big, bold, italicized font she always chose. That was her repost of my most recent post that contained Dave's video and photos.

I didn't even have to Google who Davit Nadibaidze was. A few scrolls down and a media news outlet called *Do Officiel* explained it all to me, in sixty seconds. The media news site, with 4.6 million followers, had done *something*—downloaded my video, screenshotted Angelique's post on Davit in her Stories—and made an actual video news report about it.

'Hiding in Plain Sight,' said the headline on the thumbnail in thick white letters. The video played, a cut-up of Angelique's Stories post, and my own IG post.

It was all spoken in a well-modulated, galvanizing voice-over, but I read the caption underneath the post: 'Davit Nadibaidze has been spotted! Found by one of us mere mortals on earth. Nadibaidze is the Georgian artist most famous for his obsession with the human figure and for causing one of the biggest stirs in recent art history. He has sparked a revival in figural painting with his rendition of mixed media art and raw, thought-provoking, larger-than-life portraits that has been lauded and exhibited in Berlin, Tbilisi, Zagreb, Paris, New York, Tokyo, and Singapore, among other key cities. It's been reported that some of Nadibaidze's unconventional processes include spending time in a morgue and observing plastic surgeons at work—all for him to discover and discern the nature, extremes, and possibilities of the body.'

He was represented by the Gagosian Gallery in New York and represented in all these years by other prominent galleries in Europe and the United States. His work was often in exhibitions at the Royal Academy of Art and London's Tate Britain, as well as several other contemporary art museums in Stockholm, Bergen, Amsterdam, and Gdansk. His paintings can be found in major institutions—he was a mainstay at the San Francisco Museum of Modern Art and the MOMA in New York.

It was said that his father had recognized his talent even when Nadibaidze was only seven years old, and constructed a makeshift studio for him in the tiny wine cellar they had at home. Like many Georgian families, Nadibaidze's family had a small vineyard by their house and made their own wine. Nadibaidze spent years painting in the middle of harvest season, among family, neighbours, and friends going in and out of the cellar tending to the wine fermenting inside *qvevris*—clay vessels buried on the ground. It was no wonder that Nadibaidze was famous for working in odd, busy, or dilapidated places including an old factory on the outskirts of Tbilisi, a woodworking compound and surfboard workshop in Bali, a tenement in Glasgow, train stations in Budapest. The result was artwork that was unsparing and arresting, realized naturalism with a touch of illusion and slapdash, all of which was mined and discussed constantly by the art world for its psychological translations.

Davit Nadibaidze was last seen in Venice, and it had been with his manager, who later appeared in an interview, this time sans Davit, on CNN. True, Davit had voluntarily retreated from the public eye, via a dramatic, revelatory TV interview in the same network a good five years ago. After that, it was amazing how he'd been kept visible and on the radar by his fans, pundits, and no less than the movers and shakers of the art world. But the voluntary retreat was also a concept that Davit's fans seemed to have conveniently forgotten, putting out post after post pleading for him to come back, weeks and months after his 'disappearance.' A lot of the speculations centred around his remark in that last interview five years ago, where he said that he may or may not produce any more of the style of work that he was known for. He was ready for a shift, he was craving for a change, he said. David Nadibaidze was hungry for something else—for what exactly, he wasn't ready to reveal just yet.

My video, as it was now viral, was a totally new sighting of him. It will spell a new era for the art world, announced *Do Officiel*. The online media giant was also @dofficielnews, growing rapidly at 2.1 million followers, and @dofficielworld, currently with 1.8 million followers. And as I scrolled down my feed, I realized the utter significance of it. Davit Nadibaidze—once a creator of raw, sometimes grotesque art that has always provoked—has, after five years, created *new work*. This most recent work, as innocuously revealed in my photos and video of him in Svaneti, has been declared by *Do Officiel* and several other news media as 'sharp, precise, realistic and truthful' and was 'a fresh side of Nadibaidze.' Overnight, it's been proclaimed that it was 'groundbreaking and significant' because it was a stark contrast to the style that Davit Nadibaidze has always been known. At least, that was what other accounts of *Do Officiel* have echoed, as far as its culture pages, including @dofoodies with 970K followers and @doofficielmusic, with three million followers.

In the flurry of all these, I managed to scroll and then click on another, which had 'A Davit Nadibaidze Sighting!!!' splashed on its thumbnail. Still, in a daze, I watched and listened to clips of my own video of Davit, as well as old footage of him with his gigantic paintings in Tbilisi. Often compared to Lucian Freud and his figurative paintings, he was widowed just five years after his marriage and hasn't remarried since, his work getting even bigger in scale, and more mysterious. There had been plenty of rumours—about the state of his marriage, his wife, his sexuality. Though reclusive, a documentary had already been made about his life as well as a three-volume biography by the French art critic and biographer Denis Dupont.

It was after the interview with CNN that Davit was reported to have organized an impromptu artists' retreat in a cabin somewhere in a forest near Gdansk, Poland. He had spent some time talking with the artists in the cabin, then had gone for a walk. He didn't come home that night, which sent everyone into a panic. His family was reported to have filed a report a few hours after, but was withdrawn soon. Davit, after three days, had posted something on his official Facebook page, reminding everyone of his plan to retreat from the public.

In the weeks that followed, he had sold an entire collection of paintings and at least two other series of works to gallerist Charles Bendel who owned the top six galleries in New York and London.

He was controversial, well-loved, admired, and adored yet also sneered at. But Davit Nadibaidze was a big deal. And Angelique van Leuven only acted so, because she was an artist herself. Sure, I wasn't in media or a journalist, but how did I not know about this?

I was suddenly full of questions. My mind flew back to that first meeting with Dave—Davit, I now know. It was a meeting of pure chance. Should I have talked to him more? Would it have made all this better? His name was the only thing he uttered to me, as well as that single question about the shadowing technique, and I couldn't decide if that had been a good thing or not. What would I have done had I known he was uber-famous? I had worked with big-name clients before, but not in the art world.

Everything was happening at the same time, and this was only Instagram. In my other social media accounts, my notifications, too, were non-stop—friend adds, likes, shares, comments, and tags.

I was being tagged, seemingly, a hundred times per minute.

With shaking hands, I closed the Instagram app. Only then did I notice my notifications on Facebook—132.

No.

Now this, this must the glitch I've been looking for.

Unable to stop myself, I tapped it open. The words, the profile photos, the *numbers* swam before my eyes.

567 people wanted to be added as a friend. *Do Officiel* and 16,338 other people liked a post I was tagged in.

A few scrolls down and I hit the media outlet *Art Univers*, another online news page that had more than a million followers.

There was a painting, a self-portrait of Davit Nadibaidze naked, the sinews of his muscles exaggerated.

He painted himself naked in his summer house in Racha, Georgia. Davit Nadibaidze stood before a mirror in his living room for forty-five days, *Art Univers* reported, and painted a full-length portrait of himself in the nude, with only a fur hat and boots.

I was tagged in this post. And it already had 189,000 likes.

I learned about Davit Nadibaidze's life in less than five minutes. And I learned all about the frightening power of social media in these five minutes.

For a moment, I felt rage. How on earth did I suddenly have thousands of people liking and sharing something I didn't even post?

But you posted it on Instagram, a tiny, chiding voice inside my head said. *You also performed.* I had used social media long enough to know that anything, and that meant anything that one posted could be used, downloaded, shared, taken apart, piece by piece, and put together again in a scarily different form.

It's all good, I told myself, my insides feeling weak. It was not a sex video or anything like that. It could be worse. And, isn't this good?

I had 670 friend requests.

No, it was now 821 friend requests.

I switched off my phone.

What did I have anything to do with Davit Nadibaidze? I kept asking myself. Oh right, you met him. In Svaneti. You filmed him. You took pictures like he was a sunset or something. And you posted it.

Should I blame Angelique van Leuven? No. I blame myself. I regret all this.

The thing was, it was useless to even take down that post. It had been shared, oh, tens of thousands of times already.

Reluctantly, I opened my phone again. The sight of red notifications in my apps was so unnerving, I actually went to the kitchen to look for that stray bottle of gin I keep losing in the cabinets.

There it was, a half-consumed bottle of The Botanist, stored in the cupboard under the stove. I found a clean glass, sat down on our dining table, and took a shot. It was too bitter, so I grabbed a can of soda water from Nhi's stash at the bottom of our refrigerator.

Oh my God, *Nhi!* Where was she anyway?

I took a quick swig of my haphazard gin-and-soda mixture and fumbled for my phone. There were four missed calls from Nhi, buried under all the other calls I've either ignored, missed, or declined since Angelique's post—and mine—became viral.

As if on cue, my phone lit and vibrated. Nhi!

'Babe! *O troi oi,* what's happening? What's this I'm seeing? Are you okay? I'm still at work but I've been calling and calling you—'

'I'm okay, I'm fine,' I breathed, relieved to hear a familiar voice. 'Thanks, but I'm okay.'

A pause on the other end of the line. 'Arya, babe.' Nhi's voice was quiet. 'You're not.'

My voice fell an octave. 'You're right. I'm not, Nhi.' I swallowed, feeling my throat catch, my eyes getting damp. I washed them out with another gulp of my drink.

'How can you be? I saw you, not just once but many times and randomly, on my goddamn Facebook feed! And Instagram. And Twitter—I can't even . . .' Nhi's voice took on a muffled quality as if she'd removed her phone from her ear. 'Listen,' she said, back on the line a moment after. 'I can go home and be with you and we'll figure this out, okay?'

'What? Nhi, no.' I shook my head, even though I knew she couldn't see me. I was still sitting squarely at the dining table, my hand closing in on the glass that was part gin and part soda water—a perfectly drinkable combo I've now accidentally discovered even though I've never been into cocktails. 'I know you have your event today and you can't just leave.'

'Yes, I can—'

'No,' I said, more firmly this time. 'And there's nothing we can do. It's already out there.' I took one more sip of my concoction, noting that my insides were softening. I felt warm, fuzzy at the edges. For a moment there, I could pretend that nothing big was happening online, nothing that had anything to do with me—or thousands of people I didn't even know.

'Are you sure? I'm just—I'm just a little shocked to see you with all these things.' Nhi sounded sceptical. 'And that guy, whomever he is. Whatever. Just please, tell me you're okay.'

'I'm okay,' I repeated. I didn't tell her that the gin was helping. And of course, not looking at my phone. I drew a shaky breath but forced my voice to be steady. 'I'm sure it will die down by tonight.'

* * *

How wrong I was. How *little* I knew, really, of the power, the potency, and the force that was social media.

Because two hours later, when I managed to rouse myself from my unintentional drunken, exhausted nap, where I'd been slumped, face down on our dining table, I saw my phone. And it told me everything.

While I was sleeping, the likes had multiplied by the tens of thousands. By the end of the day, my post had over 33,000 shares, had been copied and posted twice that, and when I gave up counting, had a rough tally of over 240,000 shares. I couldn't even begin to look at the comments.

I blinked and slowly placed my phone back on the furthest corner of the table. I thought of how things had been so different that morning when I was walking with Stella at the Botanical Gardens. When it was only mild curiosity that I'd felt upon seeing Angelique's Instagram Stories, where she'd reposted my video. When I had thought, as I dug into the fabulous eggs Benedict in Stella's kitchen in Bukit Timah, that it was just another day where people shared and re-shared everything, and so what was the big deal?

But then Stella, who followed me on IG, hopped on to my feed and I saw that the followers I had had grown from a thousand to . . . ten thousand, in a span of less than an hour.

That was when I thought I my IG was hacked. That was this morning. I didn't know what to call what was happening at this very moment, though. Because right now, less than twelve hours after this whole Davit thing blew up, my Instagram followers had ballooned from ten thousand to more than two hundred thousand—and counting.

Now, what would you call that?

Chapter 19

Singapore, 8.39 a.m. 'Oh hey, congratulations!'

The elevators of Isle Z had just whooshed closed behind me, and I could see Tammy in her usual spot behind reception, her animated, seemingly made-for-radio voice echoing through the narrow hall.

I smiled, a little unsteadily, as I approached the counter. 'Morning, Tammy,' I said, trying to sound light. 'Thank you.' And then, very casually—as if I was just asking for the time, I asked: 'Congratulations, for what?'

'Oh, Arya.' Tammy paused to stare at me with bright, excited eyes. 'Don't be coy,' she said, with a knowing purse of her lips. 'For going viral!'

'What?'

'You're all over my feed!' she crowed, brandishing her two mobile phones and nodding at a third one nestled in between the office phones. 'See? It's insane!'

My heart started thudding again, as it had last night when I discovered the things that had been happening at lightning speed online. This was big, coming from Tammy Paul, who was as blasé as one can get and rarely showed excitement over anything. Perhaps she'd had to be, as the head receptionist of Isle Z and who'd been fielding and managing calls for Oliver and Desmond's team right from the start.

'Believe me, I didn't want to go to work. I just wanted to be cozy with my phones and watch, you know,' she said, giving me a shrug. 'I just couldn't believe that someone who worked here would go viral. And it's you! Right here!'

I blinked. 'Oh, well—'

'But I had to get to work,' she continued, her tone both regretful and accusing.

Before I could say anything, Tammy raised a manicured palm, one hand fingering her headset. 'For Arya Alvarez?' she said in her professional voice. She cocked her head. 'Let me take a message.' I watched as she scribbled something on a bright yellow Post-it, dumping it on top of a loose pile of Post-it notes she'd apparently accumulated all morning.

'Thank you,' I said, not exactly sure how to react. 'And I'm sorry.'

'Oh dear, no.' Tammy waved her hand dismissively. 'All these calls, all morning! There are a lot of calls for you! But I told them all to message you. Thank goodness for social media. Check your accounts, okay? We can't have that clogging our lines.'

'Of course,' I said, my hand instinctively making its way inside the jumble that was my bag. I wasn't excited to check my social media accounts at all.

'What a way to see Davit Nadibaidze, eh!'

I looked at her in surprise. 'You know him? The artist?' Was it really that everyone knew him except me?

'Oh well, not really,' Tammy lifted her chin and gave me a charismatic smile. 'But he was trending on Twitter—*with you.*' She gave another emphatic nod that I knew was meant to be congratulatory. 'So I had to check him out. And I said, 'Oh my God, Arya! With Davit . . .' Her voice trailed as one of her two phones started ringing again. She picked up the office phone, listened for a moment, then nodded briskly. 'Okay.'

Turning to me, she said, 'Oliver wants to talk to you.' She handed me her little pile of notes. 'Go on,' she said, her tone softening. 'He wants you now.'

I hurried over to Oliver's office. The glass door was open, and he was typing on his laptop.

'Oliver,' I said, leaning on the doorframe, suddenly unsure what was it that I wanted to say. 'I'm sorry.' The words were out of my mouth before I could think any further. Why did I say that? Admittedly, I was so confused about what was happening, an apology felt like the only thing I could offer up right now.

Oliver looked up, concern on his face. 'Arya. Are you all right?' He closed his laptop and stood up. 'I know what's happened. I've gotten emails. Some calls.'

'What emails?'

'Media. Social media.' Oliver's tone was matter-of-fact. 'Asking for you. They've been trying to reach you.'

'They have?' I swallowed. 'Oh God,' I said, shoving my hand instinctively into my bag, where I had thrown my phone that had been put to silent and mute and everything else that I can think of, short of deleting all my apps.

For the first time since my break-up, I was afraid to look at my messages.

And then he started laughing. 'What's happened, Superstar? Who knew you actually met Davit Nadibaidze while you were in Georgia? How come I'm only hearing about this now—when I see you every day?'

I gave a feeble laugh, despite myself. 'I honestly don't know. I didn't think—I was . . .' Shit, I was so confused, really. The gin I'd ingested yesterday wasn't helping me think straight right now, either. I threw up my hands, feeling weak all over again. 'I don't know what to do, Oliver.'

'But you're all right?' Oliver paused, frowning a little. 'Arya? If this is all too much . . .'

'I'm fine.' I cleared my throat, and forced my shoulders back. I was at work, after all, and despite—or maybe, *because*—of everything that has happened, I didn't want to appear unprofessional. 'I'm fine,' I repeated. 'I'm here. I'm still in one piece.' It was true, partly. Now that I was in the room with Oliver, things didn't feel as catastrophic.

Oliver looked at me for another moment, then shook his head. 'Imagine my surprise when I opened my news sites and there you were. Or rather, there was Davit, the magnificent Angelique van Leuven, and you, Isle Z's superstar.'

'I didn't know it was him,' I said. 'I feel like a fool.'

'Don't beat yourself up too much about that,' Oliver said. 'You've been doing a great job, Arya. It's just that Davit Nadibaidze is one of the most famous contemporary artists we've had in this generation.'

'That's why.' I was mournful.

'Fun fact, Davit Nadibaidze's notorious for stalking surgeons and watching surgeries. To see those inner workings of our organs, I guess.' Oliver paused, fished out his phone and pulled up a website. It was Davit's artwork, even more recent ones that I haven't seen last night. 'Why do you think his work is so visceral?'

A tap on the glass wall. There was Tammy, gesturing for Oliver to come out of the room. 'Excuse me,' he said, and I felt the swoosh as he closed the glass door behind him.

Out of habit, I took out my phone from my bag. Already there was a message there that had found its way to my mobile number. 'You're the girl who met the elusive Davit Nadibaidze!'

I was shocked that in such a short amount of time, I was deluged with invitations. And messages, so many messages that ranged from being gushing and adoring, nonsensical to nasty. *Do Officiel* wasn't content with its pieced together videos of me and Davit—they wanted an actual, first-hand interview. *Arts Univers* wanted a video and photo shoot. There were podcast shows and Youtube vloggers. TV shows in Manila, Singapore, and Hong Kong wanted guestings. A producer from Manila had emailed me, several times, about participating in a reality game show.

I opened Instagram and Facebook. I had it on vibrate, but it was still unnerving to see the numbers move, as if it had a life of its own.

My post now had over two million views.

I laid it on the table.

My phone shivered again. And again. And *again*. And it looked funny, my old phone which I haven't even updated, buzzing continuously like that as if it were alive and calling me.

I stood up and moved across the room and away from that device. Everything felt blurry at the edges. I heard myself emit a small laugh, sounding dry and mirthless.

My own phone calling me. Wasn't that funny?

And then it didn't feel funny at all. Because it wasn't my phone calling me, like some cartoon. This was real, and this was my life. All these buzzing and shivering, all these movements and sound were the noises of thousands of people liking, reacting, and sharing. I closed my eyes and leaned my head on the wall. I told myself there was nothing they wanted from me, I was just the clueless person who posted photos and a video. And if they did want something from me—what could it really be? An image, a soundbite, a clip? A validation that I exist? These days, it could be anything. These days, your online persona can be torn and shredded into pieces, your actual body remaining intact. I wasn't sure if either was a good thing. No, I wasn't sure if any of that was a good thing at all.

Chapter 20

Singapore, 4.03 a.m. I wanted to get this over with. I wanted to clear my name, in a way. I wanted to tell the world that that was it: I saw a man, I took photos, I recorded a video.

I wanted to tell the world that I had nothing to do with Davit Nadibaidze.

Because the world seemed to think otherwise. I would learn later on that although people would start to talk about something that happened, they would also very quickly stop talking about it. Instead, they would just use what's happened to talk about the same everyday things they talk about.

Why? I suspect it's not because they want to change the world or anything. Perhaps people still, deep down, want to get their fifteen minutes of fame. Perhaps what people really want is their presence felt in the world—one comment, one post, one reel at a time.

And so here it was, the initial, shocking comments that greeted me when I first viewed them in my Instagram post.

'Is she Davit's new muse?'

'New woman! Worthy anot?'

167

'She must be Davit's new girlfriend. Romantic or platonic?'
'I smell affair. Popcorn, please.'
'Is she a photographer?'
'No, she's just a wannabe filmographer.'
'She's an influencer desperate for more followers.'
'She's a rich traveller, nothing else to do, lah.'
'She looks ugly in her IG.'
'She's a friend of celebrities.'
'Arya, the social climber. How desperate.'
'Yeah, she'd do anything for attention.'
'She's a nobody.'
'She must *be somebody.'*
'She's the next big thing.'
'She is THE thing! Right now!'

* * *

The thing with what happened, with my Davit post going viral, was that it started out under the guise of art, of discovery, even hope. It seemed, at first, as if people were just into Davit Nadibaidze, the famous painter and prolific artist, known and celebrated the world over. It was only belatedly that I realized—and so naively, that the attention would inevitably turn to me.

My social media accounts were heaving with what had become the usual—normalized in the past forty-eight hours: a deluge of comments, likes, and reactions, stitched-together Instagram reels, fifteen-second TikTok videos, and trending news articles. It was just hours after Angelique van Leuven had shared my post—not long after *Do Officiel* made that trending video of Davit, Angelique, and me—when enterprising staffers of online magazines *Bossip*, *Vice*, and *Raider Online* already managed to track down my private Facebook profile, raiding it for photos to use in their articles.

And then the whole online community started dismantling my Instagram feed. I had put it on 'Private' too late—there were already almost two hundred thousand followers in a matter of hours. What I didn't know was that these same followers had already downloaded my photos—meant to be personal and work-related—and dissected and used them. For what, I had wondered, at first. For trying to understand Davit Nadibaidze as an artist?

Turns out, it was trying to understand *me*—or rather, creating an impression of me and the work that I was doing with our celebrity clients at Isle Z.

Everyone, it seemed, suddenly had an impression of me.

A photo of me and Angelique. A photo of me and Rooki. A photo of me in a bikini . . . wait, what? Comments that ranged from nice to nasty, flowed underneath those reposted photos.

'Is it true that Rooki Sakimoto had broken up with her boyfriend?' Said one TikTok video. And then: 'Was Arya Alvarez the cause?'

It was unbelievable, the things people made up in the name of content. The same stuff—what little they could get from my sparse IG and Facebook feeds was posted and reposted, again and again, in bite-sized, easy-to-digest pieces. The repetition was unnerving. Different online media outlets, broadcasting the same news, the same impressions and assumptions—and yet it didn't make it true. I guess what disturbed me the most, was people's tendency to gather truth from familiarity.

I thanked the universe that during these initial, frightening moments, I was with Nhi. Because nothing really made sense, in those first few days. Or rather, in those first forty-eight hours. I had to remind myself that we weren't talking days any more. Days were so slow, days were so pre-Internet, days were so *yesterday*. With Facebook, Instagram, Twitter and TikTok, seconds were all it took for things to take a turn, for things to change—drastically if need be.

After my talk with Oliver, the day after the Davit post had gone viral, I tried to go on with my work as usual, as if it were another day. I had gone to my desk in a daze, trying to ignore that feeling of wanting another dose of alcohol, another dose of something, *anything*—just to escape the things I knew were happening at an unstoppable speed online.

It didn't work. Of course, it didn't. In the end, I was told by Oliver to take the day off. 'Days, if needed.' It was rare, this kind of generosity.

Nhi—bless her—had taken the day off as well.

Self-care, Nhi was convinced, was what I needed after what I've been through. 'What you're still going through,' she said, correcting herself.

It was true. The deluge of comments, the likes and the reactions, and the news items were more than I could bear. I considered changing my number, my email, my LinkedIn, my Facebook, and my Instagram. In short, I wanted to change everything.

Everything.

It was my break-up with Jake all over again. It was painful, in a way that no one—well, maybe except Nhi Tran—really understood. I had been craving intimacy, still searching for a connection with myself after my break-up, and almost as desperate as my desire to again have a connection with someone. And yet here I was now, feeling more disconnected than ever—with myself, with the online world, and perhaps even with the people I've been interacting with.

I felt paralyzed. I felt I was going nowhere, fast.

I thought of Jake. And then I thought, it was time I did something for myself, too. So many of the things I did, it seemed, always had something to do with him. Don't ask me how this thing brought me here, back to Jake *again*. But here I was. Here I am, *still*. And it wasn't exactly a healthy thing.

I paused, wanting so much to make more sense of things. And to make more sense of myself, too. What did I really want?

I wish I could say I went into hiding. But I felt like I needed to clear my name. I talked about the situation, again and again with Oliver and Desmond. There were avenues where I could do that.

Your life could change. Nhi had told me, gently.

My life could change, indeed. *I* could change my life. I could do it, as long as I was breathing. And perhaps, as long as there was the internet.

Chapter 21

Singapore, 5 a.m. It was still very dark when I got off the taxi, alighting in front of the industrial-looking studios of Channel 13, Singapore's newest TV channel, and the one that's been standing out recently and you could say fast rising in popularity, because of its bold, intriguing mix of digital coverage techniques and traditional media.

'We're going back to our roots,' Ching, the producer had told me when she first called, just a few hours after Angelique van Leuven shared my Davit video on her IG Stories. My phone and emails were still blowing up, and I was still in a weary, very confused daze. 'People are coming back to paper! To 'zines! To TV and radio—can you believe it? That's why Channel 13 is growing, and it's growing so fast. Our audiences—ugh, I love them! You, Arya Alvarez on the show would be perfect. Just perfect!'

That was the last time I heard Ching's voice because from then on, it had all been messages, and so many were they—all adding to the deluge that was happening in my DMs and inbox. There were two more TV channels that wanted to interview me. I went with Ching and Channel 13, on Oliver's advice.

And now I was here, feeling like I'd landed somewhere at the edge of Singapore in the middle of the night. But it was actually already almost 5 a.m.

The show was called *Morning Feast*, and wasn't actually about food. After Ching had called, and after I had spoken with Oliver and Desmond about this— say yes, Desmond had urged—I went on YouTube and watched a couple of *Morning Feast* past episodes. I was surprised that it reminded me of the morning shows in the Philippines, like *Good Morning, Kuya* and *Umagang Kay Ganda* which translated into 'A Beautiful Morning' and was a full-blown hour-and-a-half peppy lifestyle show that featured almost anything and everything except, well, hard news and politics. I remember catching bits and pieces of the show here and there, whenever I found myself in front of an open TV in Manila. There were traffic updates, special guests, man-on-the-street interviews, live games, restaurant and food reviews wherein restaurant owners brought their specialties to the studio before breakfast. They featured guests that ranged from artists, fashion, furniture, and jewelry designers to engineers and teachers, even housewives who had tiny businesses—anyone whom the producers believed had something interesting to say.

'Singapore is changing', Ching wrote in her messages. And yet it still needed to be at the top. 'Art is everywhere, but we're extremely interested in getting the Davit story out. Don't worry, you'll definitely see clips of the show on social media.'

The show was starting at 7 a.m., so I had to be in the studio by 5 a.m.

'This way, Arya.' It was Jackie, Ching's assistant. She was already there, holding a clipboard and two phones when I peeked inside the first door of the studio. It looked like a warehouse. Even at this ungodly hour, it was fast filling with people moving around quickly and purposefully, the atmosphere busy and charged. It struck me that it was nothing like what I'd seen on the *Morning Feast* on YouTube. Only one side of the vast room was well-lighted, with the familiar yellow, blue, and orange *Morning Feast* wall, a bright, colourful, and very recognizable installation that served as the backdrop of the show. The rest of the warehouse-like space was dark, cluttered, with rough concrete walls and lots of scaffolding. It was like two worlds existed there: one fancy and one extremely functional to the point of ugly behind the scenes. Despite myself, it still amazed me that there were things that you really couldn't see. Which was what life was about, sometimes: you have no idea what's going on on the other side of the wall.

'Is Ching here?' I didn't know why I asked; it just felt more comfortable having the people you've talked to, here in this unfamiliar place and at this ungodly hour, I guess. I'd travelled to different places with a lot of my clients, but sometimes it felt like that was just so much better, because you were both experiencing something new together. Here, I felt alone and totally like a fish out of water.

'She'll be here in a bit,' Jackie said, her tone matter-of-fact. 'If you need anything, just holler for me.'

'Will do,' I nodded. With the way the space was getting busier, hollering for someone would surely be needed. 'Listen, it's just that it's my first time appearing on TV and I'm really—'

'Just go through that door there so Agnes can do your makeup,' Jackie said, cutting me off and already frowning at her two phones. But she ushered me towards a dark corner where there was a small door, opening it slightly and gesturing me to pass through. Inside was another warehouse-looking space, where a lighted mirror was set up on a dresser-style table on one side. Laid out on one side of the table were makeup brushes, sponges, cotton balls, and a box of tissues. On the right were several opened eyeshadow palettes, rows and rows of lipsticks, a tall pile of concealers in different packaging, and tubes and bottles of liquid foundation.

'Hi there.' Agnes was at the door and was smiling, tall and lanky, and in a simple light pink T-shirt and jeans. Her face was unmade, though her hair was in a very tight fishtail braid resting on the right side of her shoulder. 'Arya? Please sit over here. Make yourself comfortable.'

I sat in the brown leather highchair, which was torn in one corner.

'I'm going to do your makeup,' Agnes began, swiping at my bare face with a cotton wet with something fragrant and cool. 'Just remember that this is for TV, so don't be shocked if it seems a little heavy at first look. The lights are so harsh at the studio you'll totally look washed out if I do a normal, everyday look.'

'Okay,' I said, not really knowing what she meant by heavy. A redder lipstick, maybe? Or darker eyeshadow? I was fine with both, actually.

Fifteen minutes later, I was looking at the thickest foundation I've ever worn in my whole life. It was so thick and yet so even and poreless that I barely recognized myself. Dark slashes of some brown-grey powder was swiped under my cheekbones, which was supposed to contour my face, according to Agnes. Dusky pink blush that honestly, I thought was just too much swirled again and again on the apples of my cheeks. The lipstick was a flattering coral pink, but Agnes mixed it with a dark red so my lips could stand out more.

'It's . . . interesting,' I said, surveying my new made-up look at the lighted mirror. It was both fascinating and repelling. All I could think of was that I might look like a clown onscreen because Agnes and I have vastly different definitions of 'heavy.'

'You like it?' Agnes seemed relaxed and very pleased with herself.

I blinked. 'Well, I've never been on TV before.' I mustered a smile. 'Thank you, Agnes.'

She nodded. 'Trust me.'

And then Jackie was at the door and ushering me towards the well-lighted set of the studio. 'Ching already told you, right? You're appearing in the segment called *Seize the Morning*. It's where we feature really current news and what's hot and trending.'

I nodded. It was in the messages and I had paid close attention to it when I was studying the episodes. 'I know. Although I really would just like to honestly say that I had no idea it was Davit—'

'She's here!' Jackie announced. I was suddenly aware of where we were. We were right on the set of *Morning Feast* and on one side of the set with velvet armchairs and a coffee table that had a plant with pink leaves on it.

Jackie was talking to *Morning Feast* host Camille Sy who was seated, looking fresh in her all-white shirt and skirt, head bent as she read from a script, her lips moving silently.

'Hi,' I said. I recognized her from the few episodes that I watched on YouTube, though there she was warm, perky, and seemed to have a million questions to ask her guests.

She didn't answer. She didn't even look up.

And then suddenly there was a flurry of people. The set was cleared of stray coffee cups, paper, and the errant headset that someone must have left. Somebody handed me a heavy gadget with a cord. 'Clip this on,' the guy said. I attached the little foamy thing that was the mike on the edge of my collar, then looked at the heavy rectangular contraption, like a walkie-talkie in my hand.

'Excuse me?' I called out, to no one in particular. Jackie was nowhere to be found, 'How do you turn this on?'

'Put it behind you,' Somebody, somewhere said. 'Press to turn it on!'

I placed it on the waistband of my pants, then tried to find where I can press the thing to turn it on. There was a button and I did as I was told. Nothing happened.

'Hello! Is this turned on?'

From my peripheral vision I could see Camille glance up, then bend down her head again. And then there was Agnes, in her apron with the brushes, holding a compact powder bigger than her palm. She tapped Camille on the shoulder. When the TV host automatically looked up, Agnes simply patted on the powder, bending down slightly to perhaps remove a smudge from Camille's makeup.

And then someone actually bounded up and pressed the button on the box in my waist, finally turning the mike on.

More lights flooded the set. Cameras in front of us moved effortlessly left and right. A spotlight glowed from somewhere above, seemingly trained solely on me. And Camille Sy, the host of the *Morning Feast*'s *Seize the Morning*, was facing front, getting ready to play to the cameras.

I wasn't ready, but I was here. What I had wanted to tell the world was that they were looking at the wrong person. I wasn't Davit Nadibaidze. This was just me.

Chapter 22

Singapore, 6.13 a.m. 'Airing in two minutes!' The floor manager called out, from somewhere in the darkened studio. The set grew quiet. 'Airing in three, two, one!'

'Good morning, good morning!' Camille's well-modulated voice filled the set, and she flashed her signature wide smile at the two cameras that was trained at us. 'Welcome to *Morning Feast*, and do you know how we start our day? We *Seize the Morning*!'

I stared at her, fascinated at the transformation. She glanced at me and gave me a bright smile. The papers she'd been holding were nowhere to be found, and thanks to Agnes, her cheeks looked well-sculpted, her skin radiant, and she had on the best cool-toned red lipstick that I've always been trying to find.

'That's right,' she continued, the words rolling easily off her tongue. 'Today we have a very special guest, as always.'

Yes, this was the Camille that I knew from my brief orientation on *Morning Feast*.

'Today on *Seize the Morning* we have the pleasure of interviewing someone really special who will be talking about one of the famous people we know. Everyone, please welcome Arya Alvarez!'

'Good morning, Camille.' I forced myself to smile at the camera that was suddenly trained on me. 'Thank you for inviting me.' My voice sounded leaden, and my throat was dry. The studio lights were beginning to feel hot.

'As we all know, Arya was the first one to spot the famous artist Davit Nadibaidze, whom we all know has shocked the art world—the world, really—when he chose to retreat from the public.' Camille leaned forward, eyes animated, the corners of her mouth pinned up—looking completely different from the limp, aloof person who'd been sitting there earlier. A true expert in her craft of hosting.

'Arya, tell us about your experience with the fabulous Davit Nadibaidze.'

I balked. The fear of being the cause of dead air and humiliating myself spurred me to open my mouth and speak. 'First of all, I wouldn't say that it was an experience,' I began. 'It was very short, and I believe I just may have been at the right place at the right time.'

'You must have known it was Davit, our missing Davit.' Camille sounded coy. 'Otherwise, you wouldn't have shared the video. Yes, this video that we all know. The one that went viral. Your thoughts on that, Arya?'

I took a deep breath,

'Let's take a look.'

I watched my video being played on the projector behind us.

What's intriguing, always, with Davit is that he gets to say something about art that still hasn't been said, but still needs to be said.

To me, it felt like groping in the dark.

Because they couldn't interview Davit Nadibaidze, they were interviewing me.

What else, really, could I tell them? That I saw Davit, thought he was a regular artist, took photos and a video, and then posted them on Instagram.

Chapter 23

El Nido, Palawan, 2.30 p.m. It was typhoon season in the Philippines and yet here I was, strapped in an airplane seat with twelve other passengers—the exact number of people this plane can carry, no more and no less.

The twelve-seater Cessna plane took a hard, sharp dip as thick ribbons of rain splashed with a resounding slap against the small oval window above my seat. I didn't need to look outside to know that there was nothing to see except opaque white clouds edged with black as rain continued pounding on the roof and windows of our aircraft. A flash of lighting lit the sky for a split second.

If I had thought that the TV appearance that I did with Singapore's Channel 13 was harrowing, then I truly had so much more to learn. Because *this* was harrowing. A little plane going up and down the skies like something made out of paper? This was terrifying on a whole new level.

I broke off from my thoughts only to realize that every single passenger, including me, was silent. Were they praying, holding on to their seats, or just asleep as this plane went through the eye of what seemed like a flash storm 15,000 feet above ground level? Were they also regretting coming on this trip, boarding this private jet as I was?

From somewhere behind me, I heard someone retch. I checked the buckle of my seat belt, closing my eyes as the plane surged forward as if carried by a mighty wind. My throat felt dry, desperate for a splash of water, even though like the others, I hadn't uttered a word since take-off, twenty-five minutes ago. A glass of something liquid was out of the question right now, of course. The lone flight attendant, a very tall Filipina who had metal braces on her teeth, was somewhere at the front and was possibly as dizzy as the others even as she was strapped on her seat by the wall.

We were en route to El Nido, a series of islands west of the Philippines, flying through the rain, wind, and dark clouds. There were no storms in that part of the archipelago—I knew this because it was taught in high school geography and because before Singapore, I had lived most of my life in this country. But no one had told us that there were storms *on the way* to this island that were heavily promoted to the rest of the world as postcard-perfect isles of white sand beaches, deep-blue waters, swaying coconut trees, and clear, sunny skies. The island of Palawan, where El Nido and the island resorts were, was out of the earthquake and typhoon belt, and only had sun and rain all throughout the year.

Another retching sound, then a fit of coughing by a woman, this time from up front. I hoped it wasn't the flight attendant.

If we survive, then we would achieve our goal of going to the party that was to be held, ironically, at a five-star resort in Palawan, named El Nido Sun Villas.

I was trying to conjure happy, calm images of sunny skies and calm waters when the man beside me spoke for the first time. 'I hope we land soon,' he said, and it was only then that I noticed that he had his shirt open almost to the navel. 'I really need to attend this party.'

Before I could reply, the captain's voice was on the speakers. 'Twenty minutes to landing. Cabin crew, please prepare for landing.'

And then the plane landed, miraculously. Beautifully, in fact. I closed my eyes again and felt my whole body flattening against my seat as it touched down with the gentlest of bumps, taxiing smoothly down the small runway until it came to a complete stop.

Everyone cheered, clapping with relief and happiness as I opened my eyes. I saw a phone with a tripod being raised from one of the seats, recording this celebratory mood. And then I looked out my little oval window, startled to see no trace of that raging, grey storm we just had during the flight. The first thing I thought was that what they say about El Nido was true: there was only sun, sand, and blue skies here.

It was also influencer party central.

* * *

We were the second batch to be flown in to Sun Villas El Nido, where international clothing brand MerciX was holding one of its quarterly influencer parties in cool destinations all over the world.

Desmond had urged me to go. Oliver was overseas, and so it was Desmond who had called me into his office and spoke about how this recent turn of events would affect Isle

Z. For a second, I had thought I would be forced to resign or something, but Desmond said something that was very, very strange: he wanted me to go and accept as many invitations from the media.

'Think of it as another part of your job,' he said. 'Because it is. Every travel manager we have here in Isle Z has a responsibility to promote the brand.'

'I know,' I said. 'I'm doing my best.'

'It will be good for our company,' Desmond said, simply. 'We're currently number three in Singapore, Arya. We can at least try to bring up our numbers.'

Our numbers. My followers had grown to half a million, even though I had not posted anything.

Admittedly, second to my flat, Isle Z had been the other place that had felt safe, the only other place that was a haven.

My mind zoomed back to two years and eight months ago, when I was hired by these two men who had a vision of providing one-of-a-kind experiences to a specific set of travellers. It was a business, first and foremost, that was true. A source of revenue and a way to profit. But there was one thing that Oliver told me was a big reason he and Desmond started Isle Z: to change people's lives through travel.

It certainly changed mine.

This was something I had realized only recently, since I moved to Singapore, on the days when I'd started, finally, to feel that I was not unlovable. That I was enough of a person—to be loved, that is. To be chosen.

Yes, it was still about Jake, and how he hadn't chosen me. Isle Z—Desmond and Oliver had. Two years and eight months ago, they hired me. Could they tell then, that I had been in the middle of a heartbreak? Maybe, maybe not. I had always thought that Desmond and Oliver had not only hired me but had, in a way, taken a chance with me.

And now my life was changing. Working at Isle Z has sometimes helped me forget about what had happened in Manila. Sometimes, I actually believed that my life has changed, truly changed. Sometimes I let myself believe that it was better, that *I* was better. Sometimes, it even felt better. I owed it to Isle Z, to my bosses, and maybe to myself— to see this thing through. Like how I handle my clients desperate for a mind-blowing, life-changing travel fix, I had to make it work.

* * *

'Arya! Miss Arya!' A heavyset woman in a blue floral long dress and a fuchsia hibiscus flower pinned on top of her very high bun was waving at me from the far end of the lobby. 'Over here!' She called again, this time doing a series of little jumps.

I raised an arm to wave back, wondering how she could recognize me from her spot that seemed almost a hundred metres away. I had just alighted from the ornamented, flower-adorned airconditioned jeepney—a luxe, tropical version of the noisy, smoke-belching raggedy jeepneys in Manila that ferried commuters all over the city—where twelve of us had piled into after taking a twenty-minute boat to the island. Like the jeep, the boat was comfortable and sleek, teeming with drinks and overflowing with food—juicy mangoes cut and carved in intricate shapes, local specialties like *kilawin* or marinated raw fish, grilled squid, and fried baby crabs. A large basket held a pile of coconuts, ready to be cut open and enjoyed. After landing, we had to take a boat to the island, then this jeep to where Sun Villas El Nido was.

The resort was a compact compound in the middle of El Nido's famed Apulit Island, and the venue for today's MerciX Glam Getaway Influencer Party. Funny that it was actually called that, but who was I to judge? I knew close to nothing about these. I had only been to familiarization tours, group travel, and private tours that had little to do with real, hardcore social media influencers. Sun Villas El Nido was smaller than most five-star resorts, but it was extremely sleek and well-designed. The lobby was vast, high-ceilinged, and open on three sides. From high above hung life-sized, sculptural chandeliers made of treated rattan in various, random dramatic shapes: human bodies, palm leaves, and stars. The lobby's only wall held a wide reception counter made of marble and topped with polished bamboo against a wall covered in an intricate, fan-like *anahaw* design.

I broke away from my group and made my way across the lobby.

'I'm so glad you made it!' The woman's cheeks were flushed. 'I'm Sandy.'

'It's my first time attending an influencer party,' I said, trying my best to sound excited. Because I wasn't, really. I wanted to get out of there, but it also felt good to be saying something true.

'Come, come!' She held my elbow and steered me towards the reception counter, where I saw the rest of my group being assigned rooms. At the entrance, I could see hotel staff wheeling in our luggage.

'You don't have to do anything,' Sandy was saying. Smiling, she motioned to one of the ladies in reception, who produced a pouch made of soft, crumpled silk from somewhere under the counter and handed it to her. She dangled the rose-coloured round bag in front of me for a second, before thrusting it in my hands.

'Everything is taken care of,' she said. 'Your key card, a scarf, and shades care of MerciX are here, in this cute bag that you can sling around your body—ready for when you are.'

'Thank you,' I nodded, taking the little pouch into my hands. 'That's very nice.'

'Oh, and there's a nifty thing there that I'd really like you to use,' she said. 'Here, give me your phone.' She reached into the bag and pulled out a piece of thin plastic, slid my phone into it, and pressed it shut. 'There. It's completely waterproof.'

She handed me back my newly-encased phone, but before I can say anything, I felt Sandy's hand on my elbow again as she steered me, determinedly, towards the other side of the lobby where I can see two pools, one decorated with translucent orange balls, and the other with gigantic floaters in the shapes of swans and rubber duckies, as well as pizza and doughnut shapes.

Two servers, one bearing a tray filled with tall glasses of bubbly and another with delicate, caviar-topped canapés, appeared. 'This is vegan,' the one with the canapés announced, handing me and Sandy a napkin each.

'I'll be back with more, so please enjoy,' said the other server, deftly putting the tray in front of us so we can take our drinks.

I thanked her, took a tiny sip form my flute and slid the buttery-salty morsel in my mouth, immediately craving for another. I hadn't eaten anything since that turbulent plane ride.

'So, Arya, tell me. How is Davit Nadibaidze?' Sandy was talking with her mouth full, her tone conspiratorial. 'Did he—did he paint you?'

'Paint me?' I asked, startled. 'You mean, as a subject? No, no, there was nothing like that.'

Before I could explain any further, a tall guy with a shock of dark curls wearing a tank and Bermuda shorts, brushed past us and did a double take. 'Oh, hey! Arya Alvarez!' He nodded at me and raised his hand as if to do a high-five. 'You found that missing famous artist!'

'No, he wasn't missing,' I began. 'He had voluntarily retreated—'

'Lucas Paolo!' Sandy exclaimed. 'Good to see you! You missed last season's MerciX party.'

'Yes, I'm Lucas.' He took my hand and gave it a few pumps, his palm feeling warm and dry. 'Don't think we haven't seen you. You're all over. And you found that missing artist for the stars, huh?'

'Arya herself works with celebrities.' Sandy was taking ample gulps from her glass.

'Is that so? Do tell!'

And so it began.

Chapter 24

El Nido, Philippines, 4.30 p.m. Everyone looked perfect, it seemed as if I've stepped into a Hollywood movie. Or a roomful of models. What it really was, was an influencer party.

'If I were given a second life, I want to be reincarnated as a MerciX influencer.'

'Paid to go on these tropical vacations, the free clothes, just to take Instagram pictures.'

'How is this real life?'

'No, this is the life!'

'I mean, fuck nine-to-five, right?'

It felt as if I'd walked into a gorgeous movie set: lush foxtail palm trees swaying in the breeze; striped, red and white umbrellas carefully positioned; a spacious tiled deck set up with quirky yet glamorous backdrops at every corner; and finally, two large swimming pools—shining a cool, bright blue that matched the sky—outfitted with the cutest swan, rubber duckie, doughnut, and pizza-shaped floaties, you couldn't not take a photo.

Or fifty, if you were an influencer and particular about your feed. At least, that was what I thought. I had no clue, actually. I may have worked and travelled with celebrities, and yes, even social media animals—but as I told Sandy, it was my first time at an influencer party. More specifically, it was my first time at the famous MerciX Glam Getaway in El Nido, Philippines.

Indeed it felt like an extremely well-curated TV or film set, and I've never felt so surrounded by so many stunning, fit, and well-dressed actors. Or dancers, I thought, surveying a group of four, dewy-skinned girls—looking not a day older than twenty-five—their complicated, cut-out swimsuits staying in place as they did an incredibly well-coordinated TikTok dance, arms flying, knees bending, and heads jerking but never losing eye contact with the phone attached to a tripod in front of them.

I wended my way through the pool area, from one chic, curated backdrop to the next, snippets of lively conversations floating above my head amidst beautiful people and their phones, compact cameras, ring lights, and furry mikes held high or secured on tripods.

This was a full-blown influencer party, and MerciX has proven that it was a master at this. The two swimming pools, with their bright-coloured floaties and accouterments, the red-striped umbrellas, and the lush mix of strategically placed palms and coconut trees that had been obviously brought in from the forests of Palawan to complete the tropical vibe, looked picture-perfect. No, it looked Instagram-perfect. This party was one big immersive photo shoot for MerciX.

Influencers in the wild, Oliver and I used to joke whenever we stumbled on people gyrating in front of their phones in the parking lot or taking what felt like a hundred selfies against some mundane-looking background for their #keepingitreal posts. Or, whatever it was that was their latest spin on things.

But this wasn't the wild. This was MerciX, a reliable, once-staid fashion label that had been around for ages, but had only lately managed to turn itself around, thanks to the extravagant influencer getaways it had started hosting in the past two years, all in exotic locations all over Asia. Iconic was now the word that was often used to describe their glam fests, held five or six times a year. Think cave parties in Indonesia, yacht soirees in Malaysia, forest tripping in Borneo—with free clothes, shoes, makeup, jewelry, gadgets, and even more trips, as long as they keep their end of the deal. That is, to upload and post using the hashtag #MercixSummer. Sandy needn't even have briefed me; one click was all it took for me to know everything about MerciX and their experiential influencer parties.

Everyone, it seemed, was making content.

On a whim, I myself raised my phone, trying to find the best angle for the scene, and snapped a wide-angle photo of the pool. Everything just seemed more manageable from a distance, I thought, as I quickly sent the photo to Nhi, who would be glad to know that despite the flights, I still had the energy to shoot and send photos.

My sudden movements had not gone unnoticed. 'Hey, it's that girl who found Davit!'

'Arya Alvarez?' A girl with blond tips and pink glitter eyeshadow had somehow sidled up to me, bending down until her cheek was on mine. Before I knew what was happening, she was putting her arms on my shoulders and raising the other for a perfectly-angled selfie.

'Say Daveeeet!' she cried, and I felt her pull the sides of her mouth back for a wide, ecstatic smile. I took a breath, mustered a smile of my own, and didn't say anything.

'Thank you, babe,' she breathed. Before I knew it, she had dropped her arms and was typing something on her phone. 'Oh, I need to fix this with a few adjustments,' she was murmuring, to no one in particular.

And then there were more people starting to crowd around me, raising their own phones, getting ready for selfies. I caught bits and pieces of what they were saying, as they tilted their heads towards mine and raised their phones for a quick snap.

'Honey, over here.' The words sounded as if uttered through bared teeth, lips that were already positioned into a bright, breezy smile. I turned to see another well-coiffed woman, brandishing a phone encased in a big, furry phone holder. 'You look familiar. A selfie, ya?'

Click, and it was done. Just like the rest, the woman had turned her back, head already bent over her phone screen.

'You were in *Do Officiel*,' I heard another say, from behind me. 'Cool.' An arm materialized on my right, holding a phone, camera set in selfie mode, of course. I saw my image on the little screen, startled at the lost expression on my face. A head appeared on my shoulder; it was that of a young guy not more than twenty. The selfie was over in a split second.

'The Davit thing,' someone was saying now. 'I shared that post, and it got, like, a thousand likes in just the first hour!'

It was another guy, who'd bent his tall body down to pose cheek-to-cheek with me.

'You're that influencer, right? What's your IG handle again?' A girl with gleaming bronzed skin and heavy winged liner on her eyes asked, not unkindly. 'Arya, is it?'

'Yes,' I said. 'I mean, no.' I wanted to laugh, but I couldn't. 'I mean, I'm Arya and no, I'm not an influencer . . .' I looked at her helplessly.

'Jesus, you're that Arya? The one who saw the missing artist? You're famous!'

I wanted to tell her that he wasn't missing, that she'd gotten it wrong, that Davit had voluntarily retreated from the public eye.

But before I could extricate myself and say anything more, there was a shout. There was a furor over by the bar, then a mad dash of people towards one of the villas at the far end.

For a moment, I felt confused, as phone-toting men and women hurried over to the same villa. Had someone been hurt?

And then the gorgeous people around me started talking.

'That's it. It's time.'

'I can't wait to see the clothes!'

'My favourite part! Are you ready?'

'Ditch your photographer. Move!'

'Arya!' Sandy reappeared from one of the cabanas. 'Let's go! It's time for the Gifting Suite!'

* * *

'Please.' Sandy, bright-eyed and alert, nodded and gestured for me to step inside, through the wide double doors of this particular villa. It had taken less than two minutes to reach it, and I noticed that this one was bigger and taller than the others. Sandy was holding my elbow again, saying hello to the rest of the guests.

People, mostly those I've seen earlier creating content by the poolside and still in their glam beachwear, were making their way inside. I smiled and followed Sandy as she turned and walked further inside, through the small foyer with the rest of the guests.

'The Gifting Suite is such a highlight,' Sandy was saying now. 'It's not just MerciX products, you know. We want variety for our influencers. We've partnered with non-competing brands. We're open to that.' She picked up a colourful pair of speakers along the way. 'You'll be surprised how many brands would pay a price tag that's in the four-digits—just for the opportunity to present and gift their products—for free, take note—to influencers attending this event.'

'It's just fabulous, isn't it?' A girl in a strapless maillot and a floppy hat was saying, as they rounded the corner.

'Why, yes,' I said. The air was charged with a mix of anticipation, celebration, and a certain giddiness. It was as if we were all on our way to watch a very entertaining, star-studded awards night where we already knew that our favourite actors, the ones we'd always rooted for, would win.

It was nothing like that, though. The scene that greeted me as we stepped off the foyer wasn't entertaining, or even star-studded.

It was bedlam.

The villa as a luxe, five-star tropical oasis of rest and relaxation slash Instagram background—was unrecognizable. Racks packed tightly with clothes were positioned two-by-two against every blank wall. Small tables, tall baskets, and open boxes overflowing with MerciX products—from headphones and mousepads to stuffed toys, pillows, and furry slippers— were on every available corner. Long metal tables, obviously brought in for the event because it looked incongruous to the rest of the room's furniture, most of which were made of wood or something natural—were placed in the living and dining area, as well as the terrace, which was easily accessed through glass sliding doors.

Influencers, the very same ones I've just seen sashaying like seasoned runway models down by the pool, or posing gracefully like celebrities by the palm trees or in front of one of MerciX's chic IG backdrops—were frantically grabbing clothes from the racks, tearing them off the hangers as if they were about to be pulled out of the room any time soon. Women in chic tropical garb, dressed impeccably for content and today's photo shoots, were rummaging through baskets and containers, occasionally holding up an item then dropping them on the shopping bags that MerciX had stacked on the tables. Three women and a guy in a floral shirt and trunks were plucking makeup from an elaborate rack that was a signature MerciX feature at the beauty counters.

'Does this make my eyes pop?' One of the women, her body poured in a soft-looking halter dress, thrust her face towards the others, turning her head slightly.

'Ugh, no,' the guy replied. He paused, looking intently at the cases of eyeshadows and foundation compacts. 'Get another one.' He reached out to the shelf, then swatted the girl's arm. 'Yikes, not that.'

'This?' I watched as the other girl, talking to no one in particular, held up a gold-encased lipstick and swipe it back and forth her lips. Then her phone was out and she took a selfie.

Someone skipped past me, three or four belts wrapped snugly around her tiny, tiny waist. She was holding up her phone. 'See here, I've chosen the best accessories to go with your MerciX outfits . . .' She trained the camera briefly on her torso, shrieking loudly—perhaps for added emphasis. 'They are all gorgeous, aren't they? I'm going crazy trying to choose. Remember, once you have your choice, tag me and use the hashtag Fashion by MerciX!'

And another, this one holding up a bunch of bright silk scarves in one hand and gripping a mini-tripod with a small camera and a furry mike on the other: 'Remember, guys. There's a fabulous MerciX giveaway for three viewers at the end of this video, so watch until the end!'

It looked more like a closing out sale than a luxe, five-star event. I stood in the middle of the room, unsure of what to do. What I knew was, whatever this is, I didn't want a part of it.

'Sandy,' I turned to where I knew she was standing behind me. 'I need to go.'

'Go?' Her eyes widened. 'Arya dear, we're just getting started! Welcome to the Gifting Suite!'

'Thanks,' I said, just as another woman brushed past me, loaded with several stiff shopping bags splashed with the MerciX logo. I felt a thin, sharp pain as the corners of the bags accidentally grazed my leg. 'It's all right,' I said, bending down and rubbing my calves. 'I—I need to work. I just remembered that I need to send an email.'

'Oh, Arya dear, please.' Sandy waved a dismissive arm. 'Stay. Try on something. Or better yet, bring something. These are all free.'

I nodded, not at all surprised. 'I know.' In fact, it just hit me that Angelique van Leuven had been telling me something about this while we were in Georgia. Another brand where she had to make an appearance and perform because she was the guest of honour.

'Please, get a dress—or ten! For yourself, dear. Do a reel. Do a giveaway. Do a 'Live'! You owe it to your followers!' Sandy got out her phone and started scrolling. 'Look at you. Almost half a million followers on IG! Please, don't forget to use the hashtags.'

I smiled weakly, also not surprised to hear that my follower count had grown again. I had muted my DMs, but I knew that there were still messages waiting for me.

A couple of women were counting their bags. 'I have twelve,' one declared.

'Oh, so it's okay if I get one more,' said the other. 'Or two!' She gave out a giddy laugh.

I needed to get out of there.

Chapter 25

El Nido, Philippines, 5.27 p.m. The resort was eerily quiet when I finally managed to slip out of the Gifting Suite, not long after I told Sandy that I needed to work. I walked quickly back to the pool area, breathing a long sigh of relief. It felt good to see the sky. It felt good to be alone. And these days, I felt I needed to be alone more than ever. Despite my line of work, I never did well in groups.

I thought of a dream I'd had, even when I was still back here. A tea shop with a garden, just like the ones I've seen in Vietnam and Japan. This lush, tropical island could certainly be an inspiration.

I paused for a moment to see the fabulously-decorated swimming pools, the well-appointed deck area. Now that it was almost empty, I could clearly see the different surfboard installations that MerciX had made: pink, red and white surfboards standing vertical and arranged like a wall, adorned with silk flowers on top and a white, cutout sign that said 'MerciX' in thick white letters. A true Instagram backdrop. Beyond that, I could see a pink lifeguard tower facing the shore.

The events that morning had happened so fast. I realized that I didn't have time to process that I was actually in the Philippines. That I was here, I was in my home country. Palawan was still part of home, even if it was an island some two thousand kilometres from Manila.

I realized that haven't gone home in more than two years. Two years and eight months, to be exact. I haven't gone back to the Philippines since I started working in Singapore.

I had a sudden craving for a mug of warm tea. I realized that I had missed my morning cup of green tea because of the rush of the early flight.

I was about to head back into the lobby and just go to my room when the faint sound of waves crashing against a rock made me look far beyond the pool, catching sight of the beach. I sucked in my breath, salty air filling the top of my lungs; I realized that I had missed the beaches in the Philippines.

I turned and made my way towards the shore. I knew I should have changed into my swimsuit, but there might be no time next time and there certainly was time *right now*. Without meaning to, I remembered Oliver's advice about grabbing what time you could, to do the things you want. Don't wait for that big chunk, Oliver used to say. Grab what little time you have—you'll see that it expands, that it wasn't as limited as you thought it was.

Frankly, I was worried that I'd be swept away with the influencers crowd again and not have the chance to fully enjoy the nature that was so lush and available on this island.

The beach wasn't that big. On one side of the island stood a massive limestone wall, part of an almost vertical mountain. On the other side, a row of sea cottages made of painted wood and cement, the roofs cleverly constructed out of curved bamboo. I took in the sight of the water, calm in most parts and a very soothing blue-green.

I took off my sandals and waded in, lifting my dress and holding up the hem to my waist so that my thighs were bare. The freebie pouch that held my phone was slung snugly across my torso. The water felt delightfully cool, the sand nubby and ticklish under the soles of my feet. I curled my toes and I felt a sudden shift in the air, a new kind of quiet as I moved forward towards the horizon and away from the beach. For a moment, I suddenly wished that I was on this island on my own, that I wasn't at some influencer gig and that I didn't have to make an appearance at the party that was happening tonight.

But this was work. My company and my bosses at Isle Z have done so much good for me. It was time that I did something back.

I thought of Jake. And then I thought: it was time I did something for myself, too. And how I wanted so much to make more sense of myself.

'Hey! Yoohoo!'

I jumped, jolted out of my thoughts. I turned back to see who was yelling. There was a man standing on one of the big, craggy limestone rocks at the side of the shore, broad-shouldered in a navy-blue sports shirt and striped shorts, the sun somehow glinting from the top of his head, which had light brown hair. He was waving widely at me. I waved back.

'Hey!' He made a motion with his hands. 'Come back!'

I frowned. Why did he want me to come back? I looked down at where I was standing, my bare feet so clear in the water that I had to squint to see just how high the water level was compared to my legs. It was low tide, so it only came below my knees. I took another step forward.

I heard a splash behind me and I turned again, startled. The guy had descended from the rock and was now splashing his way towards me.

I watched him walk, awkwardly, his feet hitting the water and I froze for a second, suddenly aware of how deserted the beach was at this time. It was just the two of us right now, and I didn't know who this man was. What was his deal? And then I thought, *I need security.* Or at least, just someone else.

I craned my neck for any guests who've decided to sunbathe, or happened to be roaming around. Or, for security guards monitoring the beach or the perimeter of the resort, though as far as I know, this resort was exclusive, known to be safe. For a split-second, I actually regretted breaking away from the crowd.

Another splash. I looked back again and frowned, not sure where exactly I could go. The man was getting closer.

'What is it?' I called out, hoping that would buy time or better yet—stop him in his tracks.

Perhaps he didn't hear me or had already given up trying to communicate, because he was still moving forward. I took a step backward. The hem of my dress had fallen into the water but I didn't care.

'Hey!' I called out again.

This time, he heard me. He started waving his arms again and started saying something. This time, I could finally make out the words: 'Be careful!'

'Oh!' I felt my jaw drop, and my eyebrows raise. Be careful? Who would someone wade all the way out here just to say that?

This man, apparently. 'Sorry if I scared you,' he panted, when he finally stopped just a few metres away from me.

'You didn't—' I began, instinctively taking another step back. But the change in direction caused the water to feel alien and heavy against my calves, that I started to wobble.

'Don't move any further!' The man raised an arm and pointed at me.

Too late. And besides, he was too far to catch me. Because I had completely lost my balance.

The next thing I knew, salty sea water was slapping against both sides of my face as I went under—with a heavy splash—for a second. Or two. I shut my eyes a moment too late, and felt myself flailing about in the knee-deep water, before managing to surface again.

Someone was pulling me up. 'I'm okay, I'm okay,' I sputtered, even as I felt solid arms haul me out and force me into a standing position. The water stung my eyes and I clutched at whatever—a shoulder, a tightly-muscled arm—with one hand. The other was trying to rub the salty water out of my eyes.

It was only then that I realized that he was saying something. 'Are you all right? Are you hurt? Are you sure you're not hurt anywhere?'

I shook my head, then gingerly opened one eye. I removed the hand that was on his shoulder, took a step back.

'Hey, hey! Don't move. You might fall again—'

I felt a surge of anger. Water was still trickling down my nose, and my dress was soaked, it sagged sticky and heavy on my body. I was wet from head to toe. And, my bag! I groped for the pouch resting heavily on my hip. Thank goodness it was still attached to my body. Got out my phone—oh, the relief that it was encased in this clever, magical plastic protection! It was lit and working, and most importantly, it was still dry.

Everything else, however, was wet. 'Look at this,' I snapped, brushing dripping hair out of my face and opening my eyes wide even as I felt a big fat bead of water land on my eyelid. 'If you hadn't gone here, this wouldn't have happened. I'm completely wet!'

'I'm sorry.' He looked around the shallow water that was surrounding us, as if searching for something.

'What is it?' I didn't bother hiding the annoyance I was still feeling. 'I didn't lose any things.'

'I wanted to warn you about sea urchins.' He ran his hand through his hair, the dark brown strands turning wet. He glanced about again. 'You haven't stepped into anything sharp and painful, have you?'

'No.' I shook my head, eyeing him suspiciously. 'Why?' I looked at my feet, which appeared intact and pain-free, bluish and wavy under water, and planted safe and solid on the sand. Sea urchins? The water was as clear as it was earlier, the sandy bottom free from seaweed and other debris. A school of tiny grey fish darted around, as if playing hide and seek. It was the cleanest water and the finest sand I've seen in years.

He pursed his lips. 'It's urchin season,' he said. 'Didn't they tell you?'

'You're not the lifeguard,' I said. 'Or from here, are you?'

'No, no.' His face took on a sheepish look, and he glanced back at the beach behind him. 'I was afraid you would step into one. That's all. Believe me, it's not fun.'

I looked down at the water as far as I could. There was no sign of any sea urchins, which I know looked like black, fuzzy, and spiny little nests on the sand. I shuddered at the thought of getting its crumbly spines under my skin.

'I was here all morning. And there was someone who stepped on a sea urchin. You wouldn't want that,' he said. 'Someone had to pee on her foot. They say it's what dissolves their spines that get under one's skin, I don't know.'

I stared at him for a moment, then looked out towards the shore. I took a step forward. 'I need to go back.'

'Here.' The guy extended a hand. 'Please, let me help you.'

'I'm fine,' I said. I gave him a tired smile. 'Maybe just let me know if there's an urchin ahead.'

He moved towards the shore as well. 'There are also baby sharks.'

'Oh, those I know,' I said. 'I've been to Club Isabelle and Dos Palmas, and a couple of other resorts in Palawan even when I was still working in Manila.' Still, I shuddered at the memory of seeing a baby shark, which was beautiful and felt deadly, as small as a loaf of bread.

'They really should have placed a sign or something,' the guy was saying now.

'Or made an announcement,' I said. The water was now down to my calves. We were almost there.

'I'll tell them later.'

We reached the shore, and I glanced at him as I shook water from the hems of my dress. It was warm and humid, but I still wanted tea. 'Yeah,' I said. 'Do that.'

'I'm Conrad.' He fumbled in his pockets and produced a pink ID with a lanyard, the same one I've seen on some of the influencers in the Gifting Suite. 'Here.' He thrust it towards me. 'Conrad Renborg.' I couldn't read the rest of the words below.

'Arya Alvarez.' I didn't say anything more. I glanced in the direction of the villas.

'I know,' he said. 'Of course, I didn't when I was being weird and calling to you out there.' His tone grew quiet. 'I recognize you now. But let's not talk about that, right?'

I nodded. 'Right.' I wanted so much to take a shower, change into dry clothes. Have my mug—or better yet, a huge pot—of tea. I remembered that I'd brought a tiny canister of genmaicha matcha, and my old travelling tea set—a handy one I got from Japan which had a strainer and a cup into one.

I felt the wet pouch bag vibrate against my hip. I fished out my well-protected phone and saw something that made me stop. No name, just a number flashing insistently on the bright screen of my phone. I've long deleted this number from my contacts, but oh, how I still knew it by heart.

Be normal, Arya, I told myself, as the phone continued its silent ringing. Why can't you be normal and answer it—or drop the call? It was better than doing nothing.

Truth was, I didn't have the heart—or come to think of it, the courage—to press 'decline'. Truth was, I was actually most likely to answer the call—and that very thought terrified me. Because what was Jake doing, calling me?

I cupped my shaking fingers around the phone and laid it facedown against my thigh, hoping that the softness of my flesh would cushion the vibrations. *Don't let one call undo everything,* I told myself. *You had worked so hard.*

Had I, really? With all that's been happening to me lately, I wasn't so sure of anything any more.

'Conrad,' I said, hoping my voice didn't betray the mix of fear, distress, and agitation I was feeling. 'I really need a hot drink. Would you like to have tea with me?'

'A tea?' Conrad blinked. 'Sure.' After a beat, he said. 'You mean tea at the café, right?'

We were near my villa. There was a separate deck made of more bamboo and wood, fashioned so it had sunken seats and an empty centre made of stone meant for bonfires. It faced the beach, of course, and was shaded by the wide, paddle-shaped leaves of *talisay* trees on both sides.

'No. I mean, tea right here.' I gestured towards the deck. 'I brought some special ones. Unless you're a pure coffee person and averse to this kind of thing . . .'

'I'll have a tea with you.' He grinned. 'Awesome.' He moved towards the deck in one swift motion. 'I'll wait for you here.'

I burst through my villa and saw that my luggage was indeed there. I closed the wooden doors behind me and quickly removed my wet clothes. The bathroom, with its long white, gold, and black marble sink, vintage-style mirrors, and glass-enclosed shower—looked glorious. What have I done? I thought as I grabbed a thick towel. My phone was silent once more, all the mute functions of my apps working to shield me from the relentless notifications I was still receiving.

And here I was, having a complete stranger over to drink tea with me, at my villa. At least it wasn't alcohol. But it was someone I barely knew. Was it really to avoid Jake, or was it actual loneliness that I was beginning to feel?

It wasn't the first time I've invited someone to share tea with me. I was an introvert, but working in the travel industry had allowed to be more forward, to not be shy when I needed it. I told myself I just felt guilty for being rude to him, when he actually had good intentions. I told myself that he felt like an interesting person, that I actually felt safe when he told me he was just looking out for me.

* * *

I found Conrad still there, bent over a sketchpad on his lap, a small flattish tin containing watercolour squares beside him. Somehow, he'd produced a small bottle of mineral water which he was using to dip his brush in. On the minuscule wooden table in front of him was his phone, clipped snugly on a thick, but folded mini-tripod. The red record button was on.

'Oops,' I said, almost bumping into the backrests of the seats as I tried to avoid being caught onscreen.

'Oh don't worry about that,' he said. 'I just film myself at random times of the day, doing random activities. Any content can be useful content.' He scooched over a little so there was more space for me to sit beside him. 'Please, come.'

I set down the tray I found in the room, with hot water, the strainer, and tea, placing it between us. He smelled of sea salt and sweat. 'What do you know,' I said, catching sight of the dark brown image on his sketchpad. 'You're drawing a sea urchin, of all things.'

He looked up, smiled sheepishly. 'The whole reason I witnessed the drama that happened at the beach this morning.' He chuckled. 'I mean, her boyfriend had to pee on her leg. Supposed to dissolve the spines.'

'I can believe that,' I said. 'Even though it's so . . . oh well, you have to do what you have to do.'

'First thing to do is to not step on one.'

At this, I laughed. A hearty, belly laugh that I haven't had in the weeks that followed Davit's viral video.

'So you're an artist—

'A travel vlogger. My channel is called Counting Countries.'

I turned sheepish. Sorry, I don't even watch a lot of YouTube.' I took out my phone. 'I can check—'

'It's fine,' he said, quickly. 'I've already discovered that the signal in the villas is close to nada. Better at the lobby and the pool area.'

There were almost zero bars on my phone, and the page wasn't even loading. I didn't forget my tea, but I've forgotten the pocket Wi-Fi I've always carried with me on trips.

'Why aren't you at the Gifting Suite?'

'That hot mess? No thanks! I'm here for El Nido. I'm based in Stockholm, where it can get very dark, believe me.'

'Definitely not a life guard, right?'

'I like drawing living things.'

'Living things?

He shrugged. 'Plants, little creatures. Sea urchins. He opened his sketchbook, which looked like my own journal.'

'Don't you get tired?' I asked. 'Your life is one whole long content. Or whatever it is you call it.'

'Not at all.'

I wished I had his energy. I glanced at the phone that was still on, recording us. 'When do you plan to turn this off?'

'Oh, that?' He grinned. 'Never.'

Chapter 26

Manila, Philippines, 6.20 p.m. The din of the crowd was deafening. Or maybe it wasn't. Maybe it just felt as if a mob, the thirty-five million fans and viewers of the reality show *Fashion Fever*, was about to descend on me—because I was frozen right there in the middle of the stage, clad in tight, strange clothing which left my leg naked and exposed, dangerously, from the side of the crotch down. That I had to look decent had become the least of my concerns.

'Ar-ya! Ar-ya!'

The studio lights were hot on my face, still tender from a sunburn I only discovered that morning, when I flew from El Nido to Manila and was immediately whisked off into the buzzing, highly-charged studios of *Fashion Fever* tucked somewhere in the confounding sprawls of Novaliches. Upon arrival at the studio, the other contestants and I had to be ushered, frantically, through a side door; the lines of people wanting to watch *Fashion Fever* live that day had grown long, winding, and dense outside the main entrance.

A reality show had been one of the things I had agreed to do, in the light of things that have happened. And as with the Merci X Glam Getaway Influencer Party, I've decided to say yes to being in *Fashion Fever* to represent Isle Z—to promote our brand, drive our boutique agency's name recall, and extend our reach.

The reality was, I wish it were as simple as that.

It had only been a week since my Davit Nadibaidze post had gone viral. And there was no question that ending up a contestant in this wildly popular reality show had been a result of that, as with getting invited to the mother of all influencer parties, the MerciX Glam Getaway in El Nido. I've attempted to extricate myself from this situation that I'd unwittingly brought on to my life by agreeing to an appearance at *Morning Feast* on TV a few days ago; that my Davit post is still alive and beating on the internet—with thousands of shares and various versions online, only meant that it had been a complete fail.

It had been about Davit Nadibaidze, at first—until it sort of wasn't. Somehow it had also become about Arya Alvarez, and the version of me they thought they knew, the version of me that people, online and perhaps in real life, want to believe in.

The internet knew me and my name, and also, they didn't. It had snowballed into something neither I nor the online community didn't—or couldn't, *not just yet*—understand. Among many other things, I had been labelled everything from being cool to cancellable, artistic to basic, adorable to hateable, good to bad, assigning me personas I've never been in my life: a messenger, an influencer, a social climber, a slut, a wannabe, an artist, a non-artist. And as long as there was the internet and its platforms on social media, as long as there were people with a keyboard and a screen and Wi-Fi, people who could type, speak, and create behind anonymous accounts and fake handles—this list, as was information on the internet, could go on endlessly.

In the week since my Davit Nadibaidze post became viral, everything about me—my physical appearance, my job, the people I worked with, the little ways and habits that could be gleaned from my social media accounts—had in some way, been viciously dismantled, taken apart, dissected, labelled, re-packaged and shared, as if I was something else and not a person. The internet had done something, and they've turned me into something else—what, I didn't know exactly. What I knew was that it didn't make me feel human.

I was going through the motions. I wanted to get back to my job at Isle Z. When this thing blew up, I had been going through something, and I needed to retrace my steps and get back on track. For myself.

I wanted to go back to myself, and go back to being me.

'Arya Alvarez! Get back out there! *Moooove!*'

From the side of the stage, Mr Production Assistant was screaming, doing frenzied jumping jacks with his arms high up and gesturing at me, his version of panic. Or murderous anger.

'*Ar-ya! Ar-ya!*'

The chant was getting louder again. And this time, it felt and sounded real.

'You're going to ruin the show!' Mr Production Assistant was yelling. *'You! Arya! Ruin! Showwww!'*

They were calling my name. They were calling me, but my name sounded alien. Of course it did.

This wasn't me at all.

I walked off the stage.

'Hey, hey! *Wait!*'

Another production assistant was calling out to me as I calmly made my way from the centre of the stage, slipping silently back into the sidelines. The opposite side—and most definitely away from where the first PA was stationed. Mr Production Assistant who, I knew, had been seething all this time and appeared ready to pounce on me for not following his meticulously-planned blocking, the instructions that had been crucial in the staging of this show.

My mike and sound cables were off from my body in less than a minute. I placed them on a vacant stool beside me.

'You, hey—*miss!*' The second PA was still calling out, stumbling over a styrofoam prop as she hurried towards me.

'Arya Alvarez, where are you going?'

I'm going back, I murmured, to no one in particular.

I didn't think anyone heard me.

Because the din was now louder than ever, a giddy, resounding cheer rising up from the audience out front and from somewhere in the cleverly hidden speakers of the *Fashion Fever* studio.

The PA stopped in her tracks, and peered out on to the stage. I stopped, too, and followed her gaze.

Strutting towards centre stage was another contestant, Alessandra Sotto, in an even more outrageous get-up—a nude body-hugging gown that had a strange, unwieldy padded tail and wide holes on the butt and hips. Vaguely, I recall Alessandra being introduced as a yoga instructor to the stars, and we all watched as she marched to the front, hiking up the offending tail, and wiggling different parts of her body until the holes seemed to be just in the right places. And then she did a split, just because she can.

The crowd went wild.

'Go Alessandra! You can do it! Go *Fashion Feverrrrrr!*' An extra loud cheer floated above the noise.

It was Mr Production Assistant. Screaming at the top of his lungs, as usual. We were on opposite ends of the stage, on the sidelines hidden from the audience. From my spot, I saw his head shift, and my stomach seized as we locked eyes—just for a split second. And then, as if I was a ghost he didn't even see, his gaze was back on the stage, and he was smiling, clapping, nodding his head.

Another contestant—the extremely flexible and apparently very entertaining Alessandra Sotto—was being fed to *Fashion Fever's* hungry audience, and Mr Production Assistant, thankfully, had finally given up on me.

Chapter 27

Santorini, Greece, 8.01 a.m. 'This is *real* travel,' someone was saying in a high-pitched, syrupy voice. 'So, we have a strict no-drama policy.'

Did I hear that right? A no-drama policy?

'It's a little too late for that,' I heard someone whisper as I carefully took my place on one of the blue and white giant cushions carefully arranged on a woven mat on the floor. It was positioned at the very centre of this well-curated rooftop café, where a group of eight girls were gathered, looking up and listening rapt to the woman speaking in front. The day was still early, the sun casting soft morning light on white-washed walls and the rooftop's light blue shutters. Not far in the distance, vibrant blue domes featured prominently in the view, towering over a myriad of flat white roofs that belonged mostly to hotels and inns and Airbnbs built on the side of the mountain. Beyond that, the Ionian Sea was like a wide, flat sheet of cool blue.

We were in Santorini, Greece, a destination so iconic and popular it was almost becoming a cliché, like Venice.

It was also still gorgeous and picturesque and dreamlike—
how could they have built all those cave houses so high up
on the side of the mountain and how could a sunset be that
sublime? It cast its melon and orange light on everything
on the island, making it always a favourite choice among
my clients despite the crowds, the tourists, the cruise day
trippers. Still a priority, despite the other Greek islands like
Naxos, Paros, Antiparos and even Symi, that I've always
recommended and believed were as unique and surreal as
Santorini. No, they want the whitewashed houses, the infinity
pools that look out to the caldera, the red and black beaches,
the whole Greek sun and sea philosophy.

The sight of the water reminded me of El Nido, which
had islands that couldn't be more different from this one.
It had been a few days since MerciX's Glam Getaway
Influencer Party and the *Fashion Fever* reality game show,
something I didn't know if I could go through again.

But because I was working for Isle Z, here I was. I had
flown in from Singapore, then Athens, then another smaller
plane to Santorini's main town Fira. An hour's bus ride took
me to Santorini's most picturesque village, Oia, where we were
now. This was where I had met, in trickles, the eight women
who had signed up for this trip. And Jia Yin Wurtzbach, who
had organized this five-day jaunt to Greece.

* * *

I couldn't tell who had made that comment but maybe it
didn't even matter, because everyone was nodding towards
the front, most with excited smiles on their faces. More than
half of the women appeared fidgety, looking around with

eager anticipation, and a couple were furiously taking photos of the speaker.

It was only eight-thirty in the morning and yet these ladies looked as if they'd opened the salons on the island and had their hair and makeup done. The dresses were something else, too—long flowy gowns in bright solid colours, or flouncy short dresses in sassy prints that seemed made for their tiny waists and narrow shoulders. They all looked like they were off to a party at 8.30 a.m.

There was no party, though. Well, not yet. We were at a briefing, led by Jia Yin Wurtzbach herself. She was clad in one of her signature goddess-like dresses in blush-pink and an asymmetrical cut, one shiny shoulder exposed and lined with gold stick-on tattoos.

Jia Yin Wurtzbach was a fashion and travel influencer whose Instagram feed—teeming with unreal photos of her perched on a cliff overlooking the Nordic fjords or twirling in front of a castle in the Loire Valley or bounding between the Pyramids in Giza all the while poured in long, flowing, flamboyant gowns she made herself—resonated with close to a million followers. It was she who had organized this trip, not Isle Z. The eight women we were travelling with her were her followers at @jiajiaworld on Instagram, each of whom had forked over $3,500, excluding airfare and transfers, to travel with her. The goal? Well, I wasn't really sure—more focused fangirling, perhaps? That and at the same time, doing exactly what your favourite influencer does on her glamorous trips: taking sunset cruises, sampling local wine, tasting the best cuisine, hitting the sights, gazing at views—all heavily documented of course, with photos, videos, clips, and reels.

I was sent here to represent Isle Z, precisely to explore this concept and find out more. All expenses were shouldered by my company, because this was supposed to bring in more business. I was still trying to recover from the MerciX party in El Nido, but I was thankful to be doing something that was more in my line of work.

The rooftop in Oia where we were at the moment, was Instagram heaven as it is—bright fuchsia bougainvillea cascading thickly from almost all corners of the low-walled terrace, nubby earth-coloured rugs and muted throw pillows placed strategically, seating and small tables facing the most amazing views of the blue domes and the caldera.

So it was strange to be talking about drama. But then this whole trip was still a little strange, even to me.

'There's no tour like this one, so you guys are all so incredibly lucky.' Jia Yin was still speaking, her voice turning purposeful. She was a svelte dark-haired woman, with blond highlights that glinted in the morning sun. When she turned, I saw her eyes widen.

'Ladies!' She called out, eyes still on me. 'We are even luckier because we have here someone who's very important, very relevant, and who has recently just gotten in touch with a famous, well-loved celebrity, the artist Davit Nadibaidze!'

As if on cue, several of the guests turned their heads and clapped half-heartedly. A couple of them gave me a little wave.

'Let's welcome Arya Alvarez,' Jia Yin trilled. 'Another influencer with such a cool job!'

'A travel manager,' I called out, trying not to look sheepish. 'I'm not really an influencer.'

'Of course you are!' Jia Yin's voice was loud and forceful. 'See, everyone here knows you!'

'Isn't this great?' One woman turned to me, eyes almost teary-eyed. 'It's thrilling to be with JY, just to be in her presence!'

'I feel like I'm living my own travel Pinterest board!'

I nodded, took a deep breath, and kept smiling. I was here for work, I kept telling myself. So just work, Arya.

* * *

The funny thing was, before the Davit Nadibaidze things got out of hand, Jia Yin Wurtzbach wouldn't have given me the time of the day.

Travelling with an influencer was now a thing, Jia Yin had told us a few weeks back, when she requested a meeting with Isle Z, to explore a collaboration. 'Think of it as travelling with your idol who happens to be a celebrity.'

Those were Jia Yin's own words when Oliver and I met with her at Isle Z a few weeks ago before all this Davit Nadibaidze business blew up. Never one to be modest, Jia Yin proceeded to tell us that influencers have truly become professional travellers: 'We know all the best spots, we know the most interesting activities, and we know how to keep safe. On top of that and the most important thing is—we know how to have fun.'

Oliver and Desmond, on the lookout for travel's next best thing, and perhaps aiming to finally win that Luxe Boutique Travel Award, had been open to the idea. In fact, they had welcomed the concept.

She had been talking with travel boards, Jia Yin said. 'Don't tell them, but their programmes? I just found them all too basic.' She had heard about Isle Z, of course. 'I had this idea. What if my followers had the chance to meet and go on adventures with their favourite influencer, learn not just travel tips from them, but also posing and photography tips? What if they had a chance to recreate the amazing photos they see on my feed?'

'I'm guessing that's the way they can really live the experience they see in your photos and videos,' Oliver said. I knew that he knew what the real score was, but it was good for Isle Z, and so he was warming to the idea.

'To be honest, I've been deluged with DMs,' Jia Yin went on. 'I keep getting all these questions, I keep getting asked by my followers if they can come travelling with me.'

I admit, I had my doubts at first. 'But Jia Yin,' I said. 'You've always promoted the travelling solo concept.'

'Oh, you know.' Jia Yin sounded offhand and breezy, waving an arm dismissively. 'We can all travel solo together!' She turned to Oliver. 'Oliver dear, it would be nice to talk about this over dinner at that *izakaya* that just opened at Keong Saik Road.'

Oliver smiled tightly. 'Well, we're here now. You can lay your plans with us, and we will try to find a way to work together.' He took a small, almost imperceptible breath, something I used to see whenever he was averse to something.

Jia Yin had actually looked disappointed. 'All right, Oliver. Next time.'

'We've seen your Instagram feed,' I prompted. 'Almost a million followers.'

'Yes, of course.' Jia Yin sighed. 'They say my feed is organically enchanting.' She said the last two words with a happy flourish.

'And travelling solo?'

'Well, since I was always travelling alone and on my own, I thought why not invite my followers to be with me?' There was an excited tremor in her voice. 'At first I wasn't into it, since the point of travelling by myself was to be, well, alone. But then I realized that we are all solo travellers, and if we can meet up and be solo together, it might be a lot of fun.'

'So yes, followers,' Jia Yin's eyes lit up. 'What do you think of followers travelling with me? I figured, there's a reason why they chose to follow me, right?'

'Well—'

'I mean, I realized that they follow me for a reason. They want to experience what I've experienced. And we can just do what I like to do. Isn't it an honour for them to be travelling with me?'

Oliver was scrolling through Jia Yin's feed. 'You always travel in these?' He held up his phone, a photo of Jia Yin at the edge of a ravine, a bright pink dress flying behind her, lifted up by an unseen breeze.

'Ah,' she smiled, looking a little smug. 'The gowns— they're my signature. They're feminine, they're fanciful but they're also adventurous. Don't you agree? And isn't that what this is all about?'

It was good business for Isle Z, once Jia Yin Wurtzback decides to book all her influencer-hosted travel with our boutique agency. Think of this as planting season, Desmond said. If we kept on, we would be fruitful in no time. If mega influencers start collaborating with Isle Z, who knows how far we could all go?

* * *

'It's only an eight to ten minute swim,' Jorge, the tour guide was saying. 'So take your photos—'

'Can they bring outfits? Another swimsuit, maybe?' Jia Yin piped up.

Jorge looked like he wanted to give her a withering stare, but chose a grimace instead. Jia Yin didn't seem to have noticed. 'Sorry no, madame, they can't. There are no changing rooms there.'

At this, a nervous chuckle rippled through the group. Our second day in Santorini, and we were on a Caldera Morning Cruise.

'Just take your photos, explore a little,' Jorge continued.

We were on a traditional-style boat, a swim and sunset cruise that Jia Yin had arranged. They had taken turns shooting photos at the bow of the boat, experimenting with posing in their dresses and swimsuits. The view from the sea, of Santorini's villages built on the side of the mountain, was spectacular.

I've been observing the whole day, and thankful that most of the women appeared loyal and smitten with Jia Yin. Everyone seemed content with the programme of activities, which was exactly what Jia Yin had predicted. This meant that she would likely be pushing through with the Isle Z collaboration, spelling business for us. Oliver and Desmond would be happy.

There was a grotto, Jorge was explaining, in the middle of a small island cove just a few hundred metres away and near where our boat was anchored. 'It is very nice. And it is a very easy swim,' he repeated. 'You won't have any problem going there and back.'

My phone rang in my bag, startling me. We weren't too far out, so there was signal out here, after all. And the boat had Wi-Fi—of course. How else would these influencers survive the day?

I plucked it from among the sunscreen and extra clothes. It was still in its nifty plastic cover, the one that was given to me at the influencer party in El Nido. I glanced at the screen. A WhatsApp call. Unknown number. I've never listed my personal phone number, but Isle Z's offices were online. I was still deluged with calls from strangers on my work phone.

I turned my attention again to the women preparing to jump out and swim. My phone rang again. When I saw the number, my insides grew cold.

As I said, I had deleted Jake's number from all my phones months ago. And yet here it was again, the number that, for years, I've known by heart. The number I've recited again and again when we booked hotels, when we signed up for things, when we filled out forms.

Slowly, even as the call didn't drop, and the phone kept vibrating, I placed it back in my bag. Then I removed my extra clothes, placed in on the seat beside me.

Around me, the women were waving giddy goodbyes to each other. Some were still taking videos, staging a graceful jump into the water. Jia Yin was nowhere to be found; perhaps she'd gone to the other side, where all the food and drinks were. Faintly, Jorge's words were echoing in my ears: just swim, see the grotto, then swim back to the boat. Easy.

There wasn't anything easy about this. I wasn't sure what I was thinking any more.

I jumped.

Chapter 28

Santorini, Greece, 8.55 a.m. The water was surprisingly warm and buoyed me up immediately after I hit the surface. The Aegean Sea was one of the saltiest in the world, and I was surprised at the lightness I felt as I swam forward towards the direction of the cove and away from our boat.

'Woo, go Arya!' I heard someone yell as I willed my arms and legs to do their thing, to push and tread water and bring me forward.

It was soothing, this movement of limbs. I surged forward, feeling empowered with every push. I didn't feel exactly healed, but it felt like moving towards something I wasn't sure was good or bad. Or maybe it was an escape— swimming away from something, as I have run away from what had happened in Manila almost three years ago.

I just wanted to get an image out of my mind. Because I could still picture it: Jake's number flashing on my phone. And then what I could picture was Jake, phone pressed to his ear, head tilted in that boyish way he had. Why was he calling?

Was it really him, calling me? But I knew it in my gut. Jake was back.

People were starting to leave the cove and swim back to their respective boats. I thought I could see our boat coming up as I swam in bold strokes towards it, giving it all my strength. I wanted to be back in time, too. I turned back and started treading.

Wait. Where was our boat?

I had been so lost in thought, I had swum in the wrong direction, towards the wrong vessel. I paused and tread water, trying to relax my arms. Trying to breathe, because my heart had beat faster in panic. My arms felt like lead. My arms crying out for rest. I didn't feel so light in the water any more. In fact, I felt as if I was about to sink any time. I didn't think I could do the few hundred metres towards the right boat.

There were people on this boat, of course. It was just a matter of catching their attention. And that was the problem, which felt monumental in this situation—treading water and lost among strange boats in Greece: no one was looking in my direction.

'Hey!' I called, hearing the stubborn reluctance in my voice. I needn't have worried about that though, because my words seemed to dissipate in the air. The water was starting to feel cool on my skin, but my legs felt like they were on fire. 'Hey there!'

I could see torsos, a bit of a head. And finally, there was someone.

'Hello!' I called again.

A guy in a hat, shirtless in white shorts. I saw him as he flashed me a grin. 'Hello, you! Do you need help in there?'

Despite the sun, the water, and the magnificent islands, I felt my face flush. I gave a vigorous nod, just to make sure he saw me. 'I can't do it!' I called out, my voice breaking.

'Hold on,' he said, looking behind him. 'Don't worry!' Then he jumped.

A splash and the guy was there swimming towards me, clutching an orange donut lifesaver in his hand.

'You all right?' His tone was light and casual, as if we had just met each other on the street, and not in the middle of the Aegean Sea. 'Here.' The orange donut was thrust briskly towards me, and I caught it, tightly.

'Yes,' I panted out. 'Thank you, thank you.' I had to stop to catch my breath. Holding that lifesaver felt like I had won the lottery; my arms and legs seemed to cry out with relief.

'You can do it?' The guy had moved away, giving space between us. 'You can swim back up? Our boat's just here.'

'Oh.' I looked up, my body bobbing up and down as I hung on to the lifesaver for dear life. 'I—I don't belong in this boat.'

He looked surprised for a moment. 'You don't? Ah, I thought you were one of my tour mates.'

'I think—' I craned my neck and squinted, trying to see if I can spot Jorge, or at least remember what our boat looked like. 'Ah, there! It's over there.' I pointed to a white and blue one around three hundred metres away, now convinced that I did see Jorge pacing up and down the boat's edge.

'Lovely,' the guy said. 'Let's go!'

He turned and started swimming, with me literally in tow in my orange lifesaver. I had a slight mishap, there was nothing to be ashamed about, but I was embarrassed all the same.

I knew I had the right boat when people started waving at me.

'You good?' That grin again.

I nodded. I wanted to ask his name, but I didn't. Too awkward. The boat was leaving anyway. And I was too embarrassed to say anything more.

* * *

I closed the door of my room behind me, making sure it was locked. The hotel I was booked in, called Athina Suites, didn't exactly have a view of the caldera and was located in one of the alleys of Oia. But I liked it. My travel mates, Jia Yin's followers, were all booked in different hotels in the same area, except for Jia Yin, who had booked herself in one of the cave hotels that Santorini was famous for.

The whole island had a pinkish glow, the cluster of Oia's mountainside white little houses dotted with twinkling yellow lights. I breathed in the warm air; it was still magical to be in the hilly streets of Santorini. Jia Yin had arranged an event for that night, at a local Greek restaurant called Naoussa. It was called 'JY's Santorini: A Degustation and Wine-Tasting' as listed in the itinerary that she had emailed us. It was possible that it may just turn out to be one long, drawn-out dinner.

Still, the women looked thrilled, because it was in one of the restaurants with a view. That night's co-host, whom Jia Yin had roped in for the dinner, was none other than Naoussa's owner, Milo.

'The ingredients you'll find in tonight's cuisine—in the dishes you're about to sample here in the restaurant—are all grown on the island's rich volcanic soil,' he said. He looked around the table, his dark features twitching into an eager smile. 'Do you feel it? The sea breezes, the Mediterranean sun—they all create sweet flavours that you can't find anywhere else.'

He continued: 'Presenting to you Naoussa's offerings, using Santorini's four important ingredients cultivated on the island: tomatoes, fava puree, white eggplant, and capers.'

Servers came from the direction of the kitchen bearing trays of stews, dips, salads, and bread, lots of bread. There were souvlakis, which looked like spicy sausages, and a dish called tomato keftedes, which looked like meatballs but were actually sweet tomatoes infused with herbs and butter.

'I still can't believe I'm here,' Simone, who was from Beijing, was saying as I joined the group already gathered around the table that was specially prepared for us.

'Oh, believe it!' Jia Yin was at the head of the table, looking tanned and smiling her red-lipped smile. 'Just don't forget to post and do your hashtags. Can you all still remember it?'

'#JYAwesomeAdventures!'

'That's right!'

I settled in my chair, soaking in the Greek songs playing from the speakers and the animated restaurant chatter, resisting the urge to take out my phone from my bag. Earlier, to take my mind off Jake's attempted call, I had typed up notes as part of my report for Isle Z, as well as suggestions that I wanted to discuss with Jia Yin on how to improve her next getaways.

My bag was resting on my lap, and as the cheerful servers poured me the first glass of white wine, I felt it vibrate. Gingerly, I took my phone out.

A message. Another DM on Instagram, on top of the many other DMs that had been there but I had not had time to read. Or had chosen not to read. And yet something told me to open it.

Hope you made it back safe to land, it read. It was from someone called @livingliam.

I was about to dismiss it as another one of those random messages that I've started getting ever since the Davit video, when something made me press on the handle, and it brought me to its Instagram feed.

It was that guy who helped me swim back to the boat. No, who *towed* me back to the right boat. My face burned as I remembered how helpless I felt.

His feed was filled with surreal images of cities around the world. I scrolled and saw photos of red-dyed incense sticks arranged in rows and clumps, looking like a field of flowers in Quang Phu Cau, Hanoi; a video of someone frolicking through the misty valleys in Lauterbrunnen, Switzerland; a sharp afternoon sun peeking roundly through a flame-coloured tree in Arashiyama Park in Kyoto, Japan; turquoise lagoons and colourful boats in Krabi, Thailand. The latest one was just four hours ago, a photo of Santorini's famous sunset, which meant that he was very active on social media.

He must have recognized me from all that coverage on the Davit video. It still felt disconcerting, to think this way. It still felt strange, and all wrong, to receive messages this way. It didn't seem right, still, to be actually recognized from something that had blown up online.

I steered myself back to the present. I should be grateful. To the 'saving' that had happened that morning, and to what was happening right now. It would have turned out more complicated, even dangerous, if not for this person and his good-natured willingness to bring me back to my boat.

I started typing out a reply, telling myself that I was doing so because I wanted to thank him. *Back safe in Oia. Thanks for being such a good sport. You saved my life.'*

And then there was another message, one that I told myself didn't matter but had wanted for so long. It wasn't through any app but through my mobile number. *'Kamusta?* I hope you are well.'

So it had been Jake who had called me earlier. It was no glitch, mistake, or any wrong number calling. I felt a surge of something—was it relief? Or was it vindication? I had hoped that by this time, it would be compassion, but I was tired, and I let my thoughts run wild. I had wanted this, really—for Jake to think of me again. For Jake to pursue me. I had thought that, if Jake didn't want me, then he must want something from me.

And then I felt angry. I had worked so hard on trying to move on. I had left Manila because of him. I had started a completely new life because I had wanted to leave the mess that I had created. The mess that Jake and I had been in. It hadn't been easy, but it had been effective and I had almost done it. I had almost forgotten him, I had almost gotten over him. I was well on my way to that.

And now, he was here again. I sagged against my chair. Who was I kidding? No, it wasn't anger that I felt. It was disappointment, and not even with Jake. This had been a concrete test and it felt as if I had failed—I was still affected. I was still curious. I still cared.

Chapter 29

Santorini, Greece, 10.19 p.m. The alleys of Oia were quiet, with the muffled sounds of partying conveniently in the distance. Soft yellow lights thoughtfully installed by residents lit the stone pathways and gave it a soft, romantic glow. I walked quickly past my hotel, Athina Suites, not even pausing for a moment. I was coming from the restaurant, where our group just had dinner, and bottle after bottle of the local white wine. The grapes, we were told, were all grown right here in Santorini.

I had originally planned to go to sleep early, as soon as the dinner was done. And yet right now, as I saw the sign at the entrance of Athina glowing with the same amber light, that thought had already been squashed as quickly as it came. I hadn't been anywhere else that night, but things had taken a different turn; I had received messages from Greece and I had received messages from Manila.

I darted through the path as fast as I could without tripping. I didn't want to be late. Or maybe, I had one too many glasses of wine? Jia Yin's fancily-named dinner and wine night had been, despite my doubts, a resounding success among our group. Jia Yin Wurtzbach, despite her flimsy philosophies, had something going on there.

He had told me to meet him at a bar near the bus station. It was one of the few that still remained open, he said. I didn't know if it had been the wine sampling, or the thought of wanting to forget Jake's messages, but I had said yes. I had said yes without hesitation.

'You came.' The guy from this morning, the one who had saved me from being left by my boat. He was wearing a loose white shirt, a crisp pair of olive-green shorts and Adidas sneakers. He looked more tanned than he was this morning, and his hair was combed back. 'It's you, finally.'

I glanced at the beer in front of him. 'It's me, Arya.'

'Arya, of course.' He extended his hand. 'I'm Liam.'

At this, we laughed. 'I'm sorry,' I said. 'I couldn't introduce myself to you properly this morning, when I thought I was drowning.'

His eyes, the colour of coffee, narrowed and crinkled up when he grinned. 'No, you weren't,' he said. 'You had it all under control. You were just tired. It happens.'

I smiled gratefully at him. It came easy—I must have downed at least four glasses of the Santorini wine at Jia Yin's dinner.

See Arya, said a little voice inside me. *You don't have to remain in that black spot in your heart.* You don't have to remain in that dark space. You can move on. Admit that you've spent more than two years unable to move on. You can still do it. It's time to honour your progress.

I should just go with the flow. I should just accept what was there. Enjoy the moment.

Enjoy this. Enjoy what was here.

'Arya, what would you like to drink?'

I gazed at the gorgeous man before me, wanting to succumb to my thoughts. Wanting the night to be normal, to be a romantic meeting where I didn't think of anyone else in my past.

My phone beeped in my hand, and I jumped. I didn't have to look at it to know that it was a Philippine number. I just *knew*. What time is it in Manila now?

Before I could think further, Liam had placed a light hand on my waist, the other handing me a glass of white wine.

I got the glass, took a small sip.

'Hey,' Liam began again. 'You were so cool, posting that video.'

The video again. I took a bigger sip this time, wanting to get rid of the anxiety I was starting to feel. 'Is that how you know me?' I asked. 'And you know Davit Nadibaidze, of course.'

'Well, not really. Everybody knows who Davit Nadibaidze is.'

'And me?' It was possible that the wine has made me shameless.

'When I saw you this morning, I didn't think of any of it. But after, I thought that you looked familiar. And then I remembered seeing clips of you on Instagram. I realized that it was you in the water—well, that was it for me.'

'Oh,' I said. I swirled my wine, slowly, watching the pale-yellow liquid fog up the globe-shaped glass.

Liam placed his head closer to mine. 'It just feels like you're everywhere.'

I didn't know what to think. But for the first time, in a long time, it felt good to let loose. It wasn't really letting go, but maybe letting loose was a reasonable start. What I was really, was tired. I was tired of holding it all in. I was tired of keeping it all in.

'Are you okay?'

I glanced up at him, as my phone started ringing again. I buried it in my bag, made a mental note to put it on 'Do Not Disturb' again. 'I'm not sure,' I said. 'Can we just talk?'

I saw a funny look cross his face, gone in a second. He sidled closer. 'You're cool. You're beautiful. You feel like an interesting person.'

I took another sip of the wine, the liquid both cool and burning as it went down my throat. And then I felt relaxed once more, heady and adventurous. 'What makes you think that?'

'You just are.' He gave a shrug, one hand on his phone.

Talking, I just wanted to talk. 'What do you do, Liam?'

He smiled. 'I'm a digital nomad. A photographer. I'm also a food and travel influencer, based in, well—everywhere. Right now I'm based in Barcelona. Which was why it was so easy for me to come here.'

'I had to do work with several hotels,' he continued. 'Do their photography, handle their digital marketing. By that, I guess I mean that I promote their business through my social media accounts.'

The words were gliding through my head. Everyone is an influencer, I thought, my brain definitely turning into mush that night. It was beginning to feel as if I was just moving, strictly, inside my own echo chamber, going in circles and not knowing any more beyond that.

'Hey,' Liam the digital nomad slash photographer slash travel influencer was saying now. 'Let's take a photo.'

I downed the remains of my wine glass. 'Okay.'

We brought our heads closer, and smiled at our images on his phone. 'I want you, Arya,' Liam whispered, his lips almost brushing my ear.

And then it was my phone again, vibrating. It was morning in Manila. It was Jake. And it just hit me why I couldn't still do it, even though I knew I was trying. I couldn't be with other men. It's been almost three years, but I couldn't move forward. Not just yet.

I wanted to want Liam. I wanted to tell him that. And I wanted desperately to say that to myself. But the truth is, I still only wanted Jake.

Chapter 30

Ghim Moh Food Centre, Singapore, 10 a.m. At first, I thought it was a prank. A phone call, from an unknown number in the early hours of the morning—4.22 a.m. to be exact—and so I had answered without really looking. When I did, no one was on the other line. Instead, I got a series of voice messages, this time on my WhatsApp.

'I would like to paint the portrait of this person who has revealed me.' It was a low, almost husky voice that sounded both smooth and lilting. A sexy voice that made me sit up, despite the ungodly hour. Somehow it didn't sound so sinister. In fact, it felt warm and charming, and despite myself, I felt drawn to it—and whoever was it, instantly.

That was the first voice message. It didn't take a minute for me, no matter how groggy I was from sleep, to know that it was Davit.

'I would like to meet you, Arya Alvarez.'

How did he know my name? How did he get my number?

I jumped out of bed, clicked on the light, and immediately pressed call back. 'Mr Nadibaidze? Davit?' I said, when

I thought I heard a click. 'Are you—are you in Svaneti? In Georgia?'

No answer. *What was that, Arya?* Flustered, I realized I didn't even know the questions to ask. I stared at my phone as it hung in limbo, and watched the screen as it ended the call automatically. And then, as if roused, it started emitting a series of beeps as more voice messages came in through WhatsApp.

'Meet me at the Ghim Moh Market. The hawker centre. Stall number fifty-seven.'

That sounded familiar. My breath caught. Davit Nadibaidze was in Singapore.

And then, as if he heard my thoughts, the next voice message was: 'I'll be there, Miss Alvarez. I expect you there, too. This morning, ten o'clock.'

And then: 'This is important.'

Did I hear that right? I played the audio message again. That was it: Davit Nadibaidze wanted to meet me, at one of the busiest spots—the hawker centre, of all places—right here in Singapore.

I felt a flash of fear, my mind racing. Was he suing me? Would I be served with a legal document? Oliver had talked me through this, but in my state of distraught, I had only half-listened. I still didn't know how these things went.

And then I felt my jaw tense, the fear replaced with something akin to anger, as another thought occurred to me: This was all a prank. Just like some of those that were mixed in with the DMs, the tweets, the emails, the comments that had been flooding my social accounts all this time.

I was ready to drop it. Ignore it like some of the messages that I've gotten so far that ranged from silly to downright nasty.

No reaction was the best reaction in these cases, was what I've started to learn since this whole thing blew up.

But I found myself taking a shaky breath as I pressed the little microphone on the left side of the messaging app, tilted my phone so the tiny speakers were close to my lips, and said: 'Mr Nadibaidze, if this really is you—how will I know this isn't just a prank? Because it really just might be. Thank you, and I'm sorry.'

For a minute or two, nothing. All was dark and silent in my room, in my and Nhi's flat.

I thought so. I had been hyped up for nothing, roused from my already erratic sleep since this whole thing went viral. I threw my phone on my pillow, and got ready to slide back into bed. I was desperate for sleep.

And then there it was. A photo of the finished painting, taken it seems, by Davit himself, that very day I was in the village of Ushguli in Svaneti, Georgia. With shaking hands, I picked up my phone again. I recognized the background, the messy palette he was working from, glistening with oil paint.

If I were to not overthink this and go with the simplest, easiest explanation, it would be that Davit had taken the photo himself, to show me that it was him.

I had no say in this. But then, I also didn't give him the chance to say anything when I posted his photo and videos, did I? I *had* to meet him.

I sent out another voice message: 'I'll be there. And I'm sorry for—for what happened.'

This time, there was no more answer. No more audio messages, and no more photos.

* * *

'Are you sure you're doing this?' Nhi asked me again, probably the third—or tenth time she'd asked me since I'd told her of the events that had transpired earlier that morning. It had still been so dark, and I had fallen back into a short, fitful, and dreamless sleep. When I woke up, I was certain that it had not been a dream at all. I pulled up the photo of Davit's finished painting and was sure, more than ever, that this was the real Davit Nadibaidze.

Or not.

I stood in the middle of the crowded food centre, wracked by uncertainty once more. I was unsure of where to look first, even as that day's early risers hurried past me, brushing hard past my shoulders on both sides. Nhi had to go to work that morning, but had offered to take the day off, just to go with me. I declined. I thought I could do this alone.

I felt exposed, as if twenty Davits were now scrutinizing me from the long queues and the thick groups of people at the many tables in the sprawling food centre. My only consolation was that this was Singapore, this was a public place, Ghim Moh was very well known to everyone in this city, and there were probably a hundred security cameras that could record everything if the situation turned dangerous.

I hope not. The danger would be me, in a lawsuit. Maybe he would have a lawyer with him. Or a bodyguard who would threaten me if I didn't do—

I turned sharply as a determined auntie barreled past me, the metal grocery cart she was dragging behind her hitting my shins.

That was when I saw him. Davit Nadibaidze, looking exactly like he did in that remote village in Georgia, sitting calmly in one of those big round hawker tables. He was in another pyjama-style outfit—in beige and gold, this time—and leather slip-ons, looking not at all out of place among the locals who were enjoying their morning fare. Beside him, slurping from wide, plastic bowls of *laksa*, was an elderly couple, both with hair completely white, and they themselves, completely oblivious.

I looked past him and around me, unable to believe that no one was paying Davit any mind. No one here recognized him.

I was by Davit's table in three strides. 'Mr Nadibaidze,' I began, bowing a little.

'Davit.' I was shocked to hear his voice again, and my brain immediately matched it with the voice message that morning. He gestured for me to sit on the stool across from him.

'What, how—how did you get here?'

'I have my ways.' He paused, made a show of glancing at the blissful uncle and aunt beside him. Then he turned back to me. 'And from what happened, it seems that you have yours, too.'

'Mr Nadi—Davit,' I began. 'I'm so sorry. I didn't mean for it to explode like this.'

He gave a small grunt. 'Explode? Explode is a big word. But maybe, yes, you are right. It exploded. And now the world knows.'

I hung my head. 'I didn't mean to expose you.'

'Ah, another word I both like and despise.' He rubbed the tips of his fingers together as if brandishing a paintbrush. 'My dear. I'm already—as you say—extremely exposed as it is.' He gave a little shrug. 'Why, I've been exposed for more than twenty years!'

The relief I felt was palpable, and I felt the knots in my stomach loosen. 'Are you alone, Mister—uh, Davit?'

'Come on.' He gave another delicate grunt. 'I'm never really alone. Maybe that's why I need the Caucasus. The mountains.'

And then I had to ask it, the most important question of all. 'Will you be pressing charges, Mi—I mean—Davit? I'm really concerned about—'

He cut me off. 'You know what I'd like to paint?' His deep voice rose above the din of the busy hawker centre. 'I want to show ecstasy in plants.'

What was that? I frowned, then said, slowly: 'Ecstasy? Do plants even feel that? Do plants feel?' It didn't sound right. And I wasn't sure where this conversation was going. 'Davit,' I said again, my voice in a rush. 'I'm really, really sorry about what happened.'

'Ah,' he said, crossing his pyjama-clad legs. 'You want to know what's going to happen. That's your concern.'

I nodded, relieved once again at this turn in conversation. 'Well, yes. Yes.'

'Thanks to you, the world now knows that I do botanical art. Plants and rare flowers, that sort of thing.' From a pocket, he took out a pair of green sunglasses, and propped them on his head. 'You have a lot of that here, in Singapore.'

I nodded again, not knowing what else to say.

'Mr Davit Nadibaidze? Is it you?'

We both looked up. A young Singaporean in an expensive-looking printed shirt and Bermuda shorts was standing before us, his face open and eager. 'I'm a fan, Mr Davit,' he said, his voice loud yet tremulous with excitement. 'I can't believe you're here!'

His phone was out in a split second. 'Can we please—can we take a selfie?'

'Of course.' Davit's smile was breezy, but he didn't move an inch from where he was sitting.

I watched as the guy bent his body, awkwardly, so his head was at the same level as Davit's. 'Thank you,' he said, sweating and breathless after he took his shot. 'I'll tag you!'

Davit and I watched as he disappeared into the crowd.

'I guess this is it,' Davit said, after a moment.

'This is what?' My voice, I was dismayed to note, still sounded fearful.

'A little goodbye.' Davit turned to face me. He pursed his lips, then sighed. 'Don't worry, Arya. I've made my decision.'

'Oh?'

'It's time I go back to the fray.'

Chapter 31

Singapore, 8.40 a.m. It took me a while to realize that what I had been working for all this time for myself, after Jake and I broke up, was neither a feeling of love nor hate—but indifference. A kind of numbing. A state of being where I still loved him but was also trying to stop loving him. A place where I didn't hate him, because I couldn't drum up hate that I didn't really feel. But to be indifferent, to be unaffected, to *not care* any more—somehow, I had placed it in my mind that that was the only way to protect myself, the only way to survive, the only way to soften the blow. I had thought that it was the only way out of this grief.

How wrong I was. Or, how forgetful.

The day after my strange encounter with Davit Nadibaidze at Ghim Moh, I had called Oliver and asked if we could meet. A good hour before we clock in at Isle Z, I said because I needed to tell him every detail of that meeting with Davit. In a way, I wanted to make sense of what happened, too.

We met at Silke, one of our morning tea spots just behind the office. Oliver was already there, pouring himself a cup from a strong pot of Alishan oolong. I waited for him as he carefully filled mine with the milky-scented, fragrant brew before I started my Singapore story on Davit, beginning from the artist's early morning voice messages.

Oliver was silent for a few moments, after I was done. 'Davit's right,' he said, finally. 'There's nothing to worry about.'

'Oh?' I took a sip from my cup, the flavours of the delicate liquid soaking my tongue. It had already cooled, rendering its taste more pronounced.

'It seems like he's decided to go back to the public eye.'

I nodded, slowly. 'I thought so, too,' I said. 'That last line he said—I think it meant that he was ready. To show his work again.'

'His new art,' Oliver looked thoughtful. 'Botanical art, by Davit Nadibaidze. What a reinvention. The art community will be ecstatic.' He grinned, his eyes lighting up. 'In a way, you helped push that.'

'I did?'

'Maybe what happened served as a wake-up call for him, too,' he said. 'Had you not posted what you posted, Davit might've stayed in hiding for another decade or so. Who knows?'

'And we wouldn't be able to benefit from his art.' I think I smiled for the first time that morning, and it felt good.

* * *

Back at the office, I remembered that I had other things to discuss with Oliver. Jia Yin and her Isle Z collaboration, for instance. Building up our little boutique agency.

I was reporting about Jia Yin and the Santorini trip when my phone started beeping. I knew, just by what's been happening in the past few days—by the calls I've been getting in Santorini—who it was. In a way, I had been waiting for it.

I steeled myself to be present, to work. And I had a lot of it in Isle Z. My email was teeming with the usual overflow of messages, and my DMs on Instagram and Twitter were unopened. I had several requests for interviews, from media outfits I didn't really recognize. I made a note in my mind to deal with it later that day.

'Jia Yin Wurtzbach has signed the contract,' I told Oliver. 'The one I ran through you to review. I know it's not the usual.' It was a contract that sealed our collaboration— Isle Z would organize four trips for Jia Yin Wurtzbach and her JY brand next year, one for each quarter—a tall order, but one that Isle Z has already done before. The direction was towards digital, online clients and the pricing had been right. Jia Yin was dead serious on making her 'Travelling with An Influencer' programme real and robust.

'No, it's great,' Oliver said. 'I know you worked with legal on this even while overseas. And I reviewed it, twice. Not a bad deal, Superstar. Technology's not such a bad thing, isn't it.'

'As long as it brings in clients, I guess that's good.'

'And we're grateful for the clients coming in this quarter.' Oliver's voice was kind. 'You did it.'

I glanced at him, a little touched by the remark. 'You know I'd do so much for Isle Z,' I said. I meant it. 'This company still has its kinks—and I know you agree with me on this. But you and Desmond have been nothing but good to me.'

'Not sure I've been good to you, ruining your teeth this way.' Oliver said, gesturing at one of the used tea cups on his desk. 'All these rich, ripe tea we're having!' Oliver, who couldn't resist a joke.

'I'm sure there's calcium in there somewhere,' I couldn't resist a small laugh. 'But really, you've taken care of me. I just hope Isle Z will take off well, you know, in other aspects.'

He turned serious, placing the cup back on the table. 'You're right, Superstar.' Oliver looked thoughtful. 'On Isle Z. There's a lot of growth to be done. That's necessary.'

'Well, I'm here as long as you'll keep me.' I drew a long breath. I felt a hard knot pressing on my right shoulder, and I felt tired. Jetlag or too little sleep. And too much happening, as usual.

'Are you happy, Arya?' Oliver still had that thoughtful look on his face. 'I mean, I still remember almost three years ago, when we first hired you. There was something about you, a kind of—well, an intense drive when you first started working here. A kind of desperation, I have to admit. Don't get me wrong, because that translated well into very hard work, if I'll be candid. You've been very active, and very creative with the work, the trips, and the clients. Your experience with your own agency in Manila gave you that confidence, and it's taught you well.'

I looked at him, my insides warming. What I liked about Oliver even at the beginning was his ability to articulate very well the things that needed to be said. He hadn't changed a bit. I wanted to tell him that if there was something or someone that needed growth, it was me.

'I'm happy,' I said, wishing that I meant it. 'I, well—there's just still some stuff I need to take care of, is all.' I gave the tiniest of shrugs. 'Everybody has, I guess.'

Oliver met my eyes for long moment, before saying: 'I know. I know it hasn't been easy on you.' He placed the tips of his fingers together, forming a tent with his hands. 'Maybe it hasn't been easy right from the start, living here on your own in Singapore. And you've had other stresses, of course.'

'This viral . . . thing.' I knew I sounded resigned.

Oliver straightened up and looked at me again. 'Listen, Arya. The way forward—well, it can be uncomfortable. I know that from experience. But this is now the way forward. Digital is where we're going with all these. The earlier you get used to it, the easier it will be for you to adapt it and embrace it. Soon, you'll be using it to your advantage— and advancement.'

'What about the traditional things, the old things that I— we like? Like, tea for example?'

'Arya, we can still have our tea,' Oliver said, gently. 'No one is keeping you from seeking your own happiness, your own joys, except yourself.'

I wish I had listened to Oliver.

Because something happened that would shake the little bubble I've built for myself in Singapore. The bubble that Oliver was trying to help me secure, so I would be on my way to solid happiness.

Jake was coming. And he was coming for me.

* * *

It started with a text, and six missed calls. *'I miss you,'* said the single line in my phone. The message was from Jake, and I didn't have to scrutinize the number to know that it was him, even though I had deleted it from my phone contact list more than two years ago. The missed calls were persistent, consistent in their frequency and the time in between calls. It demanded your attention. And they were typical Jake.

I was wrapping up work at the office, glad that it was almost five-thirty. All day, I had been negotiating with suppliers, updating my current clients via emails and calls, and tweaked some of the itineraries I was working on. By day's end late that afternoon, I ended up needing confirmation for an eight-room villa in a place called Orthez, in Southwestern France and almost at the Spanish border, and there was nothing else I could do but wait. I watched the clock, willing it to be finally six o'clock so I could lay down for that odd nap I always seemed to need whenever I didn't pay attention to jetlag. I had already thought of where I would buy food on the way home, which was at the hawker centre that I passed by every day to and from my place.

I hated to admit this, but I couldn't take Jake off my mind. My phone burned through the leather of my bag as I made my way slowly to the flat from the MRT, letting the other pedestrians hurry and pass by me.

I thought of how I had congratulated myself, in the more than two years that I've been here in Singapore, not only for executing my hasty escape from all that I'd feared in Manila—the crushing humiliation, the heartbreak, and the depression I knew I wouldn't survive—but also for my decision to cut off all ties from Jake. I had deleted my Facebook, Instagram, Twitter, even Viber and WhatsApp, and almost every social media account that I created in Manila when I left. I only started creating brand new ones a month after I moved to Singapore. And they were for work.

My years away from my own city, trying to process my break-up, felt like an assault of emotions. If there had been five stages of grief, it felt as if I'd gone through ten. A dozen.

I thought of how I had lived my almost three years in Singapore with almost no contact with Jake, which meant zero texts or calls, and only the occasional peek at his social media—as what happened in South Africa.

No contact. I wish I could say that that had solely been my decision when I finally deleted Jake Hidalgo's number from my phone, after killing all my social media presence online. Out of sight, out of mind, right? Zero contact. I had read somewhere that that was the way to go. That it was a way to get over someone and move on.

It wasn't. It was the pain—that burning, crushing, and unbearable pain that seemed to drown me every time I think of what happened to us—that made me shun any sort of communication with Jake. Simply put, it had just been too painful to maintain contact with someone I've loved, and someone I believed back then I still did—even long after we broke up. What had happened had been horrific, and what Jake had done had been unthinkable, unforgivable—but it didn't mean that I'd stopped loving him.

As for no contact—it wasn't that I wanted to do it, it was that I *couldn't* not do it. I needed it, too. Because somehow, I still needed to function. Somehow I still needed to live. I couldn't do that with pain like a fire whose flames were always threatening to singe me, every time I made contact with Jake.

God knows how many times I had wanted to text him. How many times I've wanted to ask after him. What was wrong—I'd thought again and again, and so many times—with a small 'hi,' an innocent *'kamusta?'* or a well-intentioned wish such as 'I hope you're doing well'?

How many times I had pictured us, talking again. Or even just us, texting again. Our relationship restored—as what, I wasn't really sure. I had begun thinking that maybe that even didn't matter. I had begun to feel loose, open to possibilities. Maybe there were questions that didn't really need answering.

It would open the floodgates. That was what was wrong.

I read the message again, the tenth, twentieth time I've looked at it. A myriad of questions sprang to my mind. What was he thinking? Had something happened between him and his wife? Was he still with his wife? What was he doing right now? And, did he want me? Did I still want him?

I scrolled through the empty chat space, feeling a little crazed. Jake missed me. It was right there, in black and white. In reliable words. That, then, must be the truth. Because *I* missed him. I had missed him all this time, and especially when I had just moved to Singapore. That yearning, it never really went away.

And then there was another question that niggled at me, but I pushed it aside.

'I miss you' may be a cliché, but it was from Jake Hidalgo, whom I haven't texted or spoken with for close to three years.

This time, I wanted to answer him. I wanted contact.

Chapter 32

Singapore, 7.05 p.m. I have never been afraid of heights. In all my travels, I have rarely said no to calls to clamber up hills and mountains, climb up high towers, sit on rooftops, view a city from a cliff.

Maybe that was why I told Jake to meet me thirty-three levels up a building, where we felt closer to the sky and I could see the sea and take in the sweeping, breathtaking view of Marina Bay Sands gleaming behind the pale blue waters of the South China Sea.

Yes, Jake. Twenty-four hours earlier, I never would have thought that I would see Jake again, much less talk to him. I never would have thought that I'd have the courage, the openness, the forgiveness. And maybe, the foolishness—of meeting up with my ex-boyfriend whom I'd broken up with almost three years ago because he had not chosen me. And how had he not chosen me. It had taken me a change of city and a total overhaul of my life just to be able to feel a semblance of moving on, of getting over him.

Twenty-four hours earlier, I was still just texting with Jake.

'I miss you' was what he texted.

'I miss you, too,' I wanted to write back. I swear I had my fingers ready to tap this out. I wanted to be bold. I was tired of holding it all in. I felt as if the old Arya had left my body, replaced by someone both reckless, foolish, and forgiving.

The call came in less than a minute. 'Hey. Arya?' The connection was so clear, it felt as if Jake Hidalgo was just right there, in front of me. It amazed me at how his voice had not changed at all.

I tried to keep mine even, calm. As if the person I was talking to had not rejected me, abandoned me, broken my heart. 'Jake. *Kamusta?* It's good to hear from you.'

There. I was polite, gracious, and neutral. I had the advantage of distance. I wasn't any more the crazy Other Woman. I may not be with someone right now, but at least I wasn't any more labelled a home-wrecker. A marriage-wrecker. Debbie's words may have been true, but there were things she said that weren't.

I was my own person. I was Arya Alvarez. And I was a completely different person here in Singapore.

Or so I thought.

'You there?' Jake sounded relieved, then elated. 'How have you been?'

'Oh?' I said. 'Yes, I'm here.' It took everything in me to not ask the questions I'd been desperate to ask him, questions that had formed themselves when we were not any more together and so I had given up on getting the answers to. The questions I had turned over and over in my mind for months.

'Arya. God.' His voice dropped to something grave, serious-sounding. 'I've been wanting to call you, all these months. I've been wanting to see you.'

Why only now? I wanted to ask. Still, I felt a sense of relief wash over me. That familiar feeling of almost being high. 'Jake,' I said, willing my voice to be light, casual. 'You know that I've been here the whole time.'

'Everything is good for you in Singapore?'

'Yes, all's been good.' I frowned. 'Great.'

'I saw you trending on Twitter.'

'Twitter? I don't even go there any more.'

'And I discovered your new IG account. Is it because of that guy?'

'No, no.' I protested. 'It was an accident.'

'An accident?

'That I have that many—' I stopped. I thought of Davit again, our strange meeting and what Oliver said, when I told him everything. 'Well, maybe it was a good accident.'

'Listen, Arya.' There was an urgency in Jake's voice. 'Are you well? Is everything okay with you? I've been so worried.'

I closed my eyes. Jake had been worried about me? I had no idea. There had been nothing from him in the more than two years I've been here. Or had he been trying to call me, and I had missed those calls? He didn't know my work email, but maybe he'd been emailing my old email addresses?

'Are you happy that I called you?'

'You're asking me that?' I tried to sound even, but already, I could feel my defenses going down.

'I've missed you, Arya.' Jake sounded genuinely contrite.

'Jake, I don't know what this is—'

'I need to see you.' There was that urgency again in his voice.

I swear, my heart jumped, and then it just didn't want to go back to its resting state because it kept on thumping against my chest as if I'd downed something strong and alcoholic too fast and too much.

And, how long have I longed to hear these words? How long have I told myself that these words didn't matter any more?

'I don't know what to say, Jake.'

'Say yes, Arya.'

'To what?' I didn't know where this was going.

'Arya, listen.'

'I'm listening.'

'I'm here in Singapore. Can we meet?'

* * *

Maybe that was what I wanted, this sort of impromptu meeting with Jake: some control, some distance, a new perspective. The view from high up has always made me feel that everything was more manageable. Seeing things from above always gave me that feeling of well-being, that things can go right, after all.

I met Jake at Level 33, a microbrewery in Singapore's financial district that was as famous for its craft beers and IPAs as it was for its classic views of the island state's magnificently reclaimed land: from our high table and bar seats at the terrace, we could easily gaze down at the tranquil Singapore River, the 'durians' that was the Esplanade Theatre, the Arts Museum, the iconic Marina Bay Sands.

It was nearing sunset, and I was thankful for the harsh afternoon sun that was fast waning, coating the view below with a melon-coloured glow. The service in Level 33 had always been efficient, sometimes even overreaching but genial, and servers that evening were busy going back and forth with bottles of wine and pints of beer, and trays of pungent-smelling truffle fries, braised pork belly. Most of the guests were starting dinner.

'What are you doing here?' I asked, just as a server laid down two wine glasses in front of us, and brandished a bottle for us to check. 'I mean,' I said, lowering my voice. 'What are you doing in Singapore?' I glanced at Jake and we both nodded at the bottle, and I sucked in my breath. How easy it was to remember how we had been together, doing this very same thing, in a very different city.

'Jake?' The wine had been poured, and now it was just the two of us again. I made myself look at him.

'I came to see you.'

I narrowed my eyes, tried to ignore the hard, solid thumping that was starting in my chest. How I thought I'd be calm. Or at least, unaffected. 'Jake,' I said. 'You don't travel.'

'Okay.' Jake sighed, took a swig from his glass. 'I met a potential business partner here.' He looked away, and gazed long and hard at that magnificent urban view. Then he looked back at me. 'But I've long wanted to talk to you Arya. To see you.' He reached out and took my hand.

His hand burned on mine, and I snatched my hand away. 'I'm fine here.' I cleared my throat.

'Do you think—' Jake paused.

'Has something happened?' I realized I didn't know where to begin. I was beginning to not like it, the decision that I had made. What was I doing here?

'Arya, I've left Debbie.' He looked so earnest. 'For real.'

'It doesn't matter any more.' There was an ache in my chest.

'My marriage—it's been annulled.' Jake said, softly. 'I have the papers. Signed. You can check with the statistics office if you want.'

'I told you,' I said. 'It doesn't matter any more.' I remembered how it had mattered so much. It still had, when I moved to Singapore and it had been many months after that incident. And then I had slowly realized that what I eventually needed wasn't Jake's annulment to push through—and at that time, it didn't seem that it even would, after what happened with Debbie. What I needed was closure.

It didn't happen. What happened was months—no, years—of me walking around with a wound in my chest. What happened were the feelings of unworthiness. The fear that I was not enough to be loved. That I was flawed somewhere in my person somehow, that there was a shortcoming in me that people—and even the ones I loved—couldn't accept.

It had started a fear in me that I wouldn't be loved, once someone knew me, really knew me. That I was unloveable. That I was not enough.

I felt something welling up in my throat. Slowly, I placed my napkin with both hands to my face—and then sobbed like I haven't cried in a long, long time. At the same time, something in me said—of all times to cry, why did it have to be right now, with Jake?

'Christ, Arya.' I heard the scrape of metal with concrete. The next moment, Jake's familiar arms were around me, my neck on his shoulder. He was standing in front of my seat, cradling my head on his shoulders. 'Don't cry, please.'

I felt tired. 'Jake, why are we doing this?' What was I doing here? Maybe I didn't have any business being here too in the first place.

'I'm sorry, Arya.' Jake's voice had turned soft. 'I just wanted to tell you I'm sorry. For everything.'

I didn't say anything. But my head was still on his shoulder.

'When you left, I realized I couldn't be with you. But I had to fix my stuff first. I had to right things with Debbie.'

'You chose her.' I said, my voice muffled. All the painful events of that day in Manila rose in me, threatening to drown me again as they had the first few months after I fled.

'I'm choosing you now.'

'It's too late.' I whispered. I wish I had sounded more convincing.

'It's not.' Jake was stroking my hair. 'I've changed, Arya. I really have.'

'People can't change.'

'I've righted myself. Please believe me.' Jake's tone was turning urgent.

'I do. Maybe. I need time.'

'Can we just try again? Start over? Be friends first, if you want.'

His hand on my hair felt so good. I still remember how soothing it felt, just to have someone this close, this intimate.

And then I remembered something. The woman with him in the photo that I saw on Facebook, the one whose hand was on Jake's thigh. Another woman who wasn't Debbie.

I lifted my head, and pulled away. My face burned, my chest tight as I remembered not only the shock and surprise but the humiliation I felt at seeing him, again, with another woman.

'You're with someone else.' I said, finally, hating the ways that my voice cracked and that part of my statement was almost soundless, lost in the air.

There was a split second where I thought I saw a flash of fear on his face, but it was gone before I could even register it fully in my brain. 'No,' Jake was saying, his face taut. Then he softened and looked like he was about to pull me closer. But he leaned back in his chair instead. 'Arya,' he said, his voice low. 'That's not true.'

'You're with someone,' I repeated, trying not to feel like I was pleading, hopelessly, against a brick wall. 'I can't, Jake. I can't do this again.'

Jake shook his head. 'No. I swear to you, I'm not. After Debbie . . .' his voice trailed off. 'After Debbie, I only thought of you.'

I tried to listen, carefully. Searching for what, I wasn't sure.

'Please, Arya,' Jake had.

'Then who was that?'

'Who?'

'Never mind.' That ache in my chest again, a dull but palpable soreness in my bones. My body was crying for me to just leave, to just, once and for all, cease to engage. To just walk away. All this had been a mistake. It had been futile, whatever this was. And why did I even say yes to meeting him? Had it been because I simply missed him? Because I missed having someone? Had I been so desperate for closure? Had I really wanted him? I felt tears welling up again.

'I still love you.' This was Jake. The Jake I knew and fell in love with: direct and expressive. Unafraid. 'I love you, Arya.'

I froze.

'And even if you don't love me any more, I will do everything to make you love me.' There was a fierceness in his voice that I hadn't heard before. 'It will just be like before, Arya, except for one thing.'

I gazed at his face, so earnest and intent. But I didn't answer. I swiped a single tear that had escaped from the corner of my eye.

'This time, nothing gets in the way of our relationship.'

There was something about the 'nothing' that had struck me. I brought the napkin to my cheeks again, but they were now dry.

'Thank you, Jake,' I said, gathering my things. The sun had set and the sky was awash in timid shades of pink and purple.

I met his eyes one last time, and walked away.

Epilogue

There was something to be said about being grateful for the people that caused you the most pain. About how people who've hurt you can still teach you things, help you grow, and let you evolve. This is why you can still be grateful to them because, in a way, they've made you who you are.

'Look for what you've gained, instead of what you've lost.' This was what Oliver had always told me to think in times of adversity, in times of situations you'd deem catastrophic. A simple but powerful way of seeing things.

This has been my story. For nearly three years, I had been walking with a wound in my heart that had always wanted to heal—but I didn't allow it to. I had only mostly thought of what I'd lost.

I didn't go back to Jake. For the longest time, I had believed that that was what I wanted. But it wasn't what I needed. And maybe I had just wanted the dream, not the man. Now I truly think that someone was still out in the universe, on a journey to find me as I was in finding him.

That video of Davit that went viral? Petered out after a couple of months, disappeared from the internet. Forgotten news, finally. That had already been a record, in online time. Now no one knew who Arya Alvarez was again, and that was just how I liked it.

I resigned from Isle Z and instead struck a freelancing deal with them. I said, I wanted to stay in Singapore, or the Philippines, or wherever. I wanted to stay in one place, for once. I wanted a tea shop in a garden, and I had taken my first baby steps towards that dream. Opening even a tiny shop was still no small feat. I was doing my business plan, readying the paperwork, and trying to decide if it would be in Punggol or Batangas or wherever. But staying in one place was good.

Just think of what you'd gain, instead of what you would lose. I wanted to start over.

I thought of the people, like Jake, who's caused me so much hurt, so much struggle. Now, I can only think that they have given me an opportunity. They have set me on a path to growth.

'Are you coming?'

It was Oliver. It was Sunday and we were in Singapore's Chinatown, peering at every shop we passed. We took our time like that.

'Yes, I'm here.' I stood in front of a crowded shop, just by People's Park.

'Let's have tea,' Oliver said.

I looked at the shop, fragrant with the brews but teeming with people. 'It's full.'

'Then we can go now.'

Acknowledgements

So many people have touched my life and I would like to thank those who have made this book possible.

My deep gratitude to my publisher, Nora Nazarene Abu Bakar, for her discernment, wit, and generous belief in me.

To Amberdawn Manaois, for being the best, most brilliant structural editor I've ever met, whose insight and patience have enriched this novel.

To the indefatigable marketing and publicity team of Penguin Random House SEA: Chaitanya Srivastava, Garima Bhatt, and Almira Manduriao for fabulously connecting this book to readers and letting the world know about *Sudden Superstar*.

To the hardworking folks at Penguin's editorial, art and design who've worked with me in putting together all aspects of this book.

To Joanne Ongkeko, who held my hand, unwaveringly, during my moments of struggle and success, whose shared passion for art mean so much.

Didi madloba to the Jmukhadze family: Vakho, Kote, and Elza who've let me experience the most beautiful sides of Georgia through the years.

To my friends for life, Alvik Padilla and Dinah Fuentesfina, for letting me be myself all these years, and in all these places.

I'm grateful for the writers and poets in Singapore, Malaysia, Vietnam, the Philippines, and all over the world whose words and inimitable company continue to inspire me.

To my readers, who have been with me since the beginning. I learn from you all, every single day.

And finally, to my family, Alfred and Ulric, for the immense love, selflessness, and compassion. Thank you for this life full of writing—and for giving me the courage, always, to create and continue.